The
RELUCTANT
COURTSHIP
of Madge DuPree

Other Books by Kathy Nickerson

GLORY CIRCLE SISTERS SERIES
Thirty Days to Glory
The Secret of Serendipity
Rose Hill Cottage
The Marvel House

The
RELUCTANT
COURTSHIP
of Madge DuPree

KATHY NICKERSON

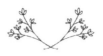

ACKNOWLEDGMENTS

Each book I write comes out of the life we live within our family and community. It isn't possible to list each one of you, but I hope you know who you are and what you bring to my life and my work. For this book, here are a few specific folks I want to thank:

The friends, family members, and readers who have encouraged me to write another book. I'm grateful for your kind words.

My long-suffering husband who puts up with the imaginary characters sharing our life and who is always the patron of my art.

Our children and grandchildren for inspiring conversations, amazing life examples, naming characters, and claiming they are never embarrassed by my writing or my public speaking.

Our church family, who are all devoted to helping people like Elmer get a fresh start in life.

Fellow writers at the HCC Writers Guild and Heart of America Christian Writers Network for supporting, encouraging, and challenging one another in art and in life.

Anna, who always brings out the better in me.

Debra, who checks my punctuation and my story arc with precision and with kindness.

Becky, who captures my stories in gorgeous paintings for book covers.

Grandpa Jim and Harriet who proved that love can blossom at any age. Well-done.

CHAPTER ONE

Marching to Zion

"What kind of stunt are you trying to pull?" Madge DuPree glared from her spot in the passenger seat of the Marvel family van. It was more of a truck, actually, and getting into the front seat had required a stepstool and a good deal of heaving and shoving on the part of Luke and Alexandra Marvel. Madge already felt like most of her dignity had been left at home. She wasn't about to surrender the rest of it by using the handicapped entrance at church.

Luke flicked the sticker hanging from his rearview mirror. "I'm taking advantage of your temporary condition to get a good parking spot."

"Oh, no you are not." Madge huffed and crossed her arms. She tried to stare straight ahead and not look at Luke's face. She hated to admit that in the few months she had been working as the Marvel family's housekeeper, she had developed a fondness for Luke. Not a fondness, exactly. Madge didn't tend to be fond of people. More than a tolerance, though. She didn't know exactly how to label the feeling. She had tried hard to ignore feelings for much of her life.

She thought Luke still watched too many sports on television, and he could be dense where his wife and girls were concerned.

But she liked him. Drat it all. She did. Outside of Pastor Cleveland, Madge didn't remember truly liking anyone from the male species before. She was thinking of that while Luke sat with the engine humming.

"Shall I help you out?" he said.

"You shall not." She pressed the button to lock her door. "Catherine and I never walked in through the side door in our lives, and I'm not about to start now."

"Madge," Alex said from the back seat, "you can't possibly manage all the steps around front. It's like walking up a mountain."

Madge supposed the Marvels had climbed a few mountains on their recent ski trip. Even so, she didn't think the front steps of Mt. Zion Church should be compared. She did remember how icy those steps could get. It was almost impossible to keep them clear. And she knew she would be out of breath before the top on a normal day. Nothing had been normal since she fell.

Alex tried again. "I think your friend Catherine would tell you to go in the side door if she were here."

"Well, she isn't here." Saying that out loud always made Catherine's death ten times worse. Madge wondered if it would always be that way. "I'm going in the front door. You people can slink in the side and go through the kitchen if you want."

They sat in silence, not even the little girls in the far back making any noise. Finally, Luke reached for the gear shift and put the car in reverse. "Okay, m'lady," he said. "We shall climb the royal stairs."

Madge turned to see if Luke was smiling or if he meant the remark as a scold. She didn't take well to being scolded. He was smiling, though, so Madge let the comment go. She didn't have much experience with men in general, and she hadn't lived with one since before they landed on the moon. She hadn't yet mastered the art of daily conversation.

Once Luke parked in front of the church, Madge descended

from the vehicle with a bit more dignity than she had shown climbing in, but with no less pain. Her broken hip had mended pretty well, but the sprained ankle and twisted knee still gave her trouble. The tall stone steps rose before her with a hint of battle.

She stood and looked at the building. Mt. Zion Community Church. She knew it wasn't the grandest building in the state of Missouri, but it always felt mighty impressive to her. Especially with all those steps leading up to the front doors.

When the Marvel family had assembled around her, she gave her handbag to Aspen, the eldest of the girls. She was the one most likely to stand with Madge in a rumble. Their relationship hadn't started out that well. Madge had never met a teenager before she showed up for duty as a nanny and housekeeper at the Marvel house. She didn't know if Aspen was typical, but she certainly had turned out to be amazing.

With Aspen ahead of her and Luke and Alex on each side, Madge scooted her walker forward and lifted it onto the first step. No good. The step was too narrow for the walker. She wouldn't be able to use it on the way up.

"Here," Luke said. "Give me the purse." He turned to Quinn, the third grader who had learned to spell under the tutelage of Madge and her friends in the Glory Circle. "Quinn, you carry Madge's purse, and Aspen, you take the walker on up to the top. Madge can lean on your mom and me." He offered his arm as he spoke.

Alex had been carrying Grace with one arm and leading Peyton with the other. She put the toddler down, nudged Peyton forward, and reached for Madge.

Grace began to wail instantly, and Madge thought about joining in. Before she could, Elmer Grigsby came up behind them.

"Here," he said. "I'll carry the pocketbook and the walker. Aspen can take the baby."

"Heavens no," Madge said. "You'll look ridiculous."

"All right," Elmer stopped with the purse in his hand. He wore the same black dress coat and hat he'd had on the first time Madge saw him. Today, they seemed to fit. He looked at the situation for another minute and then said, "I'll carry the baby." He handed Aspen the purse and took Grace in his arms.

It didn't look to Madge like the man had held a baby in about a hundred years, if ever. He didn't hold her exactly like a grocery sack, but it was similar. Grace, however, didn't protest. Instead, she reached up for the brim of his hat and grinned.

Elmer smiled back and started talking some gibberish as he walked up the steps. The little girls followed, and Aspen sprinted past all of them with Madge's purse and the folded walker.

"Okay," Luke said. "Here we go. Hold tight and stop for breath when you need to rest."

Madge needed rest on the third step, but she waited until the fifth to stop. She bent forward and tried not to gasp as she drew in air. She wondered what would happen if she just sat down on the step and quit. Or lay down for that matter. Would they send a stretcher, eventually, to carry her away? This had been one of her most hairbrained ideas. As soon as she could breathe again, she would say so. Maybe they could find a way to slide her back to the car and take her home.

A voice beside her broke the image of sledding back to Cherry Hills. "I was glad when they said to me, 'Let us go to the house of the Lord.'"

Madge recognized Aspen's voice. She must have run back down to stand beside them. Madge turned her head slightly and saw Aspen holding the Bible from Madge's purse. She nodded just enough for Aspen to know she should go on.

"Our feet are standing within your gates, O Jerusalem."

"What is that?" Alex said.

"It was on Madge's Verse-a-Day calendar. The heading said, 'A Song of Ascents,' and I wondered what that meant. So, when I got bored in the car, I looked it up on your phone."

"And?"

"And these are the songs pilgrims used to sing when they were climbing the hills up to Jerusalem on their way to worship."

Everyone stood silent for a moment. Madge felt the imagery. These words had propelled worshippers up mountains for thousands of years. Surely, they could take her up a set of steps.

"There's more," Aspen said.

"Read on." Madge gripped the arms on either side and stretched her foot toward the next step.

"I will lift up my eyes to the mountains; from where does my help come from? My help comes from the Lord."

Help from the Lord. In her seventy-five years on this earth, Madge had known a good bit of that help. She had come to recognize it pretty late in life, but she could see it now. Today, the Lord had sent a couple of strong people to walk on either side of her. That was a bonus. Two more steps done. Madge's breath came hard, but she didn't pause this time. She kept climbing.

"Unless the Lord builds the house, they labor in vain who build it."

Madge wished she could stop and think about that one. She had been laboring to help build the Marvel house for weeks. She had stumbled into the job when she overheard Alex say the family needed a temporary housekeeper and nanny. Although Madge had no experience in either role, she did have a great need for money to fix her Oldsmobile. A short-term job seemed like a great idea.

Madge did not have a history of great ideas, and this one had been no exception. Within a few hours, she had found herself in the center of a family breaking apart. She had done everything she could to apply duct tape and glue. She hoped the Almighty would make sure those efforts were not in vain.

She knew God might have some thoughts about the way she had tricked her way into the job. She had bamboozled Jack the Lawyer slicker than a used car salesman. She liked to think she hadn't actually lied. She merely omitted a few details and let him assume a few things.

Madge hadn't understood what a mess she was walking into, either. Parents splitting up. Little kids putting themselves to bed at night. Everybody upside down in the drama. Worst of all, the entire thing was happening in Catherine's house. Or, what had been Catherine's house when she was alive.

Catherine Benson's house had long been a haven in Madge's world. A glimpse into life as it might have been if Madge had married well. Or had kind parents. Or been pretty, even in old age. If she had seen the Marvel's address on the papers before she signed, she would not be climbing these steps with Luke and Alex today.

Madge took a deep breath and kept climbing. Aspen continued reading, and suddenly Madge realized she had only one more step to go. One more step and she would stand on the wide place before the tall oak doors. She stopped to catch her breath one last time.

Aspen read, "Those who trust in the Lord are as Mount Zion, which cannot be moved, but abides forever."

Madge looked up. Those same words were carved in large letters over the doorposts of the church house. She had noticed them before. She'd even helped clean bird droppings out of the carvings one summer. Yet the words had never sparkled in the sunlight as they did today.

She took the last step, and the little crowd at the top broke into applause and grins. Even baby Grace clapped her hands and laughed, although she probably had no idea what had happened.

Someone handed Madge her walker, and she grabbed it, breathing hard. She blinked hard, too, because the cold air stung her eyes and made them water almost uncontrollably for a few seconds.

Once Alex began steering the girls into the building, Luke leaned toward Madge's ear. "When we leave," he said, "we take the side door."

"You bet your sweet bippy," Madge replied.

CHAPTER TWO

Lilies of the Field

"Where are your flowers?"

Madge jerked from the dream she'd been having and felt as guilty as a fox caught sucking eggs. She didn't nap. Not even on a Sunday afternoon. She sat straighter in her soft chair and squinted at Quinn. "I don't have any flowers. It's the middle of winter."

"Technically, it is still fall." Aspen spoke with all the wisdom of a teenager as she entered Madge's sitting room. She carried baby Grace, and Peyton brought up the rear of the parade.

Aspen plopped Grace on Madge's lap and said, "Quinn means the flowers Mr. Grigsby gave you at Thanksgiving."

"Yeah," Quinn said. She wandered across the room and sat cross-legged at Madge's feet while the other girls settled in various positions around her. "So where are the flowers Mr. Grigsby gave you?"

"The get-well flowers," Peyton said. "Because you fell down and broke your leg."

"Hip, Peyton. She broke her hip." Quinn reached up and touched Madge's leg. "Does it still hurt?"

"Not much."

"I saw you fall down," Peyton said. "At Grace's school." The toddler looked up when she heard her name, but she quickly went back to sucking her thumb and cuddling against Madge's shoulder.

"Yep, I fell on the ice. These things happen." Madge wasn't sure she felt up to this particular conversation. She had intended to spend the afternoon reading and resting up from the morning of mountain climbing. Her hip was healing well, but it was taking every bit of her energy. If the Marvel family hadn't offered to keep her on, even when she couldn't do any housekeeping, she would have ended up in a nursing home for certain. Instead, she was tucked up soft and warm in the guest quarters of the Marvel house.

Talking about her ailments would be better than discussing Mr. Elmer Grigsby, though. Madge was glad the man had turned his life around, and it had been gentlemanly of him to bring flowers. She just didn't want to talk about him.

"So, I broke my hip," she said. "And I twisted up my leg and ankle pretty bad on the other side."

"Did you cry?" Peyton asked.

"I didn't dare cry. Tears would have frozen on my face, and I'm ugly enough as is."

"I cried," Peyton said. "And Quinn cried a lot. Did you cry, Aspen?" She looked at the big sister who seemed fully absorbed in the stitches on Madge's afghan.

"I didn't have time to cry. I was too busy trying to keep Madge warm with all those silly blankets from the daycare."

"They did look silly," Quinn said. "I think Jack had a Dora blanket on his head."

The girls all laughed, and Madge smiled, even though she didn't know which cartoon character was named Dora. She did know something changed between her and Jack on that sidewalk. She stopped seeing him as the snazzy, young lawyer handling the Marvel divorce. She didn't put a name on what he became. That would be sappy. She was way too old to start being sentimental now.

Which reminded her, had she sent him a thank you card? She probably should. Even now, after all these weeks. She would ask Paige if she had sent one. Paige handled everything in Jack's office and his life. She would know if Jack got a note from Madge.

"So, where are the flowers?"

Madge pulled herself back into the room. "Long gone. Fresh flowers don't last. I tossed them out with the trash."

"You should have hung them upside down and dried them," Aspen said. "Mr. Grigsby went to all that trouble to bring them to you."

"Fiddlesticks," Madge said. "He brought them for the whole family. They were just a table arrangement because your mother had him and Pastor Cleveland for Thanksgiving."

"Why did you say 'fiddlesticks'?" Quinn asked. "You always say 'balderdash.'"

"I'm cleaning up my language."

"They weren't for the family." Aspen said. "He brought them for you. He specifically said he brought them for the 'pearl of the family' because he heard she had fallen down."

Madge tried changing the subject. "Anybody getting hungry yet? I could go for an afternoon snack. If you girls help me, I think we could stir some up."

"Nah," the little girls said in unison. Then Peyton finished. "We just came to watch cartoons."

"Uh-huh," Madge said. "Because that giant television in the family room where there's a long sofa and two reclining chairs doesn't show cartoons anymore?"

"It's more cozy in here," Quinn said.

"It used to be." Madge grumbled, but she turned over the remote control to Aspen. She managed to scoot around enough to get the pressure off her hip, and she smooshed Grace down into her lap at a better angle. That left room on the other side for Peyton, who crept up without ever taking her eyes off the screen.

Quinn kept her spot at Madge's feet and Aspen leaned in on

the other side. Aspen rested her head on the arm of the chair, and Madge realized she had grown taller in the last month. Quinn's head didn't reach beyond Madge's knee, though. It was soon dropped there, and Madge thought maybe the little girl had gone to sleep.

They stayed in their bundle through two sessions of talking ponies. At some point, Madge must have dozed off because she didn't remember exactly how the rainbow pony came out of the horrible scrape she had gotten herself into.

When she did look up, Alex was standing in the doorway with a cup of coffee. "I thought I'd find the mob here. Are they wearing you out?"

"Not a bit. But I'm afraid my leg might be asleep."

Aspen turned to lift Grace off Madge's lap while Alex came into the room and roused Quinn. "Come on, girlies," she said. "Let's find some soup. We can bring Madge a tray."

"I'm not an invalid," Madge said. "I'll come to the kitchen and help. Or at least to eat."

Alex waved over her shoulder as she and the girls disappeared. Madge wiggled her toes and stretched her legs, testing for the pin pricks that come with loss of circulation. Not bad. She reached for the nearby walker and hoisted herself out of the soft chair.

The first few steps always hurt like blazes. But isn't that the way with life? The first hours after Catherine died, trying to believe her best friend was gone. The first days in this house, trying to pretend she knew how to do her job. Madge hobbled into her bedroom. She felt the stiffness retreating from her legs, and the ache grew less with every step.

She reached into the closet for a sweater and then turned to her nightstand. She slid open the drawer and was about to put her Bible inside. Instead, she stopped and let the pages fall open to the book of Luke.

Consider the lilies how they grow: they toil not, they spin not; and yet I say unto you, that Solomon in all his glory was not arrayed like one of these.

If then God so clothe the grass, which is today in the field, and tomorrow is cast into the oven; how much more will he clothe you, O ye of little faith?

She read the words over twice. They were a good reminder for someone who tended to be a worrywart. She worried mostly about her car, stuck in the repair shop. Now that she had broken her hip and become an invalid, she had no idea when she'd be able to earn enough money to get it out of hock. That car was her ticket to independence.

She did want to trust the Almighty more. And she should. He had never let her down so far.

She ran her fingers lightly over the petals pressed against the opposite page. It hadn't been a complete lie. She had thrown Elmer Grigsby's flowers out with the trash when they began to wilt. She didn't even know why she had kept this one small bloom. Such a silly, sentimental thing for an old woman to do.

Madge let her fingers linger for a moment and thought about tossing the flower the way she had tossed the idea of ever letting another man into her life. She had worked hard to develop her crochety reputation. Something of a safeguard, she supposed. Against relationships of any kind, really. Against disappointment.

Somehow, Catherine had worked her way through the bristles. And she brought all the Glory Circle sisters with her. Well, most of them. Grace Colby could be almost as cranky as Madge, probably for similar reasons.

Madge touched the flower again and started to lift it from the page. Her hand trembled for a moment. Instead of picking up the dried blossom, she moved it to the center of the page. She closed the Bible and tucked it into the drawer.

"I think I'm hungry," she said. "Can't think straight when I'm hungry."

CHAPTER THREE

The Swallow Finds a Nest

Madge wasn't responsible for the Monday morning circus any more. A broken hip had been all it took to get her out of breakfast prep and the school rush. Besides, now that Luke and Alex were living together again, they didn't need her to be the stable one. She could have stayed in her room, even in her bed, until the chaos tumbled into Luke's bus and pulled out of the garage. She didn't.

Instead, she waited until she heard the last set of feet trudge down the staircase. Aspen, probably. Then Madge grabbed her walker and forced her stiff knees to unhinge and carry her forward. She found the girls gathered around the bar in the kitchen while Alex poured cereal into bowls. Madge chose a chair in the corner and watched the action.

Aspen wandered over and picked up Madge's calendar from the windowsill. She read the daily verse almost to herself. "The swallow builds her nest and raises her young at a place near Your altar." She waited a beat and then aimed a question into the air. "Are we still a nest house?"

Madge waited to see who would respond. Alex bit first.

"A nest house?" she said. "What do you mean?"

"That's what they called us," Aspen said to her mother. "When you and dad were splitting up and the judge gave the house to us kids. People called it a nest house. I'm not sure what that means, but it sounded cool."

Luke handed Alex another cup of coffee and stepped into the conversation. "They called it a nest house because you four little birds got to live here all nice and comfy with Madge while your mom and I took turns moving in and out every other week. You stayed in the nest, while we did the flying."

Madge wished Luke would leave her out of the story. She had added a bit of fluff and feather, that was true. But she wasn't responsible for any talk about a nest.

"Who called us that?" Alex said. "And why were they talking about us in the first place?"

Madge heard the tightness in Alex's voice, and she cast about for a way to end the conversation or turn it to something else. She had nothing.

"It's no big deal," Luke said. "It just came up somewhere online, I think."

"People were talking about us in public? Who?"

"Nobody that matters," Luke said. "It wasn't even about us, really. It was about the case and about how it could set a new precedent in custody issues. Jack is the one who got most of the publicity since he was the lawyer fighting it."

Everything grew suddenly quiet in the kitchen. Aspen put her cereal bowl down, wiped a drop of milk from her chin, and said. "Jack was fighting? Like, trying to kick us out of the nest?"

Madge heard the tears at the edge of Aspen's words, but she had no idea how to help. Jack had fought the decision. That is why he and Madge started out on opposite sides. Madge had desperately needed the kids to keep the house long enough for her to earn some money. She had been counting down the paychecks until she could repair her car and get back out on her own.

Alex finally spoke up. "It wasn't like that. We wanted to sell the house, remember? That was the plan all along. Jack was just following my instructions and trying to reverse the judge's order so we could sell this house. Then you girls would have moved into an apartment with me. That's all."

Madge hadn't realized anyone else was listening until Quinn spoke from her end of the bar. "But we aren't selling the house now, and everybody lives here. Right?"

"Right," both parents said at once. Madge would have felt better if their voices had been a smidgen more confident. Fortunately, Grace saved the moment by spilling her milk.

The sisters yelled and jumped out of the way. Alex grabbed a kitchen towel, and Luke swooped over to lift Grace out of her chair before she got a milk bath.

"And is Madge staying forever, too?" Quinn asked.

Alex and Luke both looked at Madge. She raised her eyebrows, hoping one of them would pick up on the question, but nobody spoke. "Well," she said. "Not forever. You'd be sick of me by forever."

"How long, then?" Quinn asked. "Until I go to college?"

Luke laughed. "Don't worry about it right now, Squirt. Madge is for sure staying until she gets all healed up from surgery. Then she can decide what she wants to do. Now, somebody get me a towel."

Madge watched the chaos as Luke and the girls grabbed last minute supplies and hustled toward the garage. She leaned back in her chair. *Madge can decide what to do.* She liked the sound of those words, even if she didn't know the answer.

All this talk about a nest house and Quinn going off to college rattled Madge. She thought about the scripture Aspen had read. "Even the swallow finds a place."

Even the swallow. Not one of the showy, fancy birds. Just a plain old barn swallow. Even she could find a nest.

Madge considered the possibilities. The physical therapist said

15

Madge was making great progress. She might lose the walker soon and graduate to a cane. That could mean independent living within another month. Maybe two.

Once she reached that point, she supposed she would pack her small suitcase and go home. She hadn't asked lately about the progress on her Oldsmobile. It had been in the shop since the wreck with the ice cream truck more than two months ago. The work should be done by now. Maybe they were waiting on her to send the rest of the money before they finished.

All this sick leave had put a dent in Madge's savings plan. She couldn't send money even if the mechanic asked for it. Suddenly, the problem of transportation and independence rose up again. Madge looked across the kitchen to where Alex was scrubbing a pan.

"You know," Madge said, "I feel bad about my contract with you all. I was supposed to give sixty-days of service, and I came up short. Once I'm back on my feet, I'd be happy to finish out my time."

Alex turned from the sink. "I don't think you need to worry about that right now, Madge. Just concentrate on getting well. You don't have to work for us in order to stay with us."

Madge didn't know exactly how to explain that she hadn't been worried about housing. She was thinking about cash. "Oh, I don't want to overstay my welcome," she said. "I was thinking more about the business end of things. It wouldn't be good for my references if I cut out on this job early and didn't live up to my contract."

This time, Alex wiped her hands and turned around. "So, you're planning to take up housekeeping as a career? Becoming a professional nanny, maybe?"

"Well, you never know what might come up. I've got some good years left."

"Is this about your car?" Alex asked. "Are you worried you can't pay for the repairs when the time comes?"

Madge nodded. "Not to mention all those court costs they tacked on. And I suppose it will cost something to get my license back."

"Yes, probably." Alex looked at the ceiling for a moment. "Well, I happen to know a good lawyer. Maybe we should talk to Jack Oakley and see what he knows about such things."

"Maybe so," Madge said. "Heaven knows he wasn't much good to you as a divorce lawyer." She had meant that as a joke, but Alex didn't laugh. Madge started to feel uneasy, as if maybe she had touched something she should have left alone.

Just as she was about to launch into a story about her childhood to break the moment, Alex spoke up and saved her. "No, Jack was a rotten divorce lawyer. He became personally involved, and that is always a bad idea."

"Not this time, though," Madge said. "It was a great idea."

"You think?"

"Sure," Madge searched for the right words. "Jack's a friend now. Almost part of the family. It's always good to have friends." She knew the hypocrisy of the statement as soon as she made it. She was a fine one to talk about adding friends to her circle. She hadn't made a new friend since about 1985.

No, that wasn't true. Madge looked around the kitchen. She had made a handful of friends in the last two months. Something she never expected when she walked up the sidewalk and knocked on the door of the Marvel house.

CHAPTER FOUR

Let There Be Light

At supper on Monday night, Madge heard a telephone buzz just when the last of the spaghetti had been dished onto plates. Alex grabbed the phone from her pocket and looked at Madge as if phone etiquette fell under her job description now.

"It's not for me," Madge said.

Alex turned to Luke. "I know we agreed on no phones at mealtime, but I just signed up today for the sub list with the school district. This is how it works. You get calls at any time of the day or night."

Luke nodded toward the phone. "Better take it."

"It's just until the end of this school year," she said. "Hopefully, I'll get a permanent position for next year."

"It's okay. Go ahead and take the call." Luke lifted his fork and spoon above his plate and flapped his elbows out like a vulture. "The rest of the Marvel family is going to demolish this spaghetti while you are on the phone. Ready, set, go!"

The girls dug into their food with noisy gusto while Alex stepped away from the table.

Madge didn't attack her plate with exactly the same racing spirit, but she did feel hungry. That was an improvement in the past few days. And this spaghetti tasted pretty good. One benefit of Alex losing her high-powered job, the woman was learning to cook a decent meal. Sometimes.

Alex came back to the table and slid the phone into her pocket as she sat. "Sorry," she said. "It wasn't the school."

"Well, they probably don't call at supper time," Madge said.

"No," Luke agreed. "They probably wait till about daylight and give you a couple hours' notice."

"I know it won't be perfect," Alex said. "But I think I can do it."

"I think we can do it," Luke said.

"Right. We can do it."

"So, who was on the phone?" Aspen asked. "Or is it none of my business?"

"Well, it was for Madge."

Madge put her fork down and waited for more explanation. "It was Paige Rosedale checking to see if I thought you would be up to going to Prayer and Share at church tomorrow. She offered to take you."

Luke leaned back in his chair and held the bite of garlic bread aimed toward his mouth. "Paige is good people," he said. "She's way too good for Jack."

"As an administrative assistant or as a girlfriend?" Alex asked.

"Is Paige Jack's girlfriend?" Quinn asked.

"Of course, she's his girlfriend," Aspen said. "He brought flowers to her when they ate with us at Thanksgiving."

"But Mr. Grigsby brought flowers to Madge. Is Madge his girl-friend?"

Unfortunately, Madge had just taken a drink of water when this question was posed. She tried not to splutter and choke, but she ended up having a coughing fit.

"Quinn," Luke said. "Mr. Grigsby brought those flowers as a get-well gift for Madge. People do that when someone has been in the hospital. It was a very nice gesture, but it didn't mean any-thing romantic."

Madge shot Luke a grateful look, but drat the man, he winked at her.

"So, back to Paige's question," Alex said. "Jack has court tomorrow, so he doesn't need Paige in the office. She said she'd enjoy a morning with you and the ladies if you feel up to the trip. She thought you might want to go once more before the winter weather sets in and makes it difficult for you to get out."

"Well." Madge pulled herself up straighter in her chair. "I don't know why anyone thinks the winter weather will have any effect whatsoever on my ability to go to Tuesday Prayer and Share. It has never mattered a whit to me before. As to going tomorrow, sure. Let's give it a whirl."

Luke shoved his empty plate away and stretched. "I'll agree to this plan on one condition."

"As if I'm bound by whether or not you agree, Mr. Know-it-All. What's your condition?" Madge would never get used to people caring where she went and what she did. Oh, Catherine had cared. But that was different. She cared on equal footing, like one old woman looking out for the other. And Madge's nephews and their wives cared, but that was always long distance. They never poked themselves into the business of daily life. This hour by hour stuff might get old after a while. For now, though, it came with free rides, a really soft bed, and three meals that were getting better every day.

"I repeat," she said. "What's your condition?"

"You use the side door at church."

Madge used the side door. She knew she had no choice when Paige came to the door in her short purple skirt, patterned tights, and high-heeled boots. No way could she rely on Paige to support her up the front steps. Oh well, it wouldn't be so bad on a Tuesday.

She was wrong about that. When Madge opened the side door, she realized the gymnasium was totally dark. No one was in the kitchen fixing the snack for the Sunday school kids. The place felt like a cold, abandoned cavern, and she couldn't get her eyes to adjust to the dark.

They hadn't remembered the handicapped sticker, so Paige dropped her at the door and then pulled around to park in the lower lot. That left Madge to find her way forward in the nearly dark room. She pushed ahead, clapping her walker on the polished floor in front of her with each step. The echoes sounded like shouts off the walls of the Grand Canyon. Madge had never been to the Grand Canyon, but she bet it echoed this way.

"Hullo, there. Who's that?" The voice came from a back corner of the dark room.

"Madge DuPree," she yelled. "Looking for the Glory Circle sisters. Why on earth don't you have the lights on?"

A closet door swung open and the overhead light bulb revealed Elmer Grigsby with a dust rag in one hand. "Land sakes," he said. "Hold up a minute and let me get my light. You'll run into somethin'."

Madge held up. She didn't want to. Her feet twitched with the urge to keep moving. This was the second time in less than twenty-four hours that a man had told her what to do and she had done it. Her foot twitched again. Before she could give in to the urge, though, the beam of Elmer's flashlight swung across the floor. Madge saw a wide mop and bucket sitting square in front of her. To the right, a bag full of soccer balls. To the left, a rubber mat of some kind. The place was an obstacle course.

"We're cleanin' out the closets," Elmer said. "I never thought none of the ladies would come in the side door today, or I'd have flung the switches up to turn the lights on."

"Well, that was short-sighted on your part," Madge said, not even considering the pun. "We might have a visitor or something. If we're going to have a handicapped parking spot, we probably shouldn't have traps set to kill the folks once they walk in the door."

She meant it to sting, but Elmer broke into laughter. And his laugh made her smile. She stopped that as soon as it started. It surprised the daylights out of her, too. She had not expected him to have a nice laugh.

"You're right," he said. "I'll flip the lights on for Tuesdays from now on. But since they're clear yonder on the other side of the gym, you're gonna have to let me lead you across with my light today."

Madge agreed. She couldn't think of anything much more humiliating, but she knew he was right. If she stood here waiting for the old man to shuffle across the room with his rheumatism, Paige would start wondering what had happened to her. The last thing she needed was for the entire Glory Circle to come hunting and find her standing in the middle of the gym with her walker while Elmer Grigsby fumbled around in the dark.

Instead, Madge and Elmer burst through the gym doors into the bright light of the hallway at exactly the same moment as Evelyn, Grace Colby, Bess, and Erma entered the hallway from the other end. Paige came a few steps behind.

"Let there be light," Elmer said with a grin. "I think you've got it from here. I thank you for the nice little walk this morning. An unexpected pleasure."

Madge felt her neck burning and her throat getting tight as the ladies stared at her. "The lights were off," she said, more gruffly than she intended. Then she realized how risqué that sounded.

"Oh, fiddlesticks," she said as she shoved her walker forward. "Are we going to stand here gawking all morning?"

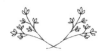

It took a while for the ladies to recover from Madge's entrance. Once they did, though, they were eager to hear how her recovery was going. She and Paige took turns telling them how well she was doing, how much Alex was helping her with therapy, and what a great idea it had been for her to stay with the Marvels for her recovery.

"But you are coming home soon, aren't you?" Bess looked at Madge with big sad eyes. "You are so far away in New York."

"It isn't New York, Bess." They usually tried to join Bess in her reality. They only corrected her if doing so would make her feel better instead of worse, and Madge thought this time it might. "Your friend, Kate, lives in New York. But I'm just over in Cherry Hills, where Catherine used to live. It isn't that far."

"Oh, visiting Catherine. Isn't that nice?" The eyes cleared, the face relaxed, and Bess returned to her normally happy self.

Madge decided to leave her there. No need to explain that Catherine had died and broken their hearts years ago. Sometimes Madge wished she could go with Bess at moments like this. She wished she could believe Catherine was just a neighborhood away instead of an entire dimension.

She didn't have much religious education, but Madge had some theories on Heaven. She had asked Pastor Cleveland once if the cartoons were true. She could not imagine Catherine wearing wings and sitting on a cloud, playing a harp. Catherine would want to be doing something to help people, even in Heaven.

Pastor Cleveland had assured Madge that although the Bible didn't give anyone a full picture of Heaven, some things were clear. We don't become angels when we die. The angels were created before the beginning of time. And whatever it looks like, it is a real place with purpose and beauty. He had said that eternal life wouldn't be much of a life if we sat around like a bunch of slugs. She liked that.

"So," Evelyn said as she brought the meeting to order, "we've been asked to take part in the Christmas tree project for the mission this year. Are we up for that?"

"Yes," Madge said. "Let's do it. We can pick out a doozy of a tree for those little kids. They never have anything for Christmas but the leftovers."

"Sounds like trouble to me," Grace said. "How are we going to transport a Christmas tree?"

"We could rent a truck," Bess said.

"Who is going to drive a truck?" Grace gave Madge a look as if daring her to volunteer.

Erma, who normally kept her opinions as close as her pennies, spoke from the corner. "Well," she said, "I'm not entirely certain of the logistics. But it seems that Madge has access to a handyman."

CHAPTER FIVE

Away in a Manger

Madge had no real intention of going back to church on Wednesday night. She still felt worn out from her Tuesday outing to Circle. Besides, the girls would have homework. She didn't want Quinn to fall behind in spelling.

By suppertime, Madge had decided on a little television, followed by an early bedtime. She was just about to say so when Aspen came into the kitchen with other ideas. She watched Alex chopping vegetables and said, "Are we eating early?"

Alex kept her eyes on the knife. "No, I'm just getting this salad done so I can concentrate on the chicken." She slid the last bit of celery into the bowl with a flourish. "Ta da! Who knew I'd learn to like cooking?"

"Yeah," Aspen turned toward Madge and made a gagging face. "Who knew?"

Not all of Alex's recipes had turned out to be entirely tasty in the weeks since she had been fired from her job as a pharmaceutical rep. While Madge thought it had been good for the girls to have her around more, they were all experiencing some culinary experiments.

"Anyway," Aspen turned back toward her mother, "I thought we'd be eating early because of the greens."

27

Alex stopped with a casserole dish in her hand. "I already chopped the greens."

"No, not eating greens. Hanging greens. Tonight is the hanging of the greens at Madge's church. I thought we were going."

"Oh, shoot." Alex let the dish slap onto the counter. She put a hand on her hip and looked around the kitchen. "You're right. I totally forgot. Looks like salad with sandwiches for supper. Go check on your sisters and make sure they have on clothing of some kind. Your dad should be home soon."

Both Aspen and Alex spun into motion before Madge had time to protest. When she finally managed to speak, Aspen had already hopped up the staircase, shouting for her sisters.

"You don't have to take me to church," she said. "I didn't plan to go. I'm pretty well tuckered out, to tell you the truth."

"Oh, but it's tradition," Alex said. "The girls have been talking about it. They heard the announcement at church, and it sounded like something magical to them."

She brushed a lettuce leaf from her arm. "The truth is, it sounded kind of magical to me. I've never been much on traditions, but this one sounded nice."

Madge stopped and considered. Nice? The hanging of the greens at Mt. Zion wasn't simply nice. When Madge started going to Mt. Zion, she mostly just attended around the edges. She arrived a little late on Sundays and disappeared the minute the last note rang out on the final hymn.

Then Catherine invited her to come and help with the hanging of the greens. On a bleak winter evening, Madge had found herself working beside Catherine, Eleanor, Erma, and Bess. She couldn't remember if Grace Colby had been there. Maybe a few others who had come and gone through the years. They decorated the sanctuary with ribbons and candles and greenery while the choir practiced carols. And they pulled Madge right into the third pew for life.

Hanging the greens hadn't been the best part, though. The best part had been the nativity. Madge had never seen such a parade for setting out nativity pieces. Members of the congregation drew lots and took turns unwrapping the large nativity figures from their velvet stoles. She had never seen anyone pray over a shepherd before setting him beside the manger. At first it seemed strange. Then it became holy.

She had drawn a wiseman that first year. She liked the look of him. Tall and dark, almost fierce in his fancy robes. So different than the shepherds who seemed to belong in the stable. She had never felt wise like this man, but she had certainly felt out of place more than once.

"So, don't you think we should go?"

Madge realized Alex had still been talking while her mind stretched back too many years. She cleared her throat as if she had been weighing all the possibilities for the evening.

"I suppose. If you really feel that way. Maybe we should."

The city had grown dark by the time they drove toward the church. Christmas lights twinkled from shop windows, and Luke turned to holiday music on the radio. The whole trip felt festive as the girls attempted to sing along. Madge tried to join in the holly jollies, but instead, she felt a bit of trepidation. She did not know entirely why.

When they pulled up to the side door of the church, Luke let the car idle and hopped out to open Madge's door. "Do you want Alex to walk you in?"

She looked at the door. Now she knew why she hadn't wanted to come tonight. The last thing she wanted was another walk in the valley of the shadow with Elmer Grigsby. If that man was lurking in a closet with a flashlight again…

"No," Madge said. "You two take care of getting the little girls unbundled. I'll meet you in the vestibule."

Luke nodded and reached for the side door. Madge blinked hard. If the room was dark, she would just barrel forward and take her chances. But it wasn't dark. The gymnasium lights were on, and the floor was clear. Madge had a straight shot to the hallway with no problems.

"There you go," said Luke. "All set?"

"Yes. All set." Madge went forward a few steps and heard the door shut behind her. She paused and listened for the sounds of anyone else in the gym or the kitchen. Or the supply closet. But all she heard was her own breathing. She pushed forward and crossed the gym floor with the walker making a loud, lonely clanking noise with each step.

When she shoved her way through the doors into the hallway, Madge expected to find people waiting. But no one was there, either. She moved on along the hall. She hardly realized she was speeding up until she felt her breath coming faster. She tried to make herself slow down, but she realized she had gotten used to the commotion of other people around all the time. Maybe she didn't like all this solitude.

With relief, Madge rounded the corner and came into the wide vestibule. People milled about, hanging up coats, chatting about the weather, chasing small children underfoot. And there, on the far side by the door, stood the Marvels.

Baby Grace saw Madge and let out a little squeal as if it had been years since they shared a rocking chair. She ran across the room with the signature ramble of a toddler. Aspen came behind to prevent a collision, and the rest of the family followed. After a few nonsensical chatterings, they all turned and started toward the sanctuary, where the real work would soon begin.

"Hello, Sister Madge." Pastor Cleveland stepped out from behind his ladder and gave Madge a hug. "I see you've brought plenty of help tonight, and we're going to need it. I've done something to this shoulder, and I don't know if I can get the wreath up where it belongs this year."

"Here." Luke took the wreath. "You just point me in the right direction, and I'll do the heavy lifting."

Pastor Cleveland chuckled. "Oh, you won't need me to do the pointing," he said. Then he nodded toward the Glory Circle sisters who were fluttering up the aisle like geese roused by the wind.

"Lord help us," Madge said. "They know a novice when they see one, Luke. Prepare yourself."

Luke could not have prepared for what followed. The next twenty minutes involved multiple discussions of whether the wreath should go "a little more to the left," "a smidge to the right," or "just a bit lower than you had it time before last."

In the meantime, Pastor Cleveland moved on to the important role of drawing lots for the assembling of the nativity. When the crowd finally quieted and gathered at the front, the lottery reveal began.

"Welcome to church," Pastor Cleveland said. "If you happen to be new to our tradition of setting the nativity, let me give you some history. This nativity scene once belonged to our beloved sister Catherine Benson. When her children were small, she wrote a prayer for each piece of the nativity. They took turns choosing a piece, reading the prayer, and putting it in place. The custom lasted many years in the Benson home. Eventually, though, the children and grandchildren all grew up and scattered. Sister Catherine decided not to mope about it. She bought herself a smaller set and donated this one to the church."

"Why does he call you all 'Sister'?" Aspen whispered to Madge.

"It's a polite way of calling us old ladies. Now listen up. One of us might get called to help with the nativity."

"I hope I get an angel," Aspen said.

"I'd rather get a cow," Quinn whispered.

"There's a pretty big crowd tonight," Madge said. "We might not get anything at all."

"I didn't put my name in anywhere," Aspen said suddenly.

"Don't worry." Madge crossed her arms and tried not to look too proud. "I listed all of us."

Pastor Cleveland had started talking again. "Okay, folks. I have the names all drawn here. I'm going to pick them in random order. When I call your name, you come to the front and select one of these objects wrapped in velvet. Then you can unwrap it. Once we've all gotten our assignments, we'll place the nativity and read our prayers."

Bess almost giggled when Pastor Cleveland called her name first. She lifted a shepherd from the wrapping and held him up like a trophy. Erma went next and behaved exactly as Madge would have expected. Pastor Cleveland had to tell everyone that Erma got the angel because she unwrapped it with her back to the crowd.

"Oh," he said as he lifted another slip of paper. "This isn't rigged, I promise, but this one is my dad, Elmer Grigsby."

Madge hadn't known Elmer was sitting behind her, but now she felt the pew shake as he gripped it to stand. Instead of shuffling out into the aisle, though, he spoke. "I beg yer pardon," he said, "but if the rules allow, I'd like to pass my turn to the person of my choice. I've already had the privilege another year."

"Well," Pastor Cleveland said. "I don't think anyone has ever asked such a thing before." He paused for a moment and then looked down at the third pew where the rest of the Glory Circle sisters sat in their usual position. Madge didn't think he was asking for official permission, but possibly for some moral support.

"Sounds good to me," she said. She looked at Grace Colby, who nodded with her usual scowl.

"Good, then, Pops. Who do you choose to represent you at the manger?"

"Miss Quinn Marvel, if you please."

Quinn stood like a woman accepting a presidential nomination and squeezed out over the knees of several Glory Circle sisters. She stopped in the middle of the aisle and turned. "Thank you, Mr. Grigsby," she said. "I've never done a nativity before."

Then she strode to the front of the church, let her hand swirl above the table full of wrapped figures for a few seconds, and finally picked up a heavy bundle and held it with both hands.

"Maybe you better help," Pastor Cleveland said to his dad.

Elmer moved a little more quickly than he had when he escorted Madge into the church. He took the bundle in his gnarled hands and waited while Quinn pulled away the blue velvet. "I got the cow," she said with a grin.

Madge wondered if a hoof might have been peeking out of that velvet somewhere. But it didn't matter. She liked seeing Quinn happy. The scene suddenly took her back to the first Christmas season with Elmer Grigsby in their church.

He had only been dried out from the drink a little while, and he was shaky when he walked. Madge remembered clearly that she had drawn the angel that year, and Elmer had drawn the donkey. She still didn't know what had possessed her to make a trade at the last second. Somehow, she had just wanted Elmer to have something a little closer to heaven than earth on his first time.

"Paige Rosedale," Pastor Cleveland interrupted Madge's thoughts, and she whirled in her seat. At least, she tried to whirl. She couldn't accomplish a full turn anymore. Instead, she twisted the best she could and saw Paige and Jack sitting toward the back.

"I'm sorry," Paige said with a wave. "I can't win. I didn't enter. I'm just visiting."

"Well, someone entered you, Miss Rosedale, because I'm holding your name right here." Pastor Cleveland held up the slip of paper. "And I think once you've attended Tuesday morning Prayer and Share more than three times, you lose visitor status."

Everyone laughed, and Paige stood. While she walked forward, Pastor Cleveland said, "And the next name is an actual visitor we are most happy to welcome to our tradition. You might as well come up with her, Mr. Oakley."

"Whoa," Jack held up both hands. Before he could state his objection, Luke grabbed his arm.

"Get up there, man. Don't ruin all my hard work. I put your name in twenty-five times." Again the laughter until Jack joined Paige and picked up the final bundle. Together, they unwrapped the figures of Joseph and Mary.

"Uh, your Honor," Jack said. "I think this deal was fixed."

"Quite possibly," Pastor Cleveland said. "But you are sentenced to carrying it out or else you have to help the Glory Circle sisters decorate the Sunday school rooms later."

Madge caught herself smiling several times as the scene unfolded. Camels and wise men, shepherds and sheep. When it was Quinn's turn to place her cow in the manger, she read from her card in a strong voice. The prayer was something about letting these gentle animals teach us to be humble and gentle, too. Madge had never liked that one. She had milked a cow more times than she wanted to count. There was nothing gentle about the old heifer that used to kick over her bucket.

Madge watched Elmer and Quinn congratulate each other on their good job while one of the young men placed the donkey. She might have stared longer, but Paige stepped forward with the virgin mother. Madge could hear the tremble in Paige's voice as she read the prayer. She made a note with the Almighty about that girl.

Jack took his turn next, and he stumbled some over the prayer. They were pretty big words about responsibility. Madge thought he ended up doing well for a guy who would rather play video games than practice law. Luke claimed Jack was turning his games into some kind of company, but she couldn't understand it.

"Now," said Pastor Cleveland, "in keeping with tradition, the baby Jesus is always placed by the youngest child in attendance. For a few years now that has been Catherine's great-granddaughter, Kate, but they are in Colorado this year. So, let's see who is our youngest this evening."

Everyone looked around at the children in the room, and it didn't take long for glances to settle on Alex holding baby Grace. "Well, well, well," Pastor Cleveland said. "I'd say this is providential. If we don't have Sister Catherine's grandbaby, we have one of Madge's little ones."

Madge blinked. She should have realized Grace would be the youngest child in the room. But she didn't belong to Madge, not really. And yet, she did. More completely than anything Madge could have ever imagined.

Alex walked forward with Grace and accepted the final bundle. Luke came from the back and helped her unwrap it and put it in Grace's chubby little hands.

"Lord help them," Madge said under her breath. "They are so clueless." She didn't mean about nativity traditions, but she figured the Almighty knew that.

Someone in the back started singing "Away in a Manger," and soon, the whole crowd had joined in. Madge dared to hum along on a few bars. Once the crèche had been completed, people scattered out to various corners to finish up little tasks. Madge wandered over toward Paige, who was twirling ribbon for Christmas eve candles. "That was something," Madge said.

"Something tricky." Paige grinned, though.

"So, is Jack your boyfriend now?" The voice belonged to Aspen, who had come up beside Madge. She took a piece of ribbon and started twirling it, too.

Paige kept her eyes on the candle. "Well, we haven't used those words, but we are spending time together, exploring the possibilities."

"So," Aspen said, "you and Jack are dating?"

"Yes, we are going on dates."

"We called that courting back in my day," Madge said. "A young man like Jack would ask permission to call upon a young lady like Paige, and then they would be courting. Completely different rules in those days."

"Better or worse?" Paige asked.

Madge examined a piece of ribbon. "Just different," she said.

"What did you do when you went courting?" Aspen asked.

Madge looked at the ceiling as if the answer from a hundred years ago might be hovering there. "I have no idea," she said. "It didn't exactly go that way for me."

The silence suddenly felt loud and uncomfortable. Madge determined to break it. "Courtship between a man and a woman, like many other things, is a total mystery to me. I wouldn't have the foggiest notion where to start if I was in Paige's shoes right now." She looked down at Paige's boots with spiky heels. "And I'd fall off them and break my other hip."

CHAPTER SIX

The Words of My Mouth

On Thursday morning, Alex got a call to substitute teach at Aspen's school, so the activity level in the kitchen rose. Just as Alex had the last backpack snagged, Aspen shouted, "We can't go yet. We haven't read the calendar."

Madge thought Alex might have rolled her eyes at the statement, but she stopped in the middle of the kitchen and motioned for Aspen to read. Madge couldn't remember when this became part of the morning ritual. Only recently, she felt sure. Might be the only Bible the girls heard outside of church, so she was glad Aspen had clamped onto the idea.

"Let the words of my mouth, and the meditation of my heart, be acceptable in thy sight, O Lord, my strength, and my redeemer," Aspen read.

Not exactly the morning pick-me-up Madge had in mind. Words had gotten her into trouble more than once.

"Okay, let's go." Alex waved and turned toward the garage.

Aspen grabbed her backpack, tucked the calendar back on the shelf, and yelled, "Psalm 19:14, in case anyone cares." As she ran past Madge's chair, Aspen dropped a sudden kiss on the top of Madge's head. "Thanks for the calendar," she said as she dashed out the door.

Madge sat back, rather shocked at the sudden splurt of emotion. Aspen didn't kiss people. At least, Madge had never seen her show that kind of affection. Well, maybe to Grace in the baby days. Nothing beyond that, though.

She was still thinking about the working of the teenage mind when the doorbell rang. It seemed to take forever to make her way to the door with her walker and the usual morning stiffness. Paige waved from the porch, but she looked slightly frozen when she stepped inside.

"Sorry," Madge said. "Haven't gotten my speed back yet."

"No problem. I just wanted to drop in on my way downtown. I have a little something for you."

Madge looked at the small handbag slung over Paige's shoulder. Little seemed like an apt description. "You want some coffee? I expect we have half a cup left in the pot."

"No thanks. I really did want to give you this. But let's sit down so you don't wear out."

Madge agreed and led the way to the family room where she and Paige sat on the sofa. Paige pulled a folded sheet of paper from her jacket pocket and talked as she unfolded it. "When I got home last night, I kept thinking about what you said, that you wouldn't have any idea where to start if a man came courting."

Madge didn't like the sound of this conversation.

"I know I'm jumping in early," Paige said. "But just in case, someday, a nice gentleman caller would happen to drop in and express an interest, I thought you could be prepared." She handed Madge a sheet of paper with a bold heading that read, "Fifty Conversation Starters for First Dates."

"What on earth…"

Before Madge could finish her question, Paige jumped in. "I know that seems silly, but it's a great idea. Lots of my friends have used things like this when they were starting out in a relationship that felt a little awkward. One of my friends used this list and married the guy. It does work. I promise."

"Well, I don't know what you mean by works, because I'm not looking for a date, let alone a husband." Madge stood and gripped her walker. "I swear, a man brings one little bouquet of get-well flowers and the whole world goes insane. I'm not the least bit interested in conversation starters, and I've got all the conversation stoppers I need. I know you thought you were helping, but heavens to Betsy, what an idea. I think I need some water."

"I'll get it," Paige said. "I'm sorry, Madge. I guess I misunderstood the situation. I certainly didn't mean to upset you. Stay right there; I'll get you some water."

"Well, I would hope you misunderstood," Madge said. "Of all the ideas. Who dreams up such poppycock? Last thing I need is a man to clutter up my life." While she rattled on at Paige, who had disappeared into the other room, Madge discreetly folded the offending paper and tucked it into the pocket of her sweater.

Paige came back with water in a few seconds and Madge took a couple of sips. They sat in silence, listening to the tick of the clock in the next room. Madge rested one shoulder against the cold leather of the sofa and wondered why a person would ever think such a thing was comfortable. Sofas should be warm and soft. This one needed an afghan over it. Maybe she should get one if they were going to sit here much longer.

"So, I guess you noticed I've been seeing Jack. Outside the office, I mean."

Yep, she definitely needed an afghan. Madge glanced around the room but didn't see anything to take the chill off her back. She sat straighter to pull away from the cold leather.

"I'm sorry. Are you uncomfortable, Madge? Is your hip hurting?"

"No, I'm fine. I just don't like this sofa much."

Paige stood and walked to the foyer. Madge heard the door of the closet open and close before Paige returned with a huge quilt.

"I have just the thing," Paige said. "I know it isn't modern of me, but I've never liked leather. I think sofas should be homey."

She tossed the quilt over the back of the sofa and tucked the ends under so everything looked neat. "There you go. Try that."

Madge leaned back. "Better. Definitely better."

"Good. I don't want to wear you out." She ran her hand along the stitching on the quilt before speaking again. "But I wanted you to know about Jack, because you're responsible for all this."

"Me?" Madge tried to look innocent, although she had tried to drop a few hints to the fellow now and then.

"Yes. Remember that day you stormed into Jack's office and tricked him into hiring you as a nanny for the Marvels?"

"You mean the day I offered my services to a family in need?"

"Yes, that day," Paige said. "That day changed my life. Until then, Jack had only seen me as office staff. But you kept putting other ideas into his head."

"Well, maybe a hint now and then." Madge tried not to feel smug, but she liked the idea that her words had made a difference. She always thought they could.

"And then when you fell, and we all spent the night in the hospital, and everything was so scary…"

"I'm glad I could arrange some drama to bring the two of you together." Madge spoke with a bit of a growl, but she didn't mean it that way. She still had nightmares occasionally about lying on the icy sidewalk, waiting for the ambulance. And the whole surgery experience was something she never wanted to repeat again.

"I'm sorry," Paige said. "I know this all sounds terribly selfish. I just wanted to say that I know you've been pulling for me all along, and it's finally working. Jack and I are seeing each other in a personal way. And we are talking about things besides work."

Madge scooted around on the sofa, still trying to get comfortable. "About time," she said. "For a lawyer, that boy is pretty clueless."

Paige stood and grabbed her coat from the nearby chair. "In some ways. But, in other ways, he is brilliant. You wait and see, Madge, he is going to surprise everyone."

CHAPTER SEVEN

Sweets for the Sweet

Snow fell again Sunday morning. Madge thought surely the family would give up any idea of church. She hated to admit it, but she kind of hoped they would call a snow day. She still didn't like all the hustle and bustle of taking a whole crew to church. She felt worn out by the time everybody found their shoes and scrambled for coats.

Quinn had started the church tradition when her parents were living apart. One morning, when Paige offered to drive Madge to church, Quinn decided to tag along. It caused quite a stir when Madge DuPree walked into the church house with a child in tow.

She thought of that again while she struggled to pull warm socks on over her stiff toes. She hoped she would never forget the picture of the ladies in the third pew staring at Quinn, all dolled up in her patent leathers and her little skirt. Madge had nothing to do with the clothes. Quinn had dressed herself. But nobody knew that. For all they knew, Madge had become a super-nanny in her old age.

Thinking of Quinn seemed to draw the girl straight into the room, because she suddenly appeared, fully dressed and ready to go. No patent leather this time. She wore warm boots and thick tights with her little sweater and skirt.

41

"Need help?" Quinn didn't wait for a response. She knelt by the chair and tugged Madge's sock the last few inches up her ankle.

"Thanks." Madge tried to sound nice, but she couldn't muster it, not even for Quinn. Nobody could be nice about needing help with their socks.

"Is that what you're wearing?"

Madge looked down at her gray sweater and her navy pants. "It's what I'm wearing right now, isn't it?"

"But to church. Is that what you're wearing to church?"

"Well, it's snowing…"

"She isn't wearing that to church." Aspen popped into the room, flipping her long hair over her shoulder the way teenagers did on that television show she liked to watch. Madge wondered if she had been practicing in the mirror. It was a pretty good technique.

"The gray doesn't bring out the best in her eyes. I'll get the light blue sweater. It will be warmer anyway." She be-bopped into the closet as if she owned the place while Madge sat wondering where her life had gone.

"And a necklace," Quinn yelled. "Does she have a necklace?"

"She doesn't have a necklace," Madge yelled toward Aspen. Then she said to Quinn, "I'm not some kind of fancy lady who wears jewelry to church. I'm just plain Madge, and we're gonna keep it that way, got it?"

"Got it," Quinn said. "But you should wear the blue sweater."

Aspen whirled back into the room at exactly that moment and flipped the sweater around with a "Ta-da!" as if it were a prize at the county fair.

"Fine. I'll wear the sweater. Now get out of here and go eat some breakfast."

The girls scattered. While Madge changed into the blue sweater, she continued to grumble about being pushed around and told what to do like a toddler. At the last minute, she reached into the drawer beside her bed and pulled out a long wooden box. She selected a small silver pin with fake sapphires in the shape of a flower and attached it to the sweater.

The weather did make for a smaller crowd than usual. Madge had to admit she was grateful for the short walk to the side door of the church. The lights were on, and the path was clear. She had wanted to ditch the walker today in favor of the new cane Alex brought home. But snow and slick sidewalks seemed a poor time to experiment.

So, she scooted her walker across the gym floor as fast as she could and then down the hallway until she rounded the corner to the empty foyer. The family came tumbling through the doorway seconds later. Boots, scarves, mittens, and coats soon flew in all directions.

Pastor Cleveland met them as they entered the sanctuary. "Glad to see some hearty souls who braved the weather," he said. "I'm afraid most of our Glory Circle sisters didn't dare get out in this. It's coming down pretty hard and supposed to keep it up all day."

"Well, we wouldn't have wanted Madge to do it if she were on her own," Alex said as she tucked her arm under Madge's. "But she is perfectly safe with us."

Madge hoped those words held true, because Elmer Grigsby was approaching. He had a look of determination on his face, and he was walking straight for them. Madge pulled herself up, stood straight, and gripped the walker for support.

"Mornin' all," Elmer said as he walked by.

"Morning, Mr. Grigsby," the girls all said in unison.

"It's good to see you," Alex said over her shoulder. She whispered toward Madge and said, "I like that man. I hear he has quite a story."

"Who doesn't?" Madge pushed forward and nudged Aspen. She wanted to get to her seat and stop all this lollygagging about. No need to chatter like a bunch of school kids in the hallway.

The third pew sat empty. She hadn't expected Bess. No one would want Bess to get out in this weather. And Erma's daughter sometimes convinced her to stay put when the temperature dropped. The daughter would have called Erma first thing this morning and warned her about the roads and the steps and the complications of broken bones.

Madge rubbed her aching leg. Erma's daughter might have a point. She glanced down the empty row again. She couldn't imagine the weather keeping Evelyn and Tom away, though. Tom drove through all kinds of weather. And they were always the first ones here. She hoped neither of them were sick. They all took it for granted that Evelyn would be in charge of things and that she would always be around. She seemed so healthy and so young. But now, sitting alone in the pew, Madge realized those things were probably the direct result of Miss Clairol and the good cut of expensive clothes.

Madge's critique was interrupted when someone shoved into her. The left side of the pew might be empty, but the right side was crowding up fast. The little girls smooshed closer together as Jack and Paige joined the Marvel family. Madge scooted down, which was not an easy task, and made room. Peyton jumped up, because she felt too crowded, and landed on the other side of Madge. Everyone had just stopped moving when Grace pushed past all the knees and held up her arms to be lifted onto Madge's lap.

"Oh, no, Gracie." Alex reached over everyone and tried to stop her. "Madge can't hold you. Her lap is sore."

"It's okay," Madge said. "I think I can do it today. Help me lift her."

And so, Madge sat in the third pew, holding baby Grace, with Quinn snuggled on one side and Peyton on the other. The last stragglers filtered into the room, followed by Pastor Cleveland and Elmer Grigsby. They were talking about something and smiling as they walked down the aisle. Elmer broke off and sat alone in the second pew while Pastor Cleveland went into the pulpit.

Madge felt a small twinge. She had sat alone in church most of her life. Even when the pew was full, she had always been alone. Until now. She felt just a tiny bit sorry that Elmer had to sit that way.

The trip had taken more out of her than she realized. The warm building, the soft child on her lap, and the comforting sound of Pastor Cleveland's voice all worked against her. Madge dozed through a good portion of the sermon. She didn't think she had snored. But she jerked awake more than once.

Afterward, Luke and Jack both told Pastor Cleveland what a great job he had done and how much they liked a specific story about some football player. Madge hadn't even heard that part. So, she leaned down and buttoned Grace's sweater to get out of the conversation.

"Can the little ladies have a Christmas sweet?"

Madge jumped at the sound of Elmer Grigsby at her elbow. She straightened and looked at him. He held out his hand with four fancy, wrapped chocolates.

"I suppose," Madge said. "That shouldn't ruin their lunch."

Elmer grinned and revealed his offering to the girls. They each thanked him and then gobbled the candy as if they had never been fed. Even Aspen had a smile in return for the candy. Grace giggled and ran down the aisle, waving her wrapper, which resulted in a race for everyone else.

"I'll get them," Aspen said.

Madge watched the ruckus for a moment before she turned to thank Mr. Grigsby. She found him still smiling and holding out another chocolate.

"I saved the best for last," he said.

"No, thank you."

"It's just a bite. Might hold you over till dinner."

"You mean lunch?"

"I mean whatever you call the meal you'll have when you leave here. A woman recovering from an injury ought to keep her strength up."

Madge huffed. But she took the candy. While she unwrapped it, Elmer reached into his pocket and pulled out another.

"I did keep one for m'self, too, because I know most folks don't like to eat alone."

She could not help herself. Madge smiled while she took the first bite. They stood eating candy for a few seconds. She didn't want to admit how good it tasted. This wasn't dime store candy. It was something exotic.

"My boy gets this from Chicago," Elmer said. "Fancy stuff."

"I guess."

"I thought it'd be a good way to introduce the next subject."

Suddenly, the candy didn't taste so good. Madge tried to swallow and breathe at the same time. She wanted very much to walk away and not hear "the rest of the story" as Paul Harvey used to say. For days now, she had seen this train coming. She had felt it in her bones that Elmer Grigsby was going to do something foolish. Yet, she had no idea how to stop him, how to go back to the place where they just exchanged a polite word now and then.

But Elmer didn't seem the least bit bothered by the scene either. He didn't seem to care if the little girls wandered back into the conversation or if Paige Rosedale stood within earshot. He looked for all the world like a man enjoying his fancy chocolate before giving a pleasant speech.

"I'd like permission to call on you," he said with no preliminaries. "Keepin' company, I think they call it."

Marge swallowed the last bite of candy. "Well, they don't call it that anymore." She pulled a tissue from her pocket and wiped her sticky fingers.

"Courtin' then. I'd like to come a courtin'." Elmer stood with one hand in his pocket, head cocked, and an easy grin on his face. As if he enjoyed this conversation.

"Oh, good grief, man. Have you lost your mind? We're a couple of old people with one foot in the grave. What on earth do you want to go doing a thing like that for?" She paused long enough for him to apologize and walk away. When he didn't, Madge said. "I think they call it *going out*."

"All right then. Let's go out."

Madge frowned. "I don't think so."

Elmer didn't wilt. He didn't even step back a little. Instead, he grinned even wider. Madge wondered how on earth he had kept all his teeth, and in such good shape, too, with all his hard living.

"We don't need to go out," he said. "I'll just come to call. Friday night around seven. Okay with you?"

Madge blinked. "I suppose. Just this once. But it has to be a secret. Don't you go blabbing to anyone that you're coming to see me."

"I won't blab," he said. "My boy will know. He already knows."

"Your boy? You mean Pastor Cleveland?" Madge grabbed her heart at the thought of the pastor thinking she was some floozy out to snag his old dad the minute he became sober and respectable.

"Yep, that's the one. He thinks it's dandy. But you know preachers are sworn to secrecy. You can trust him."

CHAPTER EIGHT

Whistle While You Work

Madge did not sleep a full hour on Sunday night. She was sure of that. All day Monday she worried and dithered about the house, unable to concentrate on anything. She wished Alex would run errands or something so she could just sit down and think. She wanted to think about how to get out of this mess she had agreed to on Sunday morning.

Elmer Grigsby could not come to call. He must be stopped. Madge had done quite well without a man in her life for nearly sixty years. Well, longer than that. She had never had a decent man in her life, other than her father. He wasn't a bad man, but he paid little attention to her. He thought girls were useless until they were old enough to cook, and she never liked the kitchen.

Now, all crippled up and dependent on people for every little thing, she certainly did not need the arm of some man. She would stand up and say so.

Madge finally broached the subject with Alex when they were on the last of the leg exercises for the day. "A strange thing happened on Sunday," she said.

"Yes?"

"Pastor Cleveland's dad, Elmer Grigsby, has evidently gotten the idea he should pay me some kind of visit. Calling on the sick,

I suppose. Maybe he's taken that on to help out his dad."

Alex kept on lifting and stretching Madge's left leg. "That's nice," she said.

"No, it isn't nice." Madge jerked her leg free. "It's silly. I don't want him to come."

"Why not?" Alex reached for the right leg. "He seems harmless, rather sweet."

"A man who has lived as hard as Elmer Grigsby could not be called sweet. And I don't want him around." She said the last part with enough emotion that Alex stopped working the leg and sat back.

"If this is bothering you so much," she said, "you should call it off. Why don't you call the church office and ask them to take you off the visitation schedule?"

Madge rubbed her thigh and looked down toward her feet. "Well, it isn't an official church visit exactly."

"Oh, I see. It's a personal visit, then? From a gentleman caller?"

"Absolutely not." Madge grabbed the arms of her chair and attempted to push herself up and walk away. Instead of stomping out in a grand exit though, she fumbled and nearly tipped over. Once she managed to stand, she said, "I think he just likes to talk, and he's looking for someone his own age. He might as well look around for a spit-and-whittle club, and I'm going to tell him so."

"Okay," Alex said. "You don't have to see him. You could leave him a note when you go to Circle on Tuesday."

Madge agreed it was a brilliant plan. She spent all afternoon working on a letter with the perfect combination of gratitude for the offer and insistence that it couldn't happen. She filled a waste basket with failed attempts. When she finally reached the last paper, Madge gave up and wrote, "Don't bother to come calling. I'm not receiving." She hesitated for a moment and then added "Sorry."

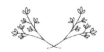

Madge's resolve held out until Paige dropped her at the side door of the church on Tuesday morning. She had the note in her coat pocket, ready to shove it into Elmer's hand the minute she saw him. Then he opened the door and offered her that grin.

"I thought you might have a bit of trouble with the door to-day," he said. "It was froze when I got here. So, I waited to help you in."

"You didn't need to do that," she said. She wanted to sound a little more growly than grateful, but she failed. Why did the man make her act like a schoolgirl? What had gotten into her? She let go of the walker and tried to reach into her pocket, but she felt suddenly shaky.

"Here," Elmer said. "Hold steady now." He grabbed onto the walker and waited for Madge to return her grip. "Are your shoes slick? I could wipe 'em down." When he reached for the rag in his back pocket, Madge found her resolve.

"Oh, for Heaven's sake," she said. "Leave my shoes alone. I'm not helpless, you know. I can get myself through doors and down hallways without somebody hovering over me. The minute this snow melts, I'm throwing this contraption away and moving on to a cane. By spring, I'll be coming up the front steps again. So, you can stop hanging around waiting for me like I'm some invalid."

Elmer straightened up, tucked the rag back into his pocket, and smiled. Madge wanted to scream. Why couldn't she make the man mad?

"Do you smile all the time?" she asked.

"I do. These days. Time was I never smiled all year."

"Well, quit smiling at me," she said. "I've nothing to do with it."

"Can't seem to quit," he said, still grinning. "Maybe I've got so many stored up after all these years I just gotta get 'em out."

"Well, as long as you understand it's nothing to do with me," she said again.

He nodded and pulled the smile back a fraction. "Oh, I understand. I see it all as clear as morning sun through those pretty windows."

"You mean stained glass?"

"I reckon. I just know they're one of the prettiest things I've ever seen. You can see the whole story drawn out in those colors."

Madge paused. She didn't remember the last time she had even noticed the church windows. Back in the day, she had taken her turn on cleaning days and sometimes washed them. But, right now, she couldn't even remember a single scene.

"Well, that's good," she finally said. "We're clear then."

"We are," Elmer said. "I'll get back to my cleanin', and you better move on into the other room where it's warm."

Madge moved. As she turned the corner, she heard Elmer start to whistle. She didn't remember ever hearing a man whistle like that before. Easy, happy, right on key. She didn't recognize the tune, but it sent some kind of feeling through her soul. She stood in the hallway and listened to Elmer whistle until she felt her shoulders relaxing. Then she gave herself a scold and scooted forward.

Circle dragged on forever. Evelyn asked for a treasurer's report. They didn't spend so much time on business most days, but they had Christmas baskets to fill, and Evelyn thought they might be short a few things. So, Erma gave the report. And that was a production.

First, she had to arrange her glasses differently on her nose. Then she had to decide whether to stand or to sit. She opened her small notebook, took a pencil from her purse, and considered the figures listed there for long enough that Madge felt sure the interest rate at the bank had changed three times.

Finally, Erma looked up and spoke. "Once we pay the bill at the market, we will have a grand total of $97.32." She sat with a thump.

"That won't be enough," Evelyn said. She tapped the table with her long, red nails, and patterned lights from her diamond bracelet danced across the ceiling. "If we want to include a few small toys, that certainly won't be enough."

"We should pass the basket," Erma said.

Madge followed the rest of the ladies and reached for her purse while Erma went to the cabinet to fetch their collection basket. She handed it to Evelyn, who handed it to Grace Colby. Madge watched the basket make its journey around the room, picking up a few bills here and a fistful of coins there. She had meant to grab a few ones from her purse, but when the basket arrived, she realized to her horror that she was holding a twenty.

She looked up to see Erma smiling at her. A real smile like Madge had not seen on her solemn friend in a long time. She dropped the twenty into the basket and shrugged. She could afford to be generous just now. Her needs were all met at the Marvel house. They wouldn't even let her pitch in for groceries while she recouped. Once she paid for her medicine this month and the few bills for upkeep on her own empty place, she should still have a good sum left over.

"Now," Evelyn said, "who wants to go along with us on Saturday to buy gifts for the children?"

Gifts for the children. Madge wilted against the back of her chair. Gifts for the children. Why hadn't she thought of that? She would still be living with the Marvels at Christmas, and the little girls would expect gifts. That would blow the budget by a mile. Not to mention the aggravation of figuring out how to go shopping. She didn't think the grocery store delivery system would work for Christmas gifts.

This being an invalid was cramping her style. Not to mention the fact that her Oldsmobile was still in the shop and her driver's license was still suspended by the judge.

Madge thought the man had gone a little strong over her small incident with the ice cream truck. No one had gotten hurt. The company probably had great insurance to repair the truck and replace the ice cream that had melted on the street.

"So, Saturday then?" Evelyn's voice interrupted Madge's thoughts. After that business was finished, they moved on to the actual share portion of Prayer and Share. Everyone had something to say today. Lots of Tuesdays were fairly quiet at this point. Today, though, everyone had a story to tell about this ailment or that surgery or another crisis somewhere in the family. Madge skipped when her turn came. She wasn't in the mood to blather.

After sharing came praying. Some of those women could bend the ear of the Almighty like nobody's business. Madge felt sure she dozed off during a few of the petitions. But she always said, "Amen," and trusted God to do the rest.

Finally, ten minutes after twelve, Evelyn banged the gavel and called the meeting adjourned. Madge always wanted to chuckle about that. They weren't a true organization with bylaws and rules of order. They didn't need a gavel to tell them when to start and stop. But Evelyn liked the tidiness of the idea. So, they used the gavel.

Madge was struggling to pull her handbag onto her shoulder so she could hold the walker when Bess approached. "I heard you talking to that nice Mr. Grigsby when I was getting a glass of water this morning," she said.

Madge jerked around, and her handbag crashed to the floor. Bess bent to pick it up. "Oh, my," she said. "Your bag is so heavy. How do you carry it?"

Madge trusted this would change the subject, so she said, "It's my favorite one, though. Holds everything plus an umbrella and extra gloves. Do you remember Catherine gave it to me for my birthday one year?"

"How nice," Bess said. "I miss Catherine. I'll be glad when she gets back from Florida in the spring."

Madge didn't know how to answer. Catherine had not gone to Florida. Bess obviously didn't remember the funeral. But Madge still could barely talk about Catherine without getting teary. So, she changed the subject again.

"Have you gotten any Christmas cards yet?"

"Oh, yes," Bess said, and her eyes sparkled. "The one from Kate in New York is covered in glitter and has a picture of roses in the snow. Imagine that. They must have some kind of magical soil in New York."

"Yes," Madge said. "They must."

"We spent that summer together," Bess said. "Kate and I. Down in Branson at my cottage. Do you remember?"

Madge remembered. She remembered that Bess had disappeared from the nursing home in Ohio where her nephew had stashed her. It took them weeks to trace her to the family cabin in the Ozarks. And when they found her, they discovered the young writer named Nora. Although, Bess called her Kate because she liked the name better. The whole thing could have been a tragedy, but instead, it had turned out to bless both women. Madge still shook her head over the whole thing.

"Well, then," Bess said. "I better catch up with Erma. She's driving me home. You have a lovely time with your Mr. Grigsby when he comes to call."

Madge touched Bess's arm. "Oh, no, you misunderstood," she said. "First, he is not my Mr. Grigsby, and second, I've told him not to call."

"That would be a mistake," Bess said. "He's a keeper." She marched out the door and down the hallway then, leaving Madge standing alone. She didn't feel entirely worried, because no one would believe Bess if she repeated this gossip. They would assume she was her usual, confused self. And yet, Madge couldn't shake the feeling that she had been caught smoking behind the barn.

Just as her head started to clear over the whole mess, the man himself stepped to the doorway. "I could be arrivin' about six on Friday if you think your family would enjoy company for supper."

Madge stared at Elmer for a few seconds. She could still hear the memory of his whistle. "Six will be fine," she said.

CHAPTER NINE

A Time for Pie

Madge heard Luke shouting from the garage when he pulled in Wednesday night. She couldn't tell what he was saying to the girls, but it had "hurry up" in the tone. He stomped into the kitchen and shook like a dog coming in from the rain. Madge thought Alex was about to scold him for the snow flying everywhere, but Quinn and Peyton came through the laundry room seconds later and stole the attention. They had found a Winnie the Pooh blanket somewhere in the back of the car and wrapped themselves up in it together. Now, they walked like a Pooh taco.

Madge felt her heart thudding. The blanket and the snow sent her flying back to that day in October. An early snowstorm had swept in, surprising everyone. Jack drove her to get the girls after school. They had made the secret arrangement when Jack learned about her license being suspended. Paige normally did the school runs, but Jack had shown up that day.

The sidewalk had been icy at the daycare. Jack carried baby Grace. The wind shrieked. Madge fell.

She did not often think of that day. Some of the memories were so muddled that she wasn't sure what was true and what was a dream. But in this moment, she remembered the cold seeping into her broken hip as she lay on the sidewalk waiting for the ambulance. She also remembered how Jack had covered her with his coat. And that Aspen had gone into the daycare and come back with every blanket that could be spared. Including a Winnie the Pooh.

"Madge?" Alex pulled her back from the sidewalk at Toddle Time.

"Yes?"

"I said that you shouldn't walk around the kitchen until I have time to get this snow mopped up. The floor will be slick."

"Right. I'll go to my room and get out of the way." She stood with some effort and started toward the hallway. As she walked, she muttered to herself about being useless and in the way. Another problem for Luke and Alex, as if they didn't make enough of those on their own.

Just as Madge stepped into her room, a small head peaked around the door frame. "Want to do spelling?" Quinn said.

Madge dropped into her chair. "You bet," she said. "Bring out *Quinn's Magic Word Search*, and let's see what this week brought us."

Suddenly, the thought of being helpless vanished. The word search had been her idea. When she realized Quinn could do a puzzle faster than the average bear, Madge had wondered if the game could help her learn to spell.

The Glory Circle sisters had come to the rescue. They created a blank puzzle grid, and every week Madge scrambled up the words from Quinn's third-grade spelling list. The child had become a star speller.

Quinn curled up at Madge's feet and produced the spelling list. Madge took a blank grid from the drawer and began scrambling words. While Madge worked, Quinn flipped through another book from her bag.

Normally, a puzzle would calm Madge's nerves, whether she was solving it or creating it. Not today. Today her thoughts felt as mixed-up as the letters she scattered across the page. No matter how she tried to avoid thoughts of a man coming to call, they danced around in her brain. She wondered if a person could call in sick for something like this. Maybe she could tell Alex her arthritis was flared up and she needed to stay in bed. Or she could get the flu. All she had to do was run a little hot water over her thermometer and the whole thing would be cancelled.

Unfortunately, Madge never found her thermometer. The calendar crept toward Friday with a relentless pace. Nothing that happened in the household offered to change the itinerary. On Friday morning, the clock suddenly speeded up beyond imagining. Madge found herself standing in front of the mirror at 5:45 p.m. staring at the old woman who looked back.

"You are a ninny," she said to the reflection in the blue sweater. "You have done some silly things in your life, but this tops them all. Now, you just be polite to the man and let him enjoy his supper. When you see him to the door afterward, you make it plain that this was a one-time call. No more of this nonsense."

She straightened the brooch on her sweater, patted at her hair as if she could tame the wild nest, and then shrugged. She reached for the fancy cane leaning against the wall. A lady's cane with a silver handle and pansies painted all down the length. The blue ones matched her sweater. The red ones almost matched her hair.

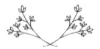

Madge heard the door knocker tap at ten minutes before six. She peeked out the family room window and saw a taxi pulling away from the curb. She felt some relief to know Pastor Cleveland hadn't driven tonight. At least she would be spared the humiliation of her pastor sitting in on the awkward evening.

Luke answered the door, and she could hear him making conversation. His tone was light, as if he enjoyed the whole thing a little too much for her comfort. Sure enough, Luke appeared in the doorway with an arm on Elmer Grigsby's shoulder.

"Look who I found at the door," he said. "This fellow claims you are expecting him. But I'll send him right on down the road if you want." Luke grinned as he spoke and so did Elmer.

"You know perfectly well he is coming for supper," Madge said. "That's why Alex has been in the kitchen since dawn."

"I hope nobody's gone to any trouble on my account," Elmer said. "I'm happy with a can of beans and the good company."

Madge crossed her arms. "Nobody eats cold beans in this house. I don't know what you bachelors are used to doing, but we put on a feed here."

"I'm sure I'll enjoy it," Elmer said. "And I'm beholden."

Luke slapped Elmer on the back and waved toward the dining room. "Let's find a seat at the table. Last time I checked the chef had things just about ready."

Madge gripped her cane and did her best to walk toward the doorway with dignity. She definitely should have practiced more. She didn't have the rhythm yet, and the effort felt jerky. Three steps in, she wobbled.

Elmer Grigsby crossed the room much faster than she would have expected for a man his age. When he reached out to steady her, Madge grabbed his hand. They stood for a second longer than necessary in that pose. She felt the warmth of his grip. Strong for a man whose knuckles showed arthritis. Yet not so firm that he made her joints ache. It was as if he knew exactly what she needed to feel stable. The thought rattled her, though, more than it comforted.

"Here ya go," he said. "Just take my arm till you get used to the new contraption."

He offered an elbow like a gentleman in tie and tails rather than a handy man in borrowed tweed. At least, she assumed it was borrowed. She didn't know when he would have ever had need of a tweed jacket with suede patches at the elbow. She hated to admit how much she liked that look.

Together, Madge and Elmer walked into the dining room where they had eaten Thanksgiving dinner only a few weeks before. Tonight, it looked like a different place. Alex and the girls had set the table with the good china, cloth napkins, and candles.

As Madge stood taking in the scene, Aspen came from the kitchen carrying a large centerpiece made of pine branches, holly berries, and silvery ribbon. She stopped when she saw Madge holding Elmer's arm.

"You look beautiful," Aspen said.

Madge pulled her arm free. "Pshaw. Now that bunch of evergreens you're holding is the beautiful thing. Where did you find it?"

"I made it," Aspen said. "Well, sort of. I got the greenery from next door. They have trees in their yard." She looked suddenly worried. "I got permission," she said. "The berries are fake. I found them with the ribbon in our Christmas stuff in the attic."

"Well, it looks mighty festive," Elmer said. He pulled out a chair and helped Madge maneuver herself into it.

Alex came into the room just then with a huge platter of something that smelled delicious. Luke followed with the salad bowl, and Quinn trooped behind him with rolls in a basket. Peyton brought up the caboose with a glass bowl that held little balls of butter. Madge was about to comment on the parade when Grace toddled from the kitchen with a bib in her hand. Everyone laughed and congratulated Grace on doing her part.

Once the clan had all gathered around the table, Luke reached out to hold hands. Madge felt a smidgen uncomfortable taking Elmer's hand at the family table. It was different than the way she had grabbed onto him to keep from falling. This was much more personal. Too personal. She thought about pulling away, but Elmer's grasp held her firm. Again, not too much pressure to make her joints throb. Solid, though. She almost liked the feel of his knobby hand against hers. She had expected his skin to be rough. Didn't men usually have rough skin? His felt tough, but not unpleasant.

Madge heard Luke say the amen and realized she hadn't pulled her hand away. She did so, but not with the jerk she had intended. Instead, she felt her fingers linger a moment. The behavior shocked her, and she immediately slapped her hands into her lap.

Elmer accepted a roll from Quinn, who had managed to snag the seat beside him. Madge thought he looked like somebody's uncle who had dropped in for a meal. Not like a man who ought to be a least a little uncomfortable under the circumstances. Instead, he talked with Luke about trucks and with Alex about going to a one-room school. "About a million years ago."

Madge didn't need to say anything during the meal because it seemed as if every member of the Marvel household wanted to learn something more about their honored guest. Or they wanted to tell him something about themselves. Or about Madge.

The little girls decided to start telling stories about the broken hip at the same time dessert appeared from the kitchen. "That isn't exactly table talk," Madge said. "I don't think Mr. Grigsby is interested in my medical history."

Alex intervened. "Maybe you and Mr. Grigsby would like to have your dessert and coffee in the family room."

"That sounds nice," Elmer said. "Though I don't know that I need any more coffee tonight. I'm gonna have trouble sleepin' for all the excitement as it is."

"No coffee for me, either," Madge said. She thought that might put an end to the infernal evening, but she was wrong.

"That pie looks mighty nice, though." Elmer nodded toward Alex. "I wouldn't turn down a bit of a slice."

CHAPTER TEN
The Best of Times

Madge didn't intend to send a panic signal across the table to Alex. Not on purpose, at least. However, when Elmer said he would be happy to take pie in the family room, Madge locked eyes with Alex.

"Well," Alex said, "maybe the girls could clear the table while Luke and I join you for some pie. And coffee. I definitely could go for some coffee."

"Sounds dandy," Elmer said. "We don't eat so fancy over at the parsonage. This is a real treat."

With that, he stood and reached over to help Madge scoot her chair away from the table. The minute she stood, Madge grabbed her cane and walked toward the next room before Elmer could offer his arm. He followed, complimenting Alex one more time on the food.

Once they were all arranged on softer chairs, Elmer spoke to the group. "Nice, mild weather we're havin'."

The others agreed.

"I don't notice it as much," Elmer said, "as when I was on my own. Weather played the dickens with me gettin' my supper sometimes. Snow was the worst. Can't push a cart through the drifts, and the lids on the dumpsters get too heavy to lift." He took a big bite of pie and sat back with a smile.

No one spoke. Madge wanted to change the subject, but she could not imagine where to take the conversation from dumpster diving. Elmer had mentioned it so casually. Like talking about the last job he had before he retired.

"That must have been hard," Alex finally said.

Elmer nodded. He didn't smile with the next words. "I don't come with much of a pedigree, that is the God's truth." He looked at Madge before he continued. "I might have amounted to something once, but I doused all that with the booze. Lost it all. My boy. My wife. My job and house. Booze is a hard master."

"What kind of work did you do?" Luke asked.

Madge felt grateful that he wanted to take the conversation somewhere positive, but she knew it was no good. She and Elmer were old, way too old to dance around the room and play games about their lives. Might as well toss it all out there on the coffee table and see if anything stood.

"My husband was a drinker," she said.

Madge thought she might have heard an audible gasp from across the room.

"Your husband?" Alex said.

"You thought I was an old maid, did you?" Madge tried to make the statement sound lighthearted, like she didn't mind, but it came out sharp.

"No," Alex said. "Not at all. I thought widowed, probably. I assumed that is why you hadn't ever mentioned Mr. DuPree."

Madge tried to decide exactly what she wanted to say about that mister. All these years of living had not softened her perspective much. She didn't want to slug him with a frying pan anymore. That was progress. They hadn't been married long enough for her to get that chance, anyway. Their whole married life lasted seven days in a smelly motel on Route 66, just outside Vegas. It had not been as glamorous as Mr. DuPree suggested when he helped her sneak out of her bedroom window one midnight.

"I was young," she finally said. "It was a long time ago. I just mentioned it to say I understand about booze."

Elmer nodded. Alex and Luke glanced at each other and then looked at the floor.

"I'm grateful," Elmer said. "More than a little grateful to your friend Catherine. They tell me she prayed for me pretty much every day for a month."

"She did," Madge said. "She didn't know it was you, of course. Just some Elmer Grigsby from the phone book. We all took turns drawing out names and praying for them a week at a time. Catherine didn't tell us she kept yours every week." Madge blinked hard to stop her watery eyes.

"So, what do you like to do for fun, Mr. Grigsby?" Alex leaned forward and hugged her knees as she spoke. Madge thought it was an awkward change of conversation, but it worked.

"Well, let's see," Elmer looked at the ceiling. "I'd have to cogitate on that a bit. Fun hasn't been on my calendar in a while."

"Cogitate," Luke said. "There's a million-dollar word."

"It's from Mr. Dickens," Elmer said. "I wasn't tryin' to put on airs. But I always liked Mr. Dickens in school. *Tale o' Two Cities*, now that is a rare one. I've not read much in the last years. My eyes are too poorly. But some things stick with you. Like the Resurrection Man who had to cogitate on a problem."

"Resurrection Man?" Madge said. "You mean Jesus?"

Elmer laughed. "No, haven't you read that one? The Resurrection Man was a grave robber."

"Good grief."

"No, it wasn't like you're thinkin'. Back in them days, a doctor had to buy up the dead bodies to study 'em. He didn't have no other way to learn about disease and surgery and the like. A Resurrection Man would dig up the grave of a body that didn't have no family. Then he'd sell it to a man of science for study. It wasn't as awful as that makes it sound."

He sat for a few moments and looked at his hands. "Time was, I'd a fit that bill about right." He looked up then. "Not as a Resurrection Man, mind you. But as one of those bodies fit only for being dug up after I died."

Madge felt the water filling her eyes again. She wasn't sure she could blink them away this time. Fortunately, Luke rescued the moment.

"Well, let's raise a forkful of pie to Saint Catherine then, shall we? She didn't know when she prayed that one day the famous Elmer Grigsby would be right here, sitting in her former parlor, eating pie, and courting Madge."

"Oh, my land," Madge said. "Nobody said anything about courting. We're just a couple of people from the same church eating supper together. Don't be making something more out of it."

She tried to sound gruff, and she tightened her shoulders to look stiff. All the while, Elmer Grigsby sat smiling on the other end of the sofa. He nodded at her as if he agreed. The smile made a liar of him, though. The man was cocky, and she couldn't imagine why. She used to think he acted shy, almost like he didn't have the right to wear good clothes or eat decent meals. She wondered when he had gotten this sudden self-confidence. She also wondered why she liked it.

"Well," Elmer said, "I 'spect I could sit here all evening and enjoy this good company. A feast for the eyes and the soul. But I reckon I ought to get along home and let you all get yer beauty sleep. Though one of you don't need it a bit."

"Can I give you a lift?" Luke spoke as he stood.

"No need," Elmer said. He rose from the sofa like a man familiar with aches and pains. He didn't groan, though, or even flinch. "I told the taxicab driver to be back about now." He looked at Madge with his best smile. "I was trustin' this thing would go well, and you wouldn't throw me out early."

"We don't throw guests out on a normal basis," Madge said. "We try to be civilized around here." She stood, too, but she couldn't stop the grimace as her knees unhinged.

Elmer reached out a hand as if to help, and she waved him away. She took a good grip on her cane and attempted to walk toward the front door with as much grace as possible. Elmer followed her, but the other two mysteriously disappeared.

Madge looked around to see if the little girls were peeking from the staircase. Evidently, they had been threatened with something dire, because no blonde heads appeared. She had been left on her own for the awkward good-byes.

They weren't awkward, though. When Madge turned back, she saw Elmer standing with his hat in his hands. He had that easy look again, as if this had been no big thing for him. She knew better.

"You have to know," he said, "that this was more than a tolerable evenin' for me."

"I expect so."

"I don't think you have any idea, truly." He looked at the hat, then back at Madge. "I've not eaten my supper in the company of a kind lady for more years than I care to remember. Longer than those two hiding in the kitchen have been alive."

Madge glanced back to see a flash of Alex jerking away from the kitchen doorway. She wanted to laugh, but the moment felt too serious.

"Well, I hope it wasn't a chore for you," she said.

"I thought it would be." Elmer seemed a little less at ease for a moment. "I expected to feel nervy and off balance."

"You didn't?"

He extended one hand as if to give hers a shake. "Not one minute," he said. "I felt like I'd stuck my feet under a fine table in my own home. Though no home I'd ever known before. It had never been nothin' like this, even at its best."

Madge accepted the handshake in silence.

"I'll say goodnight then and wait out on the stoop."

"Oh, it's too cold for that."

"Nah. I've slept all night in worse than this many a time. Besides, I'm plenty warm on the inside."

With that, he opened the door and stepped out with a little hop. Madge wondered if the man was dancing a jig on the front porch. She decided not to look.

CHAPTER ELEVEN

Kindred Spirits

Madge didn't bother getting dressed for church on Sunday. She had peeked outside during a midnight trek to the bathroom. Snow already clogged the street. More was falling, and the wind had picked up. Evidently, the snow also acted as some kind of sedative, because the family didn't rise and shine at their normal weekend time, either. She looked out the window and could see snow blowing across the wide lawn. The thought of that cold made her feel kind of sleepy, too. After coffee and toast, she retreated to her room and plopped into her comfy chair with an afghan and a book.

The book turned out to be unnecessary. She dropped off for a nap before the second paragraph. She napped off and on all day. Too much commotion this week, she supposed.

Around two, Alex appeared in the doorway asking if Madge would like a cup of soup. Everyone was kind of doing their own thing for meals. Madge accepted and even allowed Alex to bring her a tray.

She watched a little television in the evening. If anyone had asked her the plot of the show, though, she would have been lost. She just enjoyed the scenery and the nice conversations. By nine, she had tucked herself into the soft bed with mountains of pillows. It had been a wasted day, really, but Madge fell asleep feeling rather content all the same.

Monday arrived in a fury. The windows frosted completely over, but nobody thought to cancel school.

"The buses can probably run," Luke said. "It's just our side streets that haven't been plowed yet. I'll take the girls. We won't have any trouble."

Madge thought he strutted just a little as he left the kitchen. She and Alex exchanged a look, and Alex rolled her eyes. But she also smiled.

Madge had just managed to survive stretching exercises an hour later when the doorbell rang. Alex jumped to answer it and came back into the room with a guest. "Madge," she said, "I believe this is a friend of yours."

Emily stood stiffly in the dining room, looking toward Madge in the kitchen. She wore the same coat Madge had watched her hang on a peg in the old kitchen many times when she kept house for Catherine. Long brown wool with a fake fur collar. Emily had come by once before to check on Madge, but she had never crossed the threshold since the Marvels moved in. It must feel strange to see the new kitchen, not to mention the new inhabitants.

Emily drew in a deep breath and stepped forward. She marched toward the kitchen with exactly the same air she always used when she planned to tell Madge that she and Catherine were too old to be gallivanting around town in bad weather. Madge wondered if she was in for a scolding.

Instead, Emily sat in the chair Alex offered and gripped her small handbag. "Albert dropped me off while he ran some errands."

"Bad weather for getting out," Madge said. She tried not to grin.

"Yes, well, our streets had all been cleared. We didn't think about it still being bad out this way." She looked around the kitchen, and Madge decided not to poke any more buttons. Instead, she looked with Emily. It felt as if the two of them had stepped into a movie together and were imagining Catherine at the stove making tea. Emily would have told Catherine to go sit with her company. Catherine would have waved Emily away and said that she was still perfectly able to brew a cup of tea.

All the while, Madge would have been munching on chocolate oatmeal cookies fresh from the oven. Soon, the three of them would be drinking tea, eating cookies, and discussing the state of the world. Catherine had always insisted that Emily was a friend who helped her out. Not a housekeeper.

"That oven must bake cookies nice and even," Emily said.

"I expect," Madge said. "We don't bake many cookies. This is kind of a store-bought house now."

Emily responded with the shocked face Madge expected. Emily had baked her heart and soul into this kitchen during its meager days. She probably thought this big overhaul was extravagant. And wasteful.

"You bake cookies, don't you?" Emily's tone sounded like an accusation.

"I have done," Madge said. "But I'm not doing much of anything since this hip gave out."

That seemed to bring Emily back to the moment. "Oh," she said. "Sorry. I almost forgot why I'd come."

She pulled a thick envelope from her purse and handed it to Madge. The return address read Hopewell Township. Madge felt mystified. She didn't know anyone in such a place, as far as she could remember.

"It's from Elizabeth," Emily said. "Catherine's only living sister. Remember her? She came to visit about ten years ago."

Madge did remember. The sister named for a queen. That's how Catherine had always described her. She made the baby sister seem like someone rather grander than the rest of them. When Elizabeth came to visit, though, she had just turned out to be a school-teacher's wife who liked to read. She was pretty. Madge remembered that. Lots of fluffy white hair that she wore on top of her head. It was kind of like a crown, she supposed.

"Go ahead and read," Emily said. "I don't mind."

Madge looked at the envelope. "Why would Elizabeth Kirk write to me?"

"We've been corresponding," Emily said, "since...well, in the last couple of years. I boxed up some things and sent to her once the kids had gone through everything." She looked toward the dining room again and then back at the fancy kitchen.

"Anyway, Elizabeth asked about you recently. When I told her you had broken your hip, she said that made you kindred spirits, since she had done the same thing a few years ago. The next time she wrote, she included this for you. I think it is a get-well card, and I've held onto it till you almost don't need it anymore."

"Well, thank you," Madge said. "I'll read it later, if you don't mind."

"Whatever you want."

"I think I want some tea. How about you? After tea, I'll show you my rooms. Pretty impressive."

She saw Emily hesitate until curiosity won out. "That would be fine," Emily said. "Just fine."

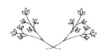

Emily didn't stay long. They heard the sound of a horn honking from the street only a few minutes after they ended the official house tour. Madge crossed her arms. "Didn't your mama teach you not to go running out the door for a boy who honked?"

She was rewarded with a small grin from Emily. "She did. But she didn't take into account a man with bad arthritis in both knees. No need to make him fetch me from the stoop on a day like this."

Emily gathered coat, gloves, scarf, and handbag without saying anything more. Finally, she looked up. "I'm glad they're taking care of you here. You should stay put through the winter." She turned and surveyed the house one more time. "This would have made Catherine happy."

Madge walked to the door and watched Emily and Albert drive away before she returned to her room. She sat with her eyes closed for more minutes than she intended, trying to process all the emotions that came with the visit. Once she felt almost normal again, she opened her eyes and picked up the envelope from Elizabeth Kirk.

> *Dear Madge,*
> *I'm not sure you will remember me, but we met when I visited my sister, Catherine Benson, several years ago. I remember you well, because I felt so glad that Catherine had a spunky friend. She could tend toward the stodgy, you know. I think you kept her lively. And she loved you.*

Madge stopped reading and reached for a tissue. She thought about closing the card and saving the rest of it for another day. A woman could only take so much. After a few seconds of blowing her nose and blinking her eyes, she persevered.

> *Emily tells me you've had a fall this winter that ended with a broken hip. How well I know the agony. You are so blessed to have a kind family in your life. I ended up in a convalescent home, which isn't quite as bad as you might imagine. But it isn't family.*

I know Catherine would be so happy that you are surrounded by the Marvels at a time like this. I trust they are as lovely as their name.

I know that Emily will get this card to you. I could have sent it to Catherine's former address. Emily explained that is where the Marvels live. What a shock that must have been to you when you applied for the housekeeping job and then discovered it was on Kensington Avenue. Somehow, I couldn't make my fingers write out that address on an envelope just yet. I'll be able to do so eventually, I'm sure.

Mostly, I just wanted to tell you that I remember you often in my prayers. Partly as a remembrance for Catherine, but also because we women-of-a-certain-age must band together. I hope you will allow me to be part of your little crew. I pray for your healing, body and soul. Because I know the soul gets weary during all this recovery time. Take care. Pace yourself. And enjoy the love around you.

I am yours in kindred friendship,
Elizabeth Kirk

Madge pulled another tissue from the box. *Enjoy the love around you.* The faces of people swirled in her mind. Catherine, of course. The Marvel sisters. Luke and Alex. Jack and Paige. Sweet Bess. Her nephews. And drat if that Elmer Grigsby didn't keep popping up in the mix.

CHAPTER TWELVE
Like a Big Pizza Pie

The sun finally awoke on Tuesday. As Madge rode along beside Paige on the way to Circle, she saw more than one Frosty the Snowman melting into a glob. They were only a couple of blocks from the church when Madge finally spoke up.

"You got any extra time today? Or does Jack have you busy?"

"I could spare an hour or so," Paige said. "What did you have in mind? Lunch?"

"Not particularly," Madge said. She didn't normally go along with those who trotted out to lunch after the Tuesday morning Prayer and Share. She liked to eat as well as the next person. Probably more than Erma or Grace Colby. While she wasn't lacking in appetite or enthusiasm, Madge did tend to lack in funds. She would never want the others to know, of course. She had remained vague about her marital status, and most of them assumed she had been widowed years before.

That was Erma's story. Widowed in her forties, no children. Her husband, though, had been a good provider and had bought an outrageous amount of life insurance from a salesman only three months before his heart attack. Erma could eat out any day she pleased. Sometimes, Madge thought that good fortune was wasted on Erma.

"So, lunch?" Paige turned the last corner.

"Well, I suppose we should eat, too, but that wasn't my plan."

"Okay." Paige pulled into the handicap lot and slowed the car.

"I need to do some Christmas shopping."

Paige threw the car into park. "Christmas shopping? That's a wonderful idea. Do you have a list?"

Madge panicked. "Not really. A list of people, I 'spose. But no idea what to get them."

"I love Christmas shopping." Paige clapped her hands. "My list isn't quite done, either, so this is perfect. I'll just text Jack and tell him I'm taking the afternoon."

"Will he mind?"

"He better not. He's on my unfinished list."

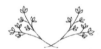

All the lights were on in the gym, and Madge glanced around expecting to see Elmer with a broom somewhere. But no. She hustled across the floor, down the hallway, and into the door of the Sunday school room without pausing. She wasn't some teenager with a crush.

"You look flustered," Evelyn said when Madge plopped into a chair. "Did you have trouble on the snow?"

"Not a bit," Madge said. "I'm just a little winded. That handicap parking isn't as handy as they make you think. Probably more steps than the front."

"But they are all level," Bess said. "That's easier."

Such wisdom from the one who didn't even know the day of the week. Madge felt rather put in her place.

"Well, you should be careful," Evelyn said. "The streets and sidewalks can still be dangerous. We don't want another fall."

Madge started to feel completely out of sorts. When would they stop seeing her as an invalid who needed watching? She gave a tap on the floor with her fancy cane.

"Stop fussing," she said. "I'm perfectly capable." With that, her huge handbag tipped off the next chair and spewed its contents across the floor. Madge stared at the mess of tissues, comb, wallet, loose change, several shades of lipstick, Quinn's spelling words, and various items she couldn't quite identify.

"Yep, perfectly capable," Grace Colby said as she bent to retrieve a compact rolling her way.

Soon, everyone except Madge was crawling on the floor picking up items and relaying them back. Paige bent to grab a bunch of papers. Madge saw her look at one piece and then tuck it behind her back.

Once all the commotion settled down and the handbag was slid under Madge's chair with all its assorted contents, Paige leaned over. She handed Madge the paper with the talking points for first dates.

Madge felt her face flush. She took the paper, wadded it into a ball, and stuffed it into her sweater pocket. Paige grinned all the way through Evelyn's opening comments.

The ladies were wound up today. They had Christmas baskets to fill and a list of families in the community who would benefit from the extra groceries. Bess had insisted they add toys to each basket. She had gone with Evelyn and Erma to select some games, books, and various gizmos.

Once the noise lowered to normal conversation, Madge clomped over to a table to help. She picked up a card game and turned it over to read the back before she tucked it into a basket. She had no idea under Heaven what to get the Marvel girls. She hoped this selection might help.

It did not. Madge could not imagine Aspen playing with a deck of cards instead of something electronic. And the idea of turning Quinn loose with a yo-yo conjured pictures of broken glassware, not to mention a few knocks on the forehead.

By the time the morning ended, Madge was beat. She wasn't sure Christmas shopping today would be a good idea at all. She started to say so when she and Paige stepped out into the hallway, but they were interrupted.

Elmer Grigsby had chosen this morning to wipe down the railings along this particular hallway. Madge did not think that was a coincidence. She wanted to be irritated about being stalked. Instead, she found it made her feel rather pleased.

"Miss Rosedale," Elmer said. He ducked his head as if tipping a hat in their direction, and Paige gave him her gorgeous smile in response.

"Mr. Grigsby. But please call me Paige."

"Afraid I can't do it, Miss," he said. "I fell a long way from my upbringin' at one time. But some of my mother's manners have stayed with me as I come back up. I shan't be calling a lady by her first name on early acquaintance."

"Well, then," Paige said. "Let's get better acquainted. Why don't you and Madge join Jack and I for dinner Saturday night?"

"We wouldn't want to intrude," Elmer said.

Madge felt the huffiness rise in her chest. The man shouldn't be tossing out words so easily. They weren't a couple. She had agreed to let him call once. That was all. He didn't need to be speaking up for her and making plans as if she just followed him around like that pesky cat of his.

"You aren't intruding," Paige said. "We're just going to a little pizza place downtown. It's called Amore. From the song."

Madge had no idea what Paige meant, but she didn't intend to say so. She wanted the conversation to end. Paige obviously didn't get her signal. She sang the first few words about the moon hitting your eye, and then she stopped. "Do you like pizza, Mr. Grigsby?"

"Sure do. 'Course, I've never had it from inside such a dining establishment," Elmer said. "My boy cooks up a frozen one now and again. And I tasted a few fancy ones in my dumpster days."

Paige stood with her mouth slightly open, as if she didn't know how to respond to such an admission. Madge felt her grouchiness evaporate in a second. Here stood a man who had, against all odds, re-entered society after decades of absence. A hermit who had crawled out of his cave, by the grace of God, and now stood as tall as a man of his age possibly could. And he had never tasted hot pizza from a restaurant. Who was she to keep the man from a gooey slice with double cheese?

"We should certainly do it," Paige said. "We can pick you both up at the Marvel house around six if that works for you."

Elmer looked at Madge with the tiniest trace of a grin. "Sounds about perfect to me. What do you say?"

Madge tried to get her thoughts together. What did she say? She could have said quite a lot if time had been allowed. She could have said that she was a fully grown woman quite content with her own company. She didn't intend to go running around town with some man at this late stage of life. She could have said that her only goal was to get healed up and back home where nobody told her what to do and nobody suggested outlandish ideas like a pizza party.

Madge could have said so much. Her brain ached with the arguments flying back and forth up there. She saw Elmer watching her, as if he could hear the debate, too. Yet, he didn't push her. He just stood with that little grin, as if he had all the time in the world for Madge DuPree to make up her mind.

Finally, Madge cleared her throat. She looked over Elmer's head instead of staring him in the face and said, "Well, I suppose."

"Alrighty," Elmer said. "You can think of it as a Christmas present for me."

Madge stuck out her chin, but she couldn't think of a response. Pretty uppity of the man to think she planned to get him a Christmas present. She certainly did not.

CHAPTER THIRTEEN

Making a List and Checking It Twice

Madge thought the mall looked like the scene of a holiday riot. She took a few brave steps toward the mob and then wobbled.

Paige reached for Madge's elbow. "Maybe we've done enough fun for one day. Let's go home and reschedule shopping for Thursday."

Madge agreed. When Thursday arrived, though, she didn't feel much bolder about the quest. The thought of all those people shoving through the aisles seemed like more than she could endure. Maybe Paige could just pick up some cards for her and she would tuck a five or ten into each one.

Then she imagined little Gracie opening a card with green stuff inside. Fiddlesticks. She would have to shop.

As they backed out of the driveway, Paige said, "I thought we might avoid the mall today. I know a small district downtown where we can find a couple of shops. They won't be so noisy, and the weather is perfect for walking on the cobblestones. It's quaint and beautiful. We could even stop for tea."

Madge nodded. She didn't know how the cane would do on cobblestones. They turned out to be more decorative than cobbled, thank goodness. Madge stepped right across the threshold of the first shop and found herself in a bookstore suitable for a fairy tale.

"May I help you?" the young clerk asked.

Madge liked the girl's curly red hair. In her green sweater and skirt, she looked like a Christmas elf. Madge held out the short list she had written, and the clerk read off the names.

"Aspen, Quinn, Peyton, and Grace. Your grandchildren?"

Madge decided she didn't have the strength for long explanations today, so she just nodded and hoped the Almighty wouldn't count it a complete lie.

"What are their ages?" the clerk asked. "That will help us select the perfect gift."

Madge knew their grades in school, but not ages precisely. She said as much. "Grace is two, though. I know that one. She doesn't move up to the Twinkle-Toes room till next year. Aspen isn't thirteen yet. She thinks she can get her ears pierced at thirteen, but I don't know about that. It's coming up soon, I think."

Once the clerk and Madge had agreed on basic ages, Paige wandered back into view. She held up a red box with black letters. "Do you know what this is?" she asked Madge.

Madge read the wording, but it meant nothing.

"This is an original version of Pac Man," she said. "Well, not original. It's the retro version. The joystick is the same, though. Jack will love it. I never dreamed of finding anything so perfect."

The elfish clerk scampered back just then and held up a baby doll with soft yellow hair. She wore a pink gown that matched her rosy cheeks. "This is a classic," she said. "No batteries needed. Just a sweet baby doll to love. Every Christmas tree needs a baby doll underneath on Christmas morning, don't you think?"

Madge had no idea. Her own Christmases growing up had been mostly practical. Shoes for school. A sweater, maybe. Once, she remembered getting a wristwatch, and she knew at the time her parents must have saved all year to afford it. If she ever got a baby doll, she didn't remember it.

The other problem was that she had never shopped for children. She always sent her nephews and their children a little cash money at Christmas. Provided she had cash to spare. Some years, it had just been a card and good wishes.

Now, she stood in this magical store and held a soft squishing doll in her hands. She felt the insane urge to cradle the toy. To rock it, even. Before such urges could manifest, she thrust the doll back toward the clerk.

"That will do for Grace," she said. She sounded grouchy, and she knew it, but grouching was always her way to cover emotions she couldn't quite name.

"Great. How about games for the two sisters in the middle?" the clerk asked.

Madge turned to Paige and raised her eyebrows for confirmation. Paige nodded.

"I think that would be perfect," she said. "They can play all through school break. Nothing with lots of small pieces, though. We don't want you tripping over things in the hallway."

The selection of appropriate games took much longer than Madge could have imagined. While Paige and the clerk debated the finer points, Madge wandered to the next aisle.

She looked over the colorful stacks of books and wondered where a person would even start to select a book for a girl like Aspen. Then, as if rising from the crowd by Narnian magic, a complete set of the *Chronicles of Narnia* glowed from a far shelf. Madge hurried over, the best she could, and examined the book covers. Not actual leather, she was sure. They looked and felt expensive, though. Madge flipped open *The Lion, The Witch, and the Wardrobe*. The picture of Lucy and Mr. Tumnus fell open, and Madge almost gasped. They both looked exactly as she had imagined.

When Madge had first come to the Marvel house, she discovered the little girls put themselves to bed every night by re-watching the farewell scene from *The Sound of Music*. The Marvel parents were always busy at bedtime doing something else. Like watching sports on television or attending dinner meetings with a client.

She knew other parents read to their children at bedtime, so she mentioned the idea to Pastor Cleveland. He had loaned her the first book in the Narnia series. She offered the book to Luke first, and he surprised her by diving right in. The first few nights, Madge stood in the hallway outside the little girls' room while Luke read. The story captured her just as it did the girls. One of her great regrets was that this broken hip kept her from climbing the steps. She had no idea what had become of Aslan after the dreadful Stone Table. She had sniffled a bit over that chapter.

Maybe, if she bought this set for Aspen, she could read Pastor Cleveland's copy for herself before she returned it. The thought startled Madge. Truth be told, she wasn't much of a reader. Certainly not children's books.

She flipped over the box and read the price on the set. Whoa. That would set back repairs on the Oldsmobile. Yet, it seemed like the perfect gift. She stood a while longer, looking at each volume on its own.

Finally, Paige poked her head around the corner. "I think we made our choice," she said. "And games are on sale. You can practically get two for the price of one."

Madge hesitated. The books cost more than she had expected to spend on the whole lot. Such extravagance would take a big chunk from her car-repair fund. It would delay her independence. She paused for one more moment and then hugged the Narnia books to her bosom. So be it. She would get the books for Aspen, even if it meant staying with the Marvels until spring.

As she and Paige walked back toward the car, Madge saw a shop with men's hats in the window. "Maybe we could drop in there," she said.

"I'll put these in the car." Paige took the bag Madge had carried over her arm. "You go on in."

A bell tinkled overhead when Madge entered, and a wrinkled little gentleman with a white mustache greeted her. "May I help you, madam?" he said. "Have you come to find something elegant for the gentleman in your life?"

Madge didn't even bristle at the thought. "I'd like a hat," she said. "A dressy one that a lawyer could wear to court."

"We have just the thing," the little man said. "Do you know the gentleman's hat size?"

That stumped Madge. The day of the snowstorm, when Jack drove her to pick up the girls and then she fell on the sidewalk, he had been without a hat. She had scolded him about it at the time, saying a man ought to wear a hat in such weather. But he told her he didn't have one.

She had no idea about his hat size. Truth be told, she didn't know hats for men came in sizes. "Kind of average, I guess," she finally said. She squinted at the clerk. "His head is probably a little bigger than yours." She hoped that didn't sound ugly. She hadn't meant the man had a tiny head, although he kind of did.

"Well, well," he said. "I think we can manage something nice for you. The gentleman is certainly welcome to come in for an exchange after the holidays if we don't get things exactly right." He walked toward the far corner as he spoke.

Madge followed and looked over the display of grey and black felt hats. She noticed one with a slight tip to the brim. "That one looks kind of snappy," she said. "Might do for a lawyer."

"It might indeed," the clerk said. "One of our best. Madam has excellent taste if I may say so."

"You may." Madge felt silly the moment those words hit the air, but she couldn't take them back.

"Shall I wrap the gift for you?"

Madge looked at her watch. "No time for that. I guess I'll fig-ure out how to wrap it myself."

The man tossed her an eager smile. "Ah, I can assist with that difficulty." He reached under the counter and whipped out a round box with green stripes. "Just the thing," he said. "Pop this bit of haberdashery into our gift box, top it with the bow of your choice, and you are ready for the tree."

"How much?" Madge asked.

The man pushed a few buttons on his register and then smiled again. "Fortunately, we have a special today. Boxes are free with the purchase of a gentleman's hat."

Madge doubted that. He probably added the price to the hat in the first place, but she was getting too tired to argue. Instead, she reached for a pair of heavy gloves from a stack on the counter. "Good," she said. "How about you throw in a fancy box for these, too?"

CHAPTER FOURTEEN

First and Forever

Elmer arrived by taxi on Saturday night, just a few minutes before Paige and Jack were due at the Marvel house. Madge was glad he hadn't come earlier. She felt like a complete fraud getting dressed up to go out for supper. Even if it was just pizza. She had never done such a thing in her life, and she could not imagine what the Glory Circle sisters would say if they ever heard about the escapade.

Aspen had insisted on helping with her hair. It had been a ridiculous attempt. Madge's hair had long ago exploded into its own orb of curls and pouf. Back in the day, she had slapped a hat on top every now and then to try and give some semblance of order. In recent years, though, she had let it go and blow about however it happened to fall on a given day.

She kept it as short as she could bear. Not that she would have minded wearing it even shorter. She just didn't want to pay for a haircut every whipstitch. So, she usually waited until it had sprouted out like a bush and was brushing the collar of her blouse before she got a trim.

The hair was in such a state now. Madge didn't mind that much. Elmer had certainly seen her mess of hair before. Aspen, however, insisted they try a scarf. Then a set of combs. If Madge hadn't protested, she would have ended up with one of those ponytail things in her hair.

Instead, she agreed to a green jeweled bobby pin. Once Aspen finished with a whiff of hairspray, Madge had to admit the look worked. The pin held back the pieces of hair that tended to flop in her face. The little sparkle of green made a nice reflection against her red hair. Even the most unruly curls seemed to bow to Aspen's insistence. They relaxed into rows that looked almost arranged.

When Elmer rang the bell, Madge was standing in the entryway patting down the last strand. She glanced into the mirror, brushed something off the shoulder of her blue sweater, and then opened the door.

He grinned like a man who had just won first prize at the county fair. No flowers this time. Madge felt relieved about that. This outing was silly enough without the man adding a dash of the ridiculous.

Just as she was about to ask Elmer in, he put his hand in his coat pocket and pulled out a package wrapped in deep blue paper. "Something for under the tree," he said. "You can't open it till Christmas morning."

Madge stepped back as if to refuse the gift, but Elmer took it as an invitation to come inside. He put the gift on the hall table next to a bowl of glittering ornaments. "No peeking," he said. "And no shaking. Promise?"

Madge nodded because she couldn't seem to make her brain form any words. What she wanted to say was that he shouldn't have brought her a present, and that he should most certainly take it back to wherever it came from first thing tomorrow and stop wasting his money on frivolity.

She could not do it, though. Partly because of the happiness on his face, and partly because of the gold initial on the top of the box. It had come from Austen's, the jewelry store where Catherine's husband had often shopped. Madge had never imagined receiving a gift from Austen's. Never.

"Mr. Grigsby, won't you come in?" Alex appeared in the entryway in time to save Madge from whatever display of emotion was about to explode. Like a true hostess, she took charge. "Here," she said, "let me hang your coat." Once Alex had the coat handled, she ushered the poor man into the dining room and then toward the family room. Alex turned before they disappeared from sight and said, "Madge? Are you joining us?"

Madge stood for another moment. She could not resist running a finger over the rich paper. "Yes," she said. "I'll be there." Once Alex disappeared, Madge pulled her purse over from its spot on the hallway table. She reached into the depths and pulled out a flat box. She should have let the man at the hat store wrap the gloves. Her job looked amateur. Too late now, though. Madge looked around to make sure no one was watching and then slipped the gift into the pocket of Elmer's overcoat.

Jack's car whipped into the driveway before Madge crossed the dining room. She heard the engine, then the doors, then the sound of the back door of the Marvel house.

"Anybody home?" Paige called from the kitchen.

General chaos came as the answer. The little girls scrambled downstairs with all the energy of children hyped up on Christmas candy. They nearly fell over one another showing Jack and Paige the loot they collected at school parties. Aspen sauntered into the room with all the elegance of a teenager trying to appear uninterested. She picked up an apple from the counter and wandered toward the noise that had centered down at the end of the bar.

Before Madge realized what she was up to, Aspen pulled something green from behind her back and waved it in the air. "Mistletoe," she announced. "Jack and Paige are under the mistletoe."

Paige jumped away from the counter. "Oh, no we are not," she said. "I'm not falling for that trick."

"Looks to me like you are alone under the mistletoe," Jack said as he slid down to another stool.

Aspen sagged onto her elbows and dropped the greenery. "Story of my life," she said.

Paige gave her shoulder a squeeze. "You have plenty of time for such things. Don't rush it."

Aspen shrugged. "I don't really care," she said. "The boys at my school are so immature."

Paige nodded. "It takes a while to grow a good one."

"Hey, should I take that personally?" Jack snagged an apple, too.

"Only if it applies," Paige said.

Madge suddenly felt tired. She did not have the energy for this kind of flirting and flitting. If that is what it was going to take to sit through supper with a gentleman caller, she was ready to ditch the whole idea. Before she could say so, she felt someone at her elbow.

"Do you need to sit a spell before we go?" Elmer said. "I don't want you to think we have to keep up with the young ones. They've got enough energy to light a Christmas tree."

Madge nodded and sank onto the nearest chair. Elmer stepped closer, almost as if to shield her from the noise across the room. "If it feels like too much excitement tonight, we can do somethin' else," he said. "Sit here by the fire if you want. Eat a cold supper of some kind."

"But you've never had fresh pizza."

He shrugged. "That wasn't the draw for me tonight. I 'spect it tastes all right, but I'm more interested in the company than the victuals."

His understanding tone sent a surge of strength and resolve through Madge. She could not imagine the life he had led on the streets before Catherine prayed him through. But she would not be responsible for denying the man an evening out at Christmastime.

"I'm good," she said. "Just needed to get my wind. I'm ready for pizza now. Although, I will warn you, the pepperoni will stay with you till morning if you're not careful."

"I'll take that into account," he said as he offered her his arm.

The pizza place was exactly as Paige had described it. A little dark for Madge's preferences, but they snagged a table in the corner under a light. The chairs were big enough to hold a person, which wasn't always the case in these trendy places. Madge leaned against the solid chair and felt herself begin to relax. She had dreaded navigating the sidewalks and crowded rooms. She need not have worried, though. Elmer's arm held steady on one side with her cane on the other. She had not realized how much it helped to lean into another body as she walked. Not that she leaned much. That wouldn't have been proper. She certainly did not intend to get dependent on a man, either. It had been a big step to let herself be lassoed into the Marvel family. Quinn had started it with the spelling.

It didn't help that baby Grace decided to like her. Never in this lifetime had a toddler liked Madge DuPree. She had hardly known what to make of it the first few weeks. Now, she hated to admit how much she looked forward to that hug at the end of the day.

She had taught Peyton to play outside. A major feat. And she had made some form of contact with Aspen, though she was not at all sure she had completed a circuit. That one seemed to short out fairly often, depending on the mood of the teenager.

All in all, though, Madge felt drawn into the circle that was the Marvel household. She had never intended to stay past her sixty days, but now she had stopped counting down.

"Madge? Are you with us?"

She looked up to see Paige holding out a menu. "I asked what kind of pizza strikes your fancy tonight."

"Oh," Madge accepted the menu. It was almost as thick as the new Christmas catalog. She flipped a couple of pages and tried to read the exotic descriptions. "Cheese?" she finally said with a question in her voice. "Or maybe hamburger?"

"Well," Elmer held the menu at arm's length. "I couldn't tell you a thing about the words on this placard, but the pictures look mighty tasty. I'm going with whatever you suggest."

"Let's get one of the specials," Jack said. "We can add a small, plain cheese in case it's too much for you, Madge."

The plan seemed good to everyone, so Jack placed the order. Once the waiter walked away, Jack picked up the conversation.

"It's hard to imagine a guy who has lived as long as you, Mr. Grigsby, and never gone out for pizza."

Elmer nodded and looked over Jack's shoulder toward the window. Christmas lights twinkled from stores across the street.

"Would it shock you if I said just a few winters ago I'd have been likely to eat supper outa the dumpster 'round back?"

"I guess it wouldn't shock me. But it is surprising."

"Life can get away from you," Elmer said. "You think things are handled, that you've got it under control, so to speak. Then, little by little, you let it get away. Jobs. Cars. Stuff. Even folks. Pretty soon, you are livin' for nothin' more than the next bottle to open. It's a sad state of affairs, and many is the man lost in it tonight, I'll tell ya."

Before Madge could say anything to ease the moment, she heard her name called from across the room.

"Aunt Madge? Is that you?"

She squinted in the dim light, and then recognized Alex's good friend Mara Lynn and her husband, Joe, standing in the doorway. Joe called her name again, "Aunt Madge? How you doin'?"

She waved back and then spoke to her tablemates. "Friends of the family." As soon as she spoke, Madge felt like a fraud. They were friends of the Marvel family, but her comment assumed she was part of that family and the friendship circle. As if to prove it true, Joe bopped his way through the crowded tables and came straight for Madge.

He reached down and gave her a big side-hug. "Hey, everybody," he said. "Mara Lynn and I are longtime friends with Luke and Alex. Well, I'm longtime. Mara Lynn is first-and-forever with Alex." He started shaking hands around the table.

"It's Jack, isn't it? The lawyer friend?" Jack stood and nodded as he shook Joe's hand.

"We've adopted Aunt Madge," Joe said, "whether she likes it or not."

Mara Lynn came up beside her husband. "I'm afraid it's true," she said. "Once Joe grabs onto you, it is impossible to get away."

"That's true," he said. "I grabbed this woman the first day I met her, and I'm still holdin' tight."

Elmer stood and bowed his head in that way Madge had seen him do before. As if he were tipping his hat in a gentlemanly kind of way. "Pleased to meet ya," he said. "I think you've shown good taste in claiming this lady."

Madge felt warmth spreading across her neck. She wasn't embarrassed by the comment. She rather liked it. But she didn't want to give in to it. She didn't want anyone to think she was getting all warm and fuzzy at this stage of life. She had a crotchety reputation to protect.

"Elmer Grigsby's the name," he continued. "I'm a friend, too." He looked straight at Madge as he spoke the last part.

She had never felt like such a schoolgirl in her life. Even when Fancy-Man-DuPree had come around spouting poetry and promises, her girlish heart hadn't pounded like this. She had run off with him more to get away from her hard life than toward any romantic notions. Now, though, she wondered if she wasn't acting more like Aspen than like herself.

CHAPTER FIFTEEN
Out of the Ash Heap

Jack stood, too, as if he had suddenly remembered manners. "Jack Oakley," he said. "And this is Paige Rosedale. Also friends of the Marvel family. I think we might have run into the two of you when Madge was in the hospital."

"That's right," Joe said. "I think we did. I just wasn't sure we had officially met."

Everyone shook hands and exchanged greetings, and then Paige said, "Let's pull up that small table and make room for you to join us. Unless you are on a date or something."

"Well," Mara Lynn said, "it isn't a real date. We just finished the last of our Christmas shopping and realized we were famished. But we don't want to interrupt."

"No," Jack and Paige said together. Paige finished by saying, "We are chaperoning these two, if you want to know the truth. I think conversation is always more lively with extra friends."

Everyone except Madge nodded their agreement. She could not manage to move a syllable from her brain to her mouth. Being out in public with a gentleman was hard enough to swallow. Now, it would practically be on the front page.

"So, go right ahead with your conversation," Mara Lynn said. "We'll catch up and jump in."

"Well," Paige looked around the table before she continued. "Mr. Grigsby was just telling us about the rather difficult life he endured before we met him."

Everyone looked at Elmer, and he picked up the story as if he wasn't the least bit embarrassed. "It's the truth," he said. "I was a bum. A drunk bum who lost everything and everyone."

Joe nodded and reached out to shake Elmer's hand again. "Welcome to the club, brother. I came close to losin' it all myself."

Madge snapped to attention at that comment. She would never have suspected Joe of being a drinker. Joe-the-Cop seemed so clean-cut and pulled together.

"When we met," Mara Lynn said, "Joe was a party animal in the fraternity. He didn't realize how hard the booze had gotten hold of him."

"She refused to go out with me," Joe said. "When she accused me of being an alcoholic, I got mad. Roarin' mad. I do believe I broke a few lamps and maybe a bookcase when I got back to my room that night."

Jack nodded. "I've known a couple of guys who could get ugly once they'd had a few. I was such a lightweight in college. I never could acquire the taste for it."

"That's a good thing," Joe said. "For guys like me and Mr. Grigsby taste didn't matter. If you poured in enough of the hard stuff, you didn't even taste it anymore."

"I hadn't thought of that," Elmer said, "but you're right. I never cared much for the taste. And, once those Glory girls got to prayin' for me, the taste turned plumb vile."

"Glory girls?" Joe and Mara Lynn spoke at once.

Elmer turned to Madge. "You tell the story," he said. "You were on the inside of it."

"Oh, not really," Madge said. "It was my friend Catherine. She drew Elmer's name when the Glory Circle sisters decided to pray through the phone book. She didn't have any idea who he was, but she kept holding onto his name every week."

The story poured out then. How Catherine had prayed for Elmer in secret and how day-by-day his brain began to clear up. The booze kept tasting worse and doing less to dull his mind.

"The real turn came when I found an old newspaper," Elmer said. "It advertised a new preacher at one of the nice churches. I recognized his face. Hadn't seen him in thirty years or more, but I knew the face. Looked just like me at that age."

"Pastor Cleveland?" Paige said.

"The very one. My only boy all grown up and preachin' from a pulpit. That picture haunted me. I couldn't toss it in the trash, and I couldn't think what to do, but slowly a plan formed. I knew they would have a big doin's on Christmas Eve. The big churches always do. I thought I'd go on down, check it out, and maybe even have the grit to introduce myself."

"What happened?" Joe said.

"I chickened out. But a week or so later, I decided I'd just go down to the church and see if I could find him on my own, when nobody was around."

"That backfired," Madge said. She hadn't meant to enter the conversation again, but she couldn't stay out now. The next scene was too good. "You can imagine," she said, "the shock for the Glory Circle when this vagabond showed up on the church steps the day of Catherine Benson's funeral."

"I remember seein' you for the first time," Elmer said. "I liked that wild, orange hair and your pretty blue coat. 'Course, you did about knock me off my feet when you stampeded by."

Madge gave him a raised eyebrow. She felt a little unnerved that he remembered her from that day. He had never said.

"So, you didn't know one another?" Paige asked.

"Heavens, no. Nobody knew who he was from Adam. And nobody knew about the prayers for him. Well, nobody except me."

Elmer turned toward her. "You knew? I never heard that part of the tale before."

Madge reached into her handbag and pulled out a beaded coin purse. She lifted a tiny slip of paper from the bag and handed it to Elmer. "Catherine told me in the hospital, just before... Well, anyway, she told me to get this coin purse out of her pocketbook. She said there was something important inside, something I needed to take care of for her if anything happened."

Elmer ran his finger over the tiny print of his own name on the paper.

"She told me how she'd been praying for you every week, even when it was time to draw a new name. 'If I leave,' she said, 'you take over. Don't stop praying for him.'"

Madge looked Elmer straight in the eye. "So, I never have."

"Well, I'll be." Elmer gave Madge such a look she could barely stand it. She had never meant to tell a soul about this promise to Catherine, about all the prayers for a man she didn't know, and here she had blurted it out over pizza.

It seemed to Madge that they sat in silence, staring at one another, for a few hours. Her mind filled with images of Elmer on the church steps in his good coat and hat while the mourners went around him. Elmer shaking hands with Pastor Cleveland and announcing his name and relationship. Elmer in the second pew the next Sunday, bent over and shaky, rarely lifting his head during the service.

The pictures shifted then. Elmer walking down the aisle with that little hop in his step. Elmer whistling in the vestibule. Elmer with flowers at Thanksgiving.

She might have sat there all night reliving every memory if Paige hadn't spoken.

"That must have been hard," she said. "To change your life-style after so many years."

Elmer didn't look away from Madge. "Not easy in some re-spects. Down at the meetin's they call it Divine Intervention."

Madge felt herself coming back into the conversation. The memories faded and the voices around her began to filter through. She heard Paige ask what Elmer meant about meetings. Joe answered. "AA," he said. "Am I right, Mr. Grigsby? Alcoholics Anonymous?"

"That's the place," Elmer said. "I go ever' week, and I've learned things 'bout myself I'd never touched before."

Joe reached into his pocket and pulled out a coin. He placed it on the table and slid it forward with one finger. "Fifteen years last month," he said.

Elmer matched the move and slid a different coin toward Joe's side of the table. "Three years last week."

Madge watched in fascination. She knew nothing about this world. She had heard of AA, but she didn't know they used a different kind of money. She felt a little nervous, as if she had stumbled into the middle of a secret lodge meeting.

Joe added another coin to the table. It had a blue stone in the center. "This is my favorite, though. This is the one I keep close all the time." He held it up and let the light shine through the stone's center. "My first twenty-four hours without a drink. That was a goal I wasn't sure I could even make."

"That's the hardest one," Elmer said. "I didn't start goin' to meetin's till later on, so I never got that one."

"You still should," Joe said. "I keep this one close to me all the time. It reminds me that I'm only one drink away from starting over. That every day is a decision. And a victory."

"Good idea," Elmer said.

"I've gone with Joe to several meetings," Mara Lynn said. "And I also go to a group for family members. I've learned a lot about myself and about this battle." She reached out to put her hand on top of Joe's and touched the twenty-four-hour coin with her fingertip. "We're fighting the good fight together."

"That's right," Joe changed his tone. Madge thought he sounded more like the college football player from back in the day. "And I'll tell you somethin' else," he said, "my higher power ain't no doorknob. I heard a guy say that at a meeting one time. That his higher power was the doorknob he had to turn to get outta the house for a drink. The doorknob kept him sober by reminding him what would happen if he went. I had to cough so I wouldn't laugh out loud."

Madge felt herself relaxing. She liked this Joe fellow.

"No, sir," Joe said. "My higher power is the Lord Almighty. He's the one that put the wooly on the wooly worm in my life. You get my meanin', don't you, Mr. Grigsby?"

Elmer nodded and Joe explained to the others. "We say that sometimes at the end of a meeting. 'Who put the wooly on the wooly worm?' Then we answer with, 'Our Father, who art in Heaven' and finish the prayer."

"That's cool," Paige said. "I've never known anything about AA, except that we kept coffee in the church basement for a group that met there on Thursday nights. It seemed like a big secret. When I was a kid, my mom warned us that if we ever saw anyone going to the church on a Thursday night, we were to keep quiet about it. Never say anything to anyone about who we saw. For several years, I thought it was an underground spy group or something."

Joe and Mara both laughed, but Madge couldn't find any humor in the situation yet.

"That is the anonymous part," Joe said. "Some guys still keep pretty hush-hush about it. Don't want their boss to know. Or their pastor. But I've always thought the more open I could be, the more chance I might help somebody else who was caught in the tangle. You know?"

"Good for you," Jack said. "That seems like the right attitude to me."

"Nothin' to be ashamed of," Elmer said. "The shame would be not gettin' the help when it was offered. I figure the good Lord lifted me outta the ash heap, like the scripture says. I'm beholden to Him and to them that prayed me through. If my story can help the next fella, so be it."

"So be it," said Mara Lynn as she lifted her water glass.

Madge was the last to join the toast. She heard the clink as they all came together above the table, and she wondered what Catherine would think if she could see the mysterious Elmer Grigsby now.

Before that thought could continue, the waitress returned with a huge pizza in each hand. She shoved them onto the table, moving forks and plates out of her way in a smooth glide. The thick smell of melted cheese mingled with the tang of tomato sauce and wrapped like a Christmas wreath around Madge's head.

Elmer breathed in the aroma. "So, that is the smell of fresh pizza," he said. "If it tastes anything like it smells, we'll be awful close to Heaven tonight, don't you think?"

He looked at Madge as he spoke, and she felt a quiver in her chest that kept her from responding.

CHAPTER SIXTEEN

'Twas the Night Before Christmas

Elmer had been right about Mt. Zion Church putting on a big doings for Christmas Eve. Most years they held a candlelight service in the evening, but this year Pastor Cleveland had suggested they do all the festivities in their morning service. Madge wondered if he was worried about all the old ladies getting out at night, and she said as much when he greeted the Marvel family in the vestibule.

"Not at all," Pastor Cleveland said. "You sisters will run circles around me any time of the year." He bent toward Peyton and Quinn. "My real motive," he said, "was to be home in my bed tonight before Santa Claus comes."

Peyton giggled and Quinn smiled. Madge thought Quinn wanted to look too big for such things, but she certainly wasn't. She had pestered everyone at breakfast wanting to make sure they didn't use all the milk, because they had to leave a glass under the tree for Santa.

Elmer stepped forward with a basket over his arm and handed Luke, Alex, and Aspen each a small white candle. Then he reached into a pocket and pulled out three plastic candles. He held the first one toward Grace. "Safer for the pint-sized," he said. "Lookee here, you just push this little button, and it lights right up." The battery-operated candle flickered with an orange glow that looked very much like a flame.

Grace took the candle and rewarded Elmer with a grin, which people didn't get too often. Peyton and Quinn each took one and thanked their benefactor. Then Elmer turned to Madge. "I've got a candle for you, too," he said.

Madge felt her cheeks burn as if he had said something personal. She told herself to snap out of it. The man was just passing out candles, not speaking love-words in code. Good grief. She snatched the candle and turned so quickly her purse whacked Peyton in the head.

Luke grabbed Peyton's hand and began to herd the clan toward the sanctuary before anything else could happen. Peyton sat beside Madge without any tears, but she rubbed the spot on her head more than once. Madge felt like a true jerk. Before she could explore that feeling, though, Alex suddenly scrunched in beside Peyton and forced everyone to scoot down several inches on the pew. As they moved, Alex looked up at Elmer passing in the aisle.

"Mr. Grigsby," she said, "won't you sit with us today? No one should sit alone at Christmas."

Elmer bowed his head in that way of his and gave Alex a smile. "Mighty kind," he said.

With that, the Marvel girls parted like the waters of the Red Sea. Madge found herself with a wide-open space on either side. Elmer stood for just a moment as if he might be asking her permission, but Madge simply could not give it. The idea of sitting with a man beside her in the third pew made her practically shiver. What would Grace Colby say, after all? She sat just a few people down the row, probably eye-balling the whole lot of them right now.

If anyone ever asked her, Madge would say she and Grace Colby were friends, of a sort. Not close, though. Maybe that is why Madge always thought of her by her full name. Grace Colby. As if the surname added some distance between them. They certainly didn't think alike on any matters of importance. Most specifically, they did not think alike on the matter of Elmer Grigsby. Grace Colby would not give him the time of day. In her eyes, he was a falling down drunk who had just managed to prop himself up for a bit.

Madge felt herself bristling and realized Elmer was still smiling at her from the aisle. She reached over, grabbed Peyton, and pulled the girl up against her. Elmer took the more-than-obvious hint and scooted in beside Alex.

Madge could feel Alex giving her a stare, but she didn't care. She would not be made a fool in church on Christmas Eve. With that, Pastor Cleveland stood and welcomed the crowd.

"We have lots of guests with us this morning," he said. "Several home folks, too. I know many of our regular crowd have traveled for the holidays. Nothing better than being with family at Christmastime." He paused and looked at the third row. "I haven't always had the benefit of my natural family or a church family for such occasions. That probably makes me extra grateful this morning to have both here with me."

He took a few seconds to clear his throat after that statement. "I'm thinking today of all the people who gathered at the manger on the first Christmas day. Oh, I know it probably didn't happen on December twenty-fifth. I even know the scholars say that the wise men and the shepherds you see in our crèche probably didn't arrive at the same time. But I like to think of it that way, just the same.

"Imagine with me, the idea of worthless shepherds, outcasts in the society of that day, kneeling beside men of great knowledge and wealth from a distant land. It must have been quite the sight. Can you smell the shepherds? Covered with smoke from their cooking fires and grease from their flocks? Now imagine the exotic fragrances of the travelers, frankincense, myrrh, and who knows what mingling with those earthy smells."

He paused as if giving everyone time to play along. Madge could stir up the shepherd's odor. She had grown up on a farm. As for the wise men, the best she could do was the strong cinnamon she sprinkled on toast for the girls. But that worked. She started to feel as if she were almost there in Bethlehem.

"Do you hear the sheep? Feel the wind blowing down from the hills?" Pastor Cleveland said. "And, in the center of it all, the soft breathing of a newborn child. It must have been a magnificent moment."

Madge had not noticed the music before. Now she realized the pianist had started to play, and the choir was humming along.

"I think God loved that moment," Pastor Cleveland said. "He loved sending His Son to rescue mankind, and He loved hearing, seeing, and smelling men of all kinds worshipping together for the first time ever."

Madge tried to get a peek at Elmer, but she couldn't see him without turning her head. So, she gave up.

"That is exactly how it will be around the throne of Heaven," Pastor Cleveland said. "And that is exactly how it should be in our churches as we wait for the great day of His return. All kinds of people worshipping together as one."

The choir took their cue and let loose with the first strains of "Oh come, let us adore Him." As the congregation rose and joined them in the song, Madge gave Peyton the slightest nudge. The two of them traded places without anyone even noticing. Madge didn't look, but when her elbow brushed against Elmer's arm, she felt certain she could feel him grinning.

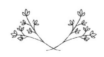

On Sunday night, Madge decided to head off to bed a little early. Not because she was waiting for Santa as Pastor Cleveland had suggested. She was worn out. As Madge tried to scoot by a group of ponies-on-parade in the middle of the room, Quinn looked up.

"What about stockings? Madge can't go to bed before we hang stockings."

Alex looked up from her phone and then around the room as if she had expected Christmas elves to take care of that task. "I'm not sure I brought the stockings down from the attic," she said. "It's been so hectic with the moving and un-moving."

Quinn scowled at that excuse, and Madge leaped in before she thought. A common problem in her nanny/housekeeping career. "When I was a child," she said, "we didn't have store-bought stockings for Christmas Eve."

Peyton frowned as she dropped a pony and looked at Madge. "What did you use?"

"Socks." Madge lifted one foot a few inches and wriggled her toes. "My mother just grabbed the heaviest sock she could find from my dad's drawer, and we pinned it to the arm of the chair by the stove."

Quinn joined Peyton in frowning. "Did Santa fill an old sock?"

"He did." The words sent Madge suddenly back to the old house with the wood stove and the loose windows. She could almost feel the wind blowing through those windows and creating small mounds of snow on the inside ledge. She could even smell the orange she pulled from the toe of her father's sock every year. "That's all children got in some families, you know. Just what came in the stocking."

"No gifts?" The little girls went from frowns to shock.

"Not one. Unless you needed underwear or a pair of shoes. Sometimes those showed up in a package under the tree."

"Never a toy?"

"Oh, I probably got a toy in my stocking some year. I don't really remember." She stopped and thought back again. "One year, I did get a wristwatch. That was something."

"I bet it wasn't as pretty as what's in your blue package this year," Aspen said.

Madge turned and raised her eyebrows at the girl. "What do you know about a blue package?"

"Well, I suppose Santa left it early," she said. "I saw it on the hall table, but I don't know where it went from there. Did you open it already?"

Madge straightened her shoulders. "I did not. It can't be opened until Christmas morning."

"Well, let's put it under the tree." Aspen jumped toward the doorway and waited with an expectant look. "I'll get it for you."

Madge started to tell Aspen to forget about it, that she didn't even plan to open the blue package. She intended to send it right back where it came from before Elmer Grigsby could get any brighter ideas than he already had. True, she had gotten him a pair of gloves. But he needed gloves. A man always needs good gloves. They were a useful gift for a gentleman who helped her in the door at church and such.

Instead of saying all those things, though, Madge waved toward the other room. "Pull open the drawer of that hall table," she said. "You might find something in there."

Aspen bopped back into the room seconds later and placed the gift under the tree in the exact center. One of the twinkling lights from the tree shone down on it like a spotlight. Madge didn't want to be impressed by the sight. She didn't want to feel her bosom warm and her heart lift at the thought of a package from Austen's under the tree for Christmas morning. She wanted to be her same old stoic, cranky self, for goodness' sake.

She failed.

As Madge prepared for bed, she thought about the story of old Scrooge. She had always thought they had a lot in common. She didn't yell "humbug" at her nephews, but she did usually manage to get around their invitations to join them for Christmas. She never outright lied. She just told anyone who asked that she had plans. She did. Plans to avoid all the hoopla and sit in her own chair on Christmas morning, eating all the cinnamon rolls she wanted. She got them from a bakery not far from the house. She normally ate a couple on Christmas Eve. If she timed her purchase just right, the rolls would still be warm and gooey, with frosting slithering off the sides and onto her fingers. She licked up every bite before she washed her hands.

On Christmas morning, when she added a cup of coffee with lots of cream and sugar, the rolls were still almost as good as fresh. Once she had downed her breakfast, she would take time opening the Christmas cards from Ben and his brother Clyde. She knew the wives fixed up those cards. Neither of the boys would ever think of such a thing. They always included a nice note and sometimes a bit of money to "go get something you like." Lately, they had been sending gift cards to eating places Madge had never heard of. She usually managed to hand those off to her hairdresser or the boy who shoveled her snow. Cheaper than a Christmas tip.

This year would be something rare. So rare Madge could not imagine it. When she climbed under her soft comforter on Sunday night, she could not imagine waking on Christmas morning in a house filled with children. She wondered if it would be like one of those Hallmark commercials.

Probably not. This wasn't exactly a Hallmark family. Luke and Alex had only been living in the same house again for a few weeks. The Christmas tree in the corner of the family room was a fake. Pre-lit, of all things. The girls had splashed some shiny balls around its edges, but the poor thing was still a sad excuse of a tree.

Not that she'd ever had much of a tree that she remembered. Her dad used to cut a spindly cedar from the edge of the pasture. It was usually small, with uneven branches and a few bare spots, but she could still smell that tree.

Her mother would pull out a box of mismatched balls, used tinsel, and a long string of electric lights. On a good year, the lights would work. If they didn't, her dad might mess with them long enough to find the burned-out bulb and stick a new one in. Madge was pretty sure they hung the lights a year or two without ever getting them to work.

She scrunched further into her mountain of pillows and remembered the last Christmas she had felt like a child. She had stood outside the hardware store that Christmas Eve and watched bubble lights explode over and over on a perfectly trimmed tree. She had never seen anything so magical, and she stood on the sidewalk until her toes started getting numb. For those few minutes, she forgot the ugly tree at home and the stocking she knew would be mostly empty the next day. She even forgot that her dad had lost his job and their Christmas dinner would come from a charity basket her mother had managed to sneak through the back door when he was sleeping.

She pulled the cover up a smidge higher and gave a sigh. Should have thought of all that a week ago. The Marvel tree could have done with some bubble lights.

CHAPTER SEVENTEEN
God Bless Us Every One

Scrooge stayed with Madge in her dreams. She couldn't have repeated the scenes clearly, but she knew they were filled with more humbugs than bubble lights. She forced herself out of bed at daylight and tried to dress without making noise. If she managed not to bang a drawer or squeak a door, she might get a whole cup of coffee before the madness descended.

The dining room clock seemed to click louder than usual as Madge scuffed into the kitchen. For the first time, she decided that automatic timer on the coffee machine was a good thing. She filled her cup halfway and then added almost as much creamer and sugar. Real cream would have been nice, but she hadn't thought to order any. She had taken back her role of chief-grocery-shopper right after Thanksgiving. Paige had taught her months ago how to shop at Barker's online and get boxes of food delivered straight to the house. It was the only duty she performed these days, and it helped her feel a little less like a free loader.

Madge gripped her cup and hoped she could make it into the family room without sloshing. Her cane did not make for a smooth transport. Even so, she planned to sit in front of the less-than-gorgeous Christmas tree and savor a few minutes of caffein-ated silence.

She had not counted on the four blonde heads peeking from between the spindles on the staircase.

"We're waiting for the music," Quinn whispered.

"What music?"

"The Christmas music that says Santa has been here, and we can come downstairs."

"Oh." Madge stood holding her coffee, her cane, and a whole load of misgivings about the traditional expectations of the girls. She did not expect Christmas morning to go as it had in the past. Months of separation had taken a toll on Luke and Alex. They were trying to make things work, but Madge didn't think either of them were quite in the swing of life yet.

She looked toward the family room, then back at the staircase. "Let me check," she whispered.

She left her coffee on the dining room table and crept toward the family room. "Lord Almighty," she prayed silently, "we could do with another Christmas miracle right now. Let there be gifts under that tree."

Madge suddenly understood how Mr. Scrooge felt when he finally woke up on Christmas morning. The spindly tree glowed like a magnificent blue spruce in the darkened room. Gifts large and small spilled out from beneath its branches in glittering glory. Four of Luke's golf socks hung from the mantel, fat with promise. The cookie plate held only crumbs, and the coveted glass of milk sat empty. It was Hallmark after all.

Madge looked at the music machine across the room. She had absolutely no clue how anyone ever made the thing work. So many dials and buttons. She wanted the girls to come sit in this moment with her, though. In true Scrooge style, she wanted to share.

Madge hadn't sung in front of other people since she had been humiliated by an eighth-grade teacher. Well, that wasn't true. She had sung a verse under her breath just this year. The first time baby Grace sat on her lap at church. It had been a day of firsts. But singing was not something Madge did. Even so, she pulled in a breath and then croaked out, "Hark the herald angels sing, glory to the newborn King."

From the staircase, Aspen's sweet, clear voice echoed back, "Peace on earth, and mercy mild."

The girls ran down the staircase, but when they entered the room, they stood perfectly still.

"God and sinners reconciled," Madge sang the words in as close to a whisper as her raspy voice would allow. She didn't even care how she sounded. She felt overwhelmed at the reality of what the words meant. Here she stood, an old sinner come late to the faith. Barren in every imaginable way, yet so full in this moment that the emotions threatened to spill out in actual tears.

Grace saved the moment. She made a dash for the nearest gift and pulled off a huge bow before anyone could stop her. The chorus of no's that followed broke the spell. The girls dropped to the floor and wriggled as close to the tree as possible. Aspen held Grace and whispered to her that they had to wait for mama.

"That's right, isn't it?" she said to Madge. "We should wait for our parents?"

Madge considered. A part of her had been wanting to spank the two adults in this house all along. She wasn't sure they deserved this perfect moment after the way they behaved the past year. Threatening to split up their family. Going all the way to court to get it done. Talking mean to each other, right in front of the girls.

Then Madge remembered the stab of mercy she had felt for her own rotten life just five minutes ago. "Maybe you should turn on the music," she said to Aspen.

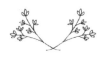

Chaos followed.

Luke and Alex arrived, both looking as if they needed strong coffee and a few more hours in bed. Instead, they plopped down on opposite sides of the room and attempted to smile at their eager daughters.

"Well," Luke yawned and rubbed his eyes. "Looks like Santa came."

"That one's mine," Peyton yelled. "I see my name."

"Indeed, it is," Luke said. "But I was thinking we should start a new tradition this year."

"What's that?" Quinn said.

Luke picked up a Bible from the end table beside him. Madge had never seen a Bible in that spot before. In fact, she hadn't seen a Bible anywhere in the whole house.

"I thought we could read the Christmas story," Luke said. "The real one. Not the one where 'you'll shoot your eye out.'"

The little girls giggled. Alex stretched and nodded. "Maybe I could get some coffee first?"

"I'd take a cup," Luke said. Then he motioned for Grace to come sit on his lap. Quinn and Peyton scooted closer to Luke's knees, but Aspen stayed in her spot near the tree.

When Alex returned, Luke opened the Bible to a place that had been marked with the attached ribbon. "And it came to pass in those days," he began.

Madge closed her eyes and listened to the familiar words in this unexpected setting. She thought, quite possibly, that nothing could ever feel nicer in this world.

She was wrong.

Within a few minutes, the storybook room turned into a scene worthy of the nightly news. It looked as if a hurricane had come through. Or maybe an earthquake. Grace hugged Madge's baby doll and gave it multiple kisses during the melee. Even Aspen seemed impressed with her books. She thanked Madge more than once.

The little girls had already strung one of their games across the floor when Luke said, "I see an envelope in the tree branches with your mama's name on it. Must be from Santa."

Alex put her coffee cup on the end table and pulled back the tree branch near her side of the couch. Sure enough, a white envelope tied with a red ribbon fell to the floor. She picked it up and looked at Luke with a frown.

"I thought we said no gifts."

"We did. I'm telling you, that one must be from Santa."

Madge couldn't tell whether Alex was happy or mad about the gift. Sometimes her face was hard to read.

Aspen curled up on the sofa and peeked over Alex's shoulder while Alex pulled the ribbon loose.

"Read it out loud," Madge said once Alex held the note.

"It's a trip," Alex said. She kept staring at the paper instead of looking at Luke.

"Where?" Madge thought Alex was being pretty secretive about the whole thing. Just get on with it, woman. Breakfast was waiting.

"To Aspen." Alex dropped the note in her lap and let the ribbon slip to the floor.

Madge raised an eyebrow. Aspen. The honeymoon location for Luke and Alex. The place where Aspen Marvel got her name. Madge had heard them say they hadn't been back for many years. That Luke had some moves. She started smiling and winked across the room at him. But Luke was watching Alex.

"You want to go, don't you?"

"Well, sure, but how can we afford it?"

Aspen reached over and touched the paper. "It's for all of us," she said. She looked at her dad as if he just might be Santa Claus.

"What about Madge," Alex said. "We can't leave her alone."

Madge crossed her arms. "I've been on my own more years than you have been alive. Stop fussing over me. Get out of here and have fun at Aspen, wherever that is."

"It will be fun," Luke said. "Snow, skiing, hot chocolate in front of the fire."

Alex hesitated one more minute. "Okay, I guess Joe and Mara could look in on you, Madge. And you could call them if you need anything."

"Sure," Madge said. "The truth is, I'll enjoy the peace and quiet."

"I'm packing right after breakfast," Aspen said. She jumped from the sofa and waded through the knee-deep sea of wrapping paper as if she were skiing. She made a full circle in the room and ended in front of the Christmas tree. She reached for Madge's blue box and held it out like a sacred offering.

"You have one more to open," she said.

Madge fingered the soft robe she had unwrapped and glanced at the box of cherry chocolates from the little girls. "Oh, I've had so much already," she said. "Maybe I ought to wait on that one."

"I don't think so," Aspen said. "You have to open it on Christmas morning like he said."

That statement drew looks from everyone in the room. They all turned and gave Madge the attention she had hoped to avoid. Aspen placed the gift carefully on Madge's knees.

Madge waited a few more seconds, and then she opened the tiny envelope attached to the box. "From Elmer and Aspen," it said. Madge realized her mouth was hanging open when she looked up at Aspen.

She shrugged. "I didn't put any money in on it. I told him to leave me off. But he says the whole thing was my idea, so I had to go in on it with him. You'll understand when you open it."

Madge did not understand. She slid her finger under the edge of the paper and slowly peeled it back. Inside, she found a blue velvet box with the gold monogram from Austen's on top. That would have been gift enough, to tell the truth. She lifted the hinged lid as slowly as she could while everyone else watched.

Pearls. A luxurious strand of what Madge realized must be real pearls. She started to slam the lid shut, but Aspen intervened.

"Remember," she said, "when I did the painting of our family, and I put you in the center? I painted a pearl necklace on you because your real name, Margaret, means pearl."

"And you are a pearl to us," Quinn shouted. "I remember."

Madge remembered, too. How could she forget? And she remembered that Elmer Grigsby and Pastor Cleveland had been sitting with them at the Thanksgiving table when the picture was unveiled.

"What you don't know," Aspen continued, "is that Mr. Grigsby held onto that thought. He says that he can't make himself call you Madge. He doesn't think it fits. But that Margaret is too stuffy. So, when he saw the picture, he knew in a second that he would always and forever call you Pearl."

Madge felt something almost giddy rising in her as Aspen spoke.

"He doesn't say it out loud. He only told me so I'd understand why it was important that we give you pearls for Christmas this year. He probably didn't even want me to explain it, but I had to, because you should know."

"Well," Madge said. "It's a nice thought." She tried to clear her head. "I know you meant well, and this is about the nicest thing I've seen in my whole life. You tell him that when you give them back." She held the box out to Aspen.

"I'm not giving them back," she looked at Luke for backup, but he seemed as stunned as Madge. She turned to Alex.

"Mom?" Aspen said, "We can't give them back, right?"

"Well, that is a pretty extravagant gift," Alex let the thought dangle, and Luke suddenly recovered.

"It is the perfect gift," he said. "Don't over think this, Madge. Just be grateful and let a friend indulge you a bit this year. It isn't an engagement ring or anything."

117

"Oh, Lord in Heaven," Madge said. "What kind of person do you think I am? Engagement ring? Good grief, man. I'm an old woman and Elmer Grigsby is an old man, and we don't have any business going around giving each other gifts and acting like young lovers. An engagement ring." She huffed a little harder than necessary after that speech, and she knew it.

Alex came over and took the box. "Why don't we just put these pearls in your room for now? You can think it over for a few days and decide how you want to handle it."

Madge nodded and Alex kept talking as she walked away. "Or Aspen can help you try them on, and you can look in that mirror over the sofa to see what you think." She stopped at the door with her back to the room.

Madge considered. She was surprised that she couldn't make herself disagree with that idea right away. While she tarried, Aspen crossed the room in two leaps and retrieved the box.

"You have to try them on," she said. "Even if you give them back later, you should try them this morning."

Madge pulled herself up and turned to look in the huge mirror. Aspen took that as permission and pulled the necklace from her box. When the pearls touched Madge's neck, she took in a big breath. They were smooth and cool against her skin, yet she felt warm, almost feverish. She reached up and touched the pearls, watching herself in the mirror.

She looked like a red-headed Barbara Bush standing there with her morning hair flying all over the place.

"Well," she said as she continued touching the pearls. "God bless us, every one."

CHAPTER EIGHTEEN

Multitude of Counselors

On Tuesday morning, Madge waved good-bye to the Marvel family as they set off for their grand adventure in the mountains. She stood a little longer than necessary at the edge of the drive and watched Luke's big vehicle disappear down the street. After a few minutes, she realized a light snow had started. Flakes landed on her nose as she turned to hobble back into the house.

The big. Empty. House.

Madge wandered around the kitchen, straightening this and wiping that. Even with her cane, she made quick work of the job. She looked at the family room where the Christmas tree sat empty of any presents. It looked more sad than festive now. She tried to remember how it had looked on Christmas morning with a family around the tree.

Madge's own childhood had never included siblings. Her much-older brother left home before she started to school. At his funeral, Madge realized she barely knew the man. His sons had made a good attempt at staying in touch with her since then.

Madge had often wondered how it would feel to have a sister. Maybe that is why Catherine had meant so much to her. And why she liked watching the Marvel sisters together.

Madge heard her purse ringing. She couldn't remember exactly where she had left the thing. Maybe on the hall table. It was on about the tenth ring before Madge managed to dig the tiny phone out of her gigantic purse.

"Madge? Oh, good. I thought you might have gone visiting or something."

"Who is this?" Madge pushed the phone harder against her ear.

"It's Paige. Rosedale."

"You could have left off the last name. You're the only Paige I know."

"I hope you had a merry Christmas," Paige said.

"Tolerable." Madge knew she had started this conversation with a huffy tone, but she could not pull herself back.

"Well, I'm back in town already, and I wondered about Circle. Will we have it today?"

Madge wondered about the term "we." Paige was a little young for the Glory Circle sisters. In her defense, though, she had been a regular attender since Madge started needing a driver. She didn't know how to answer the question of whether or not they would have Circle today. A little snow. Close to the holidays. She couldn't remember what they had decided about all that.

"I'd have to call Evelyn to find out," she said.

"Why don't you do that," Paige said. "I'll go ahead and start your direction. If Prayer and Share is cancelled, we can just have a cup of cocoa in front of the fake fire. If Alex doesn't mind."

"Alex is on her way to Aspen. The town. Or the mountain. Or something."

"Oh," Paige stayed quiet long enough Madge thought she might have lost connection. Finally, Paige spoke again. "Are you all alone? Were you alone on Christmas?"

"Of course not. I mean, I'm alone now, but everyone was here for Christmas. It was a jolly old time." Madge knew her cranky voice didn't sound jolly.

"I'll be there in a few," Paige said. "Don't go outside by your-self."

Madge started to tell Paige exactly what she thought of that advice, but Paige had ended the call.

Madge faced herself in the mirror that hung above the hall table. She pulled at the neck of her sweater and stretched it to one side, then the other. She wanted to make sure the silly pearls didn't show.

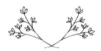

Paige whipped her little car into the handicap parking lot of Mt. Zion Church just minutes before nine. Madge had caught a glimpse of Evelyn's car around front, but she wondered if anyone else would brave the cold. She didn't think any of the Glory Circle sisters had left town for Christmas.

She still dreaded going through the side door. Not only did it go against her grain, but she had to worry about whether or not Elmer Grigsby would be lurking around. He might have flowers or something the way he had been behaving.

Elmer did not assault her when she entered the room. The lights glowed bright above the wooden floor, making it almost glow in return. Madge scooted across the expanse as fast as her hobbly leg would take her.

The hallway was empty, too. The sound of her cane echoed a little even with the muffle of the carpet. She was glad to finally reach the Sunday school room and not feel so much like she had been left behind on the planet or something.

Paige met her at the door, and they entered to the clatter of women all talking at once. Comparing Christmas stories, dis-cussing who tried what new recipe, and which great-grandchild said the cutest thing.

It was the normal post-Christmas meeting of the Glory Circle sisters. Usually, Madge sat in silence while everyone cackled on.

Today, though, she could join the conversation. Once she had shrugged off her coat and stowed her handbag under her chair, Madge made a little noise like clearing her throat.

"We had quite the to-do at our place," she said.

The room grew quiet, and Evelyn turned toward Madge. "At the Marvel house?"

"Well, yes, that's where I'm staying until my leg gets all healed."

"Oh," Bess clapped and smiled as if she were following the conversation. "Such a lovely name for a house. Is it magical?"

"Marvel doesn't mean magic," Grace Colby said. "And it's just the name of the people Madge works for."

Bess looked distressed until Madge spoke up again. "I expect you would have called it magic, Bessie. Those little girls were a sight in their Christmas pajamas and all their new toys."

"Kids are spoiled to death these days." Grace Colby pulled a tissue from her purse and touched her nose as if she could smell the rottenness of entire generations.

"Well, aren't you just Scrooge himself today?" Madge crossed her arms and poked out her chin. "The Marvel girls are not spoiled. They've been through a terrible time, and if they got to enjoy a little frill on Christmas day, I say 'so be it.' One baby doll isn't going to spoil a child for life."

"Oh, a baby doll for Christmas." Bess had returned to her former jolliness. "Every house should have a baby doll for Christmas."

"Well," Madge sat straighter, "I thought so."

"I think it's lovely," Paige said, "that Madge had a family for Christmas this year." She must have realized how that sounded, because she covered herself quickly. "I mean, she's always had a family. Just not always little girls. At Christmas, I mean. It must have been nice…"

The poor girl let the sentence dwindle under the scowl of Grace Colby. Evelyn, always the smooth one, came to her rescue.

"And what about you, Paige? Did you go to your family for Christmas?"

"Oh, at Martha's Vineyard isn't it?" Bess had mistaken Paige for Jackie Kennedy the first time they met, and her illusion seemed to have returned with the Christmas jollies.

"Well, no," Paige said. She looked around the room as if asking someone else to step in. When they didn't, she said, "President Kennedy's family does live there, I think. My family is here in the Midwest. Plain old farmers."

"Nothing wrong with farming." Erma spoke from her corner with more determination than Madge had heard from her in a while. "My people were farmers for generations."

"And did you take Jack to meet your parents?" Evelyn held the perfect pose, as if she were just making conversation and not digging for information. She sat with legs bent to the side, ankles crossed, and one hand on top of the other in her lap. Madge thought of it as her queenly pose. She was a nice queen, but still. The position of her hands showed off the new ring Santa had brought for Christmas this year. Madge didn't know much about gems, but the red stone must be a ruby. Surrounded by what must have been diamonds.

Madge tucked her own hands into the pocket of her sweater. The pressure of the pearls against her skin started to feel heavy and she wished she had left them at home in the blue box with the velvet lining. Such soft velvet.

"I said, 'What did you get from Clyde this year?'"

Madge jerked and realized Evelyn had switched the conversation and was talking to her.

"Oh, the usual. Nice card. A puzzle book." She didn't mention that Clyde had included a gift card to some fancy eatery. She had tucked that into an envelope with a note for Paige, but she hadn't presented it yet.

"Well, I'd say we've had a lovely Christmas," Evelyn said. "Let's start thinking about our New Year's projects, shall we?"

"Project One should be to turn the heat on in this room," Grace Colby said.

"It does seem a bit nippy," Erma agreed.

Bess chose that moment to enter today's reality and said, "Somebody should go check on that Mr. Grigsby and see if he has the thermostat turned down."

Everyone turned to Madge in one movement. As if they had been watching a tennis match and the ball had been batted her way.

"What? I don't know if the heat is on."

"Oh, I'd say the heat is on." Paige giggled as soon as she spoke, and several of the ladies joined her.

Madge wagged her head. "I don't know what you're getting at, Paige Rosedale."

"She's getting at you," Grace Colby said. "Crazy notions for a woman of your age, Madge. But we shouldn't be surprised."

Paige spoke up with what Madge would describe as a nice tinge of sassiness.

"It isn't crazy at all," Paige said. "I think it's lovely that Madge has a gentleman friend. She is perfectly able to make such a decision."

"Ha." Grace Colby turned one shoulder toward Paige and spoke in Erma's direction. "A man that age couldn't be looking for anything except a nurse."

"Or a fortune," Bess said. "In the stories, rich widows are always taken for their fortunes by shady gentlemen. You should be careful."

Madge didn't suppose anyone in the room fully understood that she was neither a widow nor rich. She mumbled so only Paige could hear, "Wrong on both counts."

To Bess she simply said, "Don't worry." Then she jerked a thumb toward Paige. "This lot will make sure nobody comes after my worldly possessions or my virtue."

Paige bumped her shoulder against Madge and winked just as Bess gasped. She pointed over Paige's other shoulder toward the door, where Elmer Grigsby stood with his hat in his hands. Madge had no idea what he might have heard as he stood there. She tried not to look him in the face, but when she looked down, she saw the gloves she had given him for Christmas poking out of his coat pocket. She suddenly felt like she had cheated on him the way she talked to the ladies. Before she could think what to do, he spoke.

"I'm terrible sorry, ladies. Looks like the furnace is actin' up a bit. I know it's cold in here, but I've got a heater in the back closet, and I'm gonna fetch it so you can go on with your meetin'. Sorry to be a bother."

Madge felt a hot stab in her chest. A quick heat like when she ate pepperoni too late at night. Before she could think of anything to say, Elmer was gone. She could hear his footsteps in the hall, but he wasn't whistling.

CHAPTER NINETEEN
The Solitary in Families

Madge insisted she could walk to the door on her own when she and Paige arrived back at the Marvel house Tuesday afternoon. They had stopped for lunch, and Madge could feel the ache in her bones about to turn into a throb by the time they got back to Cherry Hills.

When she used to drive over here to pick up Catherine, Madge never thought of Cherry Hills being so far from Mt. Zion. Once she came to stay with the Marvels, though, the distance seemed to grow. Maybe it was all the heavy traffic now. New stores popping up on streets that used to be empty. Madge had never craved a return to country living, but this was a little too much culture to suit her.

She came through the side door and entered from the kitchen side of the house. Back in the day, Catherine's kitchen had been a homey spot. A little outdated, maybe, but the kind of room that seemed to reach out and offer to wrap itself around you. Now, Luke and Alex had turned it into something worthy of a magazine. And about that cold.

The red light on the coffee pot seemed to be the only warmth in the room. Madge scolded herself for forgetting to turn it off. She hustled across the room and took care of that chore. The dining room looked equally stark in the afternoon light. It didn't get much sun. Madge turned toward the family room instead. She could have napped in her own room. Instead, she plugged in the tree lights and sat in Luke's chair.

With an afghan over her legs, she sank into the cushions and sighed. She waited a few minutes for her own body heat to warm the chair and for the afternoon contentment to settle in. It normally did after she had spent a morning with the Glory Circle sisters. No matter if Bess was daft and Grace Colby was grumpy. She wasn't bothered because Erma was shy and Evelyn was polished. Madge just liked being with them, and she could admit that to herself. Usually, she could get a nice nap afterwards and feel almost happy.

Today, however, happy land failed to appear. So did her nap.

Instead, Madge tossed about in the chair trying to find a comfortable spot. Finally, she had to admit to herself that she was also trying to get rid of a certain picture in her mind. The picture of Elmer Grigsby carrying her Christmas gloves in his pocket. They looked good with his coat.

In the next minute, though, she remembered the look on Evelyn's face. Madge had expected Grace Colby to look down on Elmer. Grace looked down on just about everybody. Evelyn had more mercy, though. She usually covered up her disgust even if she felt it. Madge had noticed a strange look on Evelyn's face, though, when Elmer stepped into the room. She wasn't sure exactly what it meant, and she wasn't sure she had the spine to go against Evelyn's disapproval.

None of that mattered, though. She had probably hurt Elmer's feelings if he overheard her rattling on about money and virtue. She didn't plan to let this thing go any further, but she didn't want to make him feel bad, either.

"Lord," she finally prayed. "You better just get me outta this mess. I don't know why in the name of Heaven I've fallen in with such a fellow. It's time You do something about it."

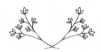

Madge evidently slept after she turned things over to the Almighty, although she didn't remember falling asleep. When she next opened her eyes, darkness had arrived. And with it, the softening of Christmas lights on the lonely family room.

Alex had tried to clear away most of the debris from Christmas morning, but a few stray wrapping papers still lingered in the corners. The rest of the room looked completely put together. Tidy. Matching. She supposed some would say elegant. And completely empty.

Madge roused herself from the sofa and looked into the darkened dining room. She had been alone in this house many days while everyone else was at school or work. She had learned to be comfortable that way. This aloneness felt different. Empty.

She supposed it was because she had grown used to the sound of little girls chattering all the time. Or the washing machine rumbling. Or Luke's ball games on television. It certainly was not because she missed anyone else. Especially not the man who had given her these pearls. They were about to choke her to death.

Madge managed to undo the clasp, which was a real trick with stiff fingers. The trip to her bedroom to put the pearls back in their velvet bed took more vigor than she had expected. She bumped into a chair in the dining room and wished she had turned on a light. She couldn't quite bear to look at the empty house in light. The dark helped her pretend everyone was already upstairs asleep.

They were not. And the game didn't help her one bit as the evening wore on. She peeked out a window once and saw snowflakes falling hard. They didn't look festive now that Christmas was over. Just cold. And slick.

The jangle of her phone from the kitchen made Madge jump higher than she knew she could. Elmer Grigsby's voice on the other end did nothing to calm her soul.

"I jest wanted to check that you made it home alright. It's a-snowin' here like sixty."

"It's snowing some here, too. Didn't start till after I got home, though." Madge had long ago stopped worrying about the fact that she called the Marvel house her home.

"I'd kinda planned to offer to take you for pie and coffee after meeting tomorrow night, but I'm not expectin' to see you get out with this storm."

Madge pulled back the curtain on the window over the kitchen sink. Snow had turned the swing set into something like an ice palace. A streetlight made it sparkle like magic. Evidently, Elmer had covered her thoughtless words much like the snow had covered the lawn.

"Thanks," she said. "I'll probably not get out tomorrow."

"Well," Elmer paused, "I hope the house doesn't feel too lonely while you're caught there."

"Not a bit," Madge said. She hunched her shoulders and pulled into herself as if to prove the point. "I've got everything I need. I could last till spring."

"Could you now?"

She could practically hear the smile in his voice, and she wanted so badly to be irritated by it. Instead, she smiled back.

When Madge woke on Wednesday morning, she felt sure the clock had broken in the night. She had never slept past six for as long as she could remember. The clock pointed to eight-thirty.

"Liar," she said. "Batteries must have gone out last night and I didn't notice." She reached over to find the battery slot and discovered the cord instead. It was firmly attached to the outlet on the wall.

Madge ignored her dressing gown and slippers. She didn't even take time for her cane but simply padded toward the dining room on her bare feet. She used the walls for support. She squinted at the ticking clock on the far wall. Eight-thirty.

"Well, my heavens," she said. "I must be sick."

She felt her forehead but couldn't find any fever. She couldn't imagine that the small exertions of the day before could have worn her out so much. Of course, there had been the Christmas to-do. And staying up late on Christmas Eve. Plus, the pizza supper on Friday night. And shopping with Paige before that.

Madge realized she had done more in the past week than in all the time since her hip surgery. Maybe she was just worn out. She went back to the bedroom and plopped into her chair. She picked up her Bible and opened to the psalms. That was always a good place to brighten the day. "God sets the solitary in families," she read aloud. She stopped mid-sentence. Was that what God had done to her? Was it the reason she suddenly felt lonely when she had lived alone for more than half a century? As if bidden by these thoughts of connections, Madge's telephone buzzed.

She managed to retrieve the phone from her purse before it stopped, and she was surprised to hear Ben's wife, Nancy, on the other end.

"Is it snowing at your place?"

"Has been. I've not looked out yet today."

"Oh, I'm sorry. Did I wake you?"

"I don't sleep the morning away like the teenager in this house," she said as she reached over to part the curtains. "Good glory," she said. Snow had piled so high it covered half the window.

"I guess it's a blizzard," she told Nancy.

"Well, that's what we heard on the news. Are you all okay? Do the Marvels have other heat if the electricity goes out?"

Madge was stuck, and she knew it. In their Christmas Day phone call, Madge had not told Clyde that the Marvels were leaving for a few days. She hadn't wanted him to worry, since he and Nancy had left town for the holidays. She didn't know a thing about the fireplace in the living room. She thought it had a real flame, but she didn't know how that worked. Gas, maybe? She supposed there was a switch somewhere to turn on the flame.

"Oh, I'm just hunky-dory," she said. "Toasty warm. Safe inside. Plenty of food. Don't you worry about me."

"Well, we are certainly glad you stayed with the Marvels a little longer than expected. I'd worry if you were all alone in your little house."

"Yep, not a thing to worry about," Madge said. "You all go on and have a great time. I'm hunky-dory."

Once they exchanged a few more pleasantries and said their good-byes, Madge plunked down on her chair. She remembered all too well that Catherine nearly froze to death in this house during an ice storm. It had a new furnace since then, but if the electricity went out, she expected the heat would go, too.

With all the strength she could muster, Madge started gathering afghans and blankets and carting them to her room. She thought it would give her the best chance of staying warm if it came to that. She wanted to go upstairs and pull the puffy comforters off the girls' beds, but she knew she couldn't handle the climb. Maybe she should check the dryer. Alex might have washed some bedding before they left.

Madge pulled a stool into the laundry room and dropped onto it with more of a thud than she intended. This pulling and pushing and fetching and toting had done her in. She opened the dryer door and reached in to pull out something that looked like sheets.

They were sheets. White sheets covered in vines. From the green room upstairs. Madge sat back and considered. Why would Alex be washing the sheets from a room nobody had used? Because somebody was using it. With a sudden jolt, Madge realized Alex and Luke were still in separate rooms. She wasn't the only person living alone in this family.

CHAPTER TWENTY

Winter Wonderland

Mara Lynn called on Friday afternoon. The electricity had held together despite the wind bashing against the house like a madman trying to get in. Madge didn't want to admit how much she hated the sound. She had never liked wind, and now it got on her last nerve. She wasn't sure why. She had lived alone more years than she had ever lived with other people. She liked living alone. Yet, she had obviously grown soft since coming to stay at the Marvel house. She was glad to hear Mara Lynn's voice on the phone, even though she didn't recognize it and had to be told.

"We promised Luke and Alex we would check in on you while they're gone. I had a text from Alex yesterday, and she said they were losing cell service, so we probably won't hear from them."

"Okay. I'm fine." She wondered how many times she had used that word recently.

"Plenty of food in the house?"

"Sure."

"Warm enough?"

"Toasty."

Madge waited for the next question, which she planned to bat across the air with one word. Instead, she heard a scramble and then Joe's voice came across the speaker.

"Aunt Madge? This is Joe. You better quit bein' all brave over there and tell the truth. Are you lonesome?"

Madge sucked in a breath. That question had not been on the roster in her mind. If anyone else in the world had asked it, she would have shrugged it off. Growled something smart aleck right back at them. But something about the way Joe said it, as if he had the right to ask and might even have a way to fix things.

"Could be," she said. "A person gets used to the commotion, I guess."

"That's what I thought. We're still snowed in over here. Plows haven't been near our street. But just talkin' to somebody helps sometimes."

Madge hated to admit that she felt lighter. "Who'd have thought it?" she said. "I never needed to talk to anybody that I remember before now." She wasn't sure she had uttered those words out loud. They had come to her mind, and she might have blurted them.

"Well, things change. You get used to people being around, and when they're gone, you feel lonesome. It's natural." He paused as if to let her think about it. "It's good. Real good to let people into your life. Even if they make you lonesome when they leave."

Madge blinked to clear the mist from her eyes. She was about to tell Joe exactly what she thought of his philosophy when she heard a strange, scritchety sound at the door.

"Hold on," she said to Joe.

Maybe a limb had fallen against the house in the night. She pulled her bathrobe closed in case any of the neighbors were also out checking things, and she hoped the snow wouldn't bury her when she opened the front door.

Madge did almost get a blast of snow in the face, but it came from a shovel heaved just past her head.

"Whoa! I didn't see you there." Emily's husband, Albert, lowered the shovel and wiped the back of his sleeve across his eyes.

Once he had caught his breath, he said. "Emily's waiting in the car. We didn't aim to bother you."

"I'm not bothered." Madge folded her arms across her chest and wished she had grabbed a coat to cover her robe.

"Well, we wanted to get out and about if we could today. Just check on things, you know." He stood with both hands on the shovel as if waiting for a report.

"Things are okay here," Madge said. "If that's what you're checking."

"Oh, not particularly." He swung the shovel up over one shoulder and nodded toward the cleared sidewalk. "Just thought the mailman might appreciate a path to your front door."

Madge looked over Albert's shoulder and saw Emily sitting in the passenger seat. "Tell Emily I'm just dandy. No need to be checking around on me. Heat's on. Lights, too. Plenty of food in the house."

"Uh huh." He turned a little, as if he might walk away. "We did hear a rumor that you're all on your own. The folks have left town for a bit."

Madge pulled herself up and pushed out her chin. "You tell Emily and anyone else who noses about my business that I've been on my own for more years than I care to count. I don't need looking after."

Albert shrugged. "I'm sure you don't need looking after," he said. "I was just thinking of the mailman."

Madge regretted that she had been quite so grouchy about the whole thing. The man was freezing his fingertips to get her a clear path to the street.

"Thank you for the scooping," she said. "The mailman will be glad."

When she stepped back inside and closed the door, Madge heard a noise from the hall table. Drat if she hadn't dropped her phone when she opened the door.

"Aunt Madge? You still there? What's goin' on over there? Do I need to send a car?"

"Don't send any cops," Madge said. "I just had company at the door."

"Company?"

"Oh, just Emily, the former housekeeper, and her husband. He still likes to shovel these walks sometimes. Can't get out of the habit."

She managed to convince Joe and Mara Lynn that everything was in order. A job she'd had to do more times than she liked in the last twenty-four hours. If Paige or Jack called, she just might hang up on them.

Instead, she took a nap. She got dressed first. The idea of lying about in nightclothes all day made her feel like an invalid. She didn't bother with matching her pants and sweater. She never had cared much about it before, and she wasn't sure why she had started thinking of it recently. She pulled on the first thing she grabbed and added double socks with her slippers.

She decided on Luke's reclining chair for naptime, but she covered it with one of her afghans first so it wouldn't feel cold. She planned to say a few prayers for folks before she slept. Especially for the Marvels on their trip.

When Madge awoke, she couldn't remember if she had finished her prayers, so she threw up a "God bless" for the whole family. She looked out the front window once her knees loosened up. The streetlights had begun to flicker. She had slept until nearly dark.

As she turned from the window, the sound of the doorbell made her jump. She shouldn't have been surprised to see Elmer Grigsby standing with hat in hand. But she was. Especially after Joe said their streets were still blocked.

"What on earth?" she said. "How did you get out here to Cherry Hills in the likes of this weather?"

Elmer poked a thumb toward the driveway where a shiny silver car sat with its engine purring. A young man with a slouchy beret sat in the driver's seat, but he was staring at his phone and paying no attention to Elmer.

"Mr. Uber," Elmer said as he grinned. "Neatest thing you've ever seen. You just poke a few buttons on them little telephones, and this fellow will take you anywhere you want to go in the city. Right reasonable, too."

Madge wasn't too sure about Mr. Uber. Catherine had often called for a town car instead of a taxi. The only difference Madge had ever been able to tell was that the driver wore a uniform and the car had a smidge more leg room. Catherine insisted it was safer. You never knew what you'd get with a taxi. What would she think of this arrangement?

Suddenly, Madge realized Elmer had started to shiver. "You better come in," she said. "Before you catch pneumonia."

"Oh, no. That wouldn't do. You being a gentle lady at home alone. What would the neighbors think?"

Madge thought about telling him the neighbors were too far away to see who was at her door. That was one of the perks of a house with a long drive and deep lawn. She also thought about mentioning that none of them paid any attention to comings and goings. If they did, they wouldn't think twice about Madge entertaining a gentleman caller. She knew that much about how the world had changed.

Instead, she said, "Well, you better get back into the car with Mr. Uber, then. You're freezing."

"Get your coat," Elmer said. "And boots if you've got 'em."

"I don't." Madge turned and reached behind the door for the Mizzou jacket that always hung there.

"That looks right smart." Elmer offered his crooked elbow to her as if he were a gentleman in a top hat and tails.

"What?"

"Let's go. I've got a treat waitin' for you in the car."

"I'm not going anywhere in that car."

"Just a little ride around the neighborhood," he said. "The fancy lights are all still up and they are a sight. You'll like 'em."

How Elmer Grigsby had a clue what she would or would not like, Madge did not know. Even so, she reached for his arm and held on for dear life as they walked toward the car. She didn't intend to break the other hip.

"Now, don't you worry about your reputation," Elmer said as he opened the door. "Mr. Uber will be our chaperone."

Madge didn't feel the cold anymore. In fact, her face felt completely warm. She slid as far over on the back seat as possible and waited for Elmer to climb in. She had not ridden in the back seat with a man since... well, pretty much since ever. She expected she should feel nervous. Instead, she felt warm.

"Alrighty, then." Elmer removed his gloves, the ones she had given him, and placed them on the seat with gentle care. Then he reached down at his feet and opened a little thermos bag. He pulled out two cups with lids.

Madge felt the heat wrap her fingertips when she accepted the drink. "A little hot chocolate for the ride."

With that, Mr. Uber pulled into the street.

Madge sipped her cocoa. She hated to admit it was perfect. And the lights! With the mounds of snow in all the yards, displays that had been pretty earlier in the month were now majestic. She caught herself giving an "ooh" or an "ah" now and then.

Elmer grinned like a boy the entire ride. He pointed out various spots along the route. When they came to a sparkling corner where it looked as if each homeowner had tried to outdo the other, he slapped his knee. "Lights of Glory right there. Do you see 'em, Pearl?"

Madge sucked in her breath, and Elmer looked caught.

"I hadn't meant to say it out loud."

Madge waited. She didn't even know how to respond.

"It's just," he picked up the gloves and worried the edges. "Well, it's like this, you see." Finally, he replaced the gloves and turned to face her. "You just aren't a Madge. It doesn't suit you. Aspen told me your real name is Margaret, but that feels too stuffy. None of those names roll just right to suit me."

Madge tried to keep her face neutral. She didn't know whether she should admit that she knew this story or not.

"So, then I thought of Thanksgivin', of Aspen's painting. And I thought, 'That's it. That's the right name for her. She is a Pearl, exactly right.'"

He took another sip of cocoa and then said, "I've been thinkin' of you as Pearl since before Christmas, but I 'spect I should ask your permission to call you that out loud. I'm sorry if I riled you."

"I'm not riled," Madge said. She scooted around on the seat trying to get comfortable, although she couldn't say exactly what ached. "You can call me whatever you want. It's a free world."

Elmer chuckled. "Yes, it sure is that. Didn't always feel that way to me, but it sure does now. Yes, siree, it sure does."

They had reached the driveway of the Marvel house by the time the conversation came to that point. Elmer helped her out and walked her back to the house with the same offer of his arm.

Once again, Madge was surprised at how strong he felt. How steady. When they reached the front door, Madge took one step inside and turned. Heavens to Betsy, she hoped the man didn't plan to try kissing her. She'd slug him.

Elmer removed his hat, stepped forward, and gave a little half-bow. "All right, then," he said. "Truth is I just wanted to come by and see if your streets were clear enough to pass. Make sure you were okay. The cocoa was my boy's idea."

"Well, now you know the streets and I are both hunky-dory." Madge knew she sounded cross when she answered with short words, but her own feet were starting to go numb from the cold. Her mind whirled with thoughts, emotions, and memories of bright lights. She could barely keep it all straight.

"Good," he gave her that grin. "I'll send Mr. Uber 'round to fetch you for church on Sunday."

He whirled and once again took a little hop step as he started down the sidewalk. Madge wanted to shout after him that she didn't need a ride to church. She certainly didn't need an old man doing hippity-hops on her slick sidewalk and ending up in the hospital with a hip like hers.

Madge did not say those things, though. She watched him go and felt her soul unclench a tiny bit from its hard grasp on solitary life. She whispered so low nobody could have heard her if they had been standing nearby. "Thanks, you silly old thing."

CHAPTER TWENTY-ONE
Side by Side

Mr. Uber arrived exactly on time Sunday morning. Madge saw him pull into the driveway, because she had been peeking out the window every ten minutes for a good hour. Before she could finish pulling on her coat and gloves, he rang the doorbell.

Madge swung the door wide and stared at the young man with his scruffy face. Not a beard. Just whiskers.

"You give door service?" she asked.

The young man doffed his hat and then slapped it back on his head. "Not as a rule. The gentleman who called for your ride asked if I would escort you since it might be slick."

He reached for her arm, and Madge waved him away.

"Balderdash. I can walk on my own two feet." As she spoke, she took the first step onto the sidewalk. Her feet immediately chose to go in opposite directions. Madge swung her arms like a whirly-gig and bashed the poor Uber man in the head with her purse before she managed to grab onto him from the back.

"Whoa," he shouted. "Hold still or we'll both go down."

Madge held still with great effort. Mr. Uber turned and hooked his arm under her elbow.

"Now," he said, "let's take it slowly."

Madge held back the many things she wanted to say as they walked. Instead, when the young man handed her into the car, she said, "Is Mr. Grigsby paying you extra to walk to and from?"

"He is." The driver touched the tip of his hat.

Madge gave a response that was something between a harrumph and a growl. She leaned into the soft seat, though, and did feel a smidgen grateful that she hadn't needed to skate to the car on her own. She wondered how long it would be before a winter walkway no longer reminded her of sirens, snow, and Winnie-the-Pooh blankets over her feet.

The drive out of Cherry Hills was slow. Only a few of the streets had been cleared, so the driver had to pick and choose. Once they reached the main roads, though, the streets were completely dry. Madge looked at the mountains of snow along the sides and realized someone had been working all night to make this path to church for her. She felt grateful, suddenly, for the unknown men in the big machines who made the way. She was not accustomed to feeling gratitude.

When the Uber driver stopped in front of the church and looked at the tall steps. "You able to make that climb? It looks like it could have some slick spots."

Madge wrested with her answer. She hated going in through the handicap parking when she rode with Paige or Luke. No way could she make herself admit to Mr. Uber that she couldn't climb the church steps yet. Just as she was ready to blurt it out, someone knocked on the window. Madge jerked and turned to see Evelyn and Tom.

When the driver rolled down his window, Evelyn said, "If you drive up that side street and come in around the back, you will find a nice parking spot in the upper lot. Much easier to navigate on a snowy day."

The driver nodded and gave Evelyn a wave.

Madge waved, too, but not quite so nicely. She had to admit Evelyn's style came through, though. She didn't even use the handicapped word. Just the upper lot. Why hadn't Madge thought of that before? It sounded classy. By the time they had parked, Madge had begun to feel almost glad for the shortcut. She would have liked to tell Catherine about the new name.

Before she could think further about that, the back door of the church flew open and Elmer Grigsby stepped out.

"Many thanks," he told the driver, "for delivering my package with care."

The driver looked over the back seat at Madge. "I'll admit this is the most unusual drive I've ever arranged. We see some interesting things in this job, but I've never been a chaperone before, and I've never delivered a gentleman his lady."

"Oh, balderdash," Madge said. "This isn't some movie, and I'm nobody's lady." She realized that was twice in one day that she had fallen back on her bad language habits. But these things simply required a strong word. She climbed out of the car and ignored Elmer's arm while she pulled herself up straight.

"Didn't mean to offend," he said.

Madge gave him a side-eye, expecting to see a little humility in the man. Pretty forward letting the driver assume such things. Elmer Grigsby did not look humble. His eyes crinkled at the edges from the grin he was trying to hold back.

Madge stood straight and hoisted her handbag onto the shoulder nearest Elmer. The giant bag made it impossible for him to offer his arm again, and Madge felt like she had won a point somehow. In the next second, she wondered why on earth she kept trying to beat the man. For that matter, why did she keep letting him into her life in any manner whatsoever? This silliness must stop, and now was as good a time as any.

She turned to tell him so, but Elmer no longer stood beside her. Madge felt a slight nudge and turned to see that he had slipped behind her and moved to the other side. He held out his arm.

"I'm not walking into church on your arm."

"Why not?"

"Because. What would people say? What would the girls think?"

"You mean the ladies in the third pew?"

"I do."

"Well, I 'spect they would think it was a good thing you had somebody to help you navigate into the church while the Marvels are away."

Madge stood uncertain for a few more seconds. "I don't think so," she finally said. She gripped her cane and started the walk across the gym floor. It became the longest walk of her life. She could feel Elmer following her, probably within touching distance. But she was determined to ignore him.

When she was within two steps of the hallway, Elmer stepped ahead of her and pushed open the heavy door. He nodded as she passed through, but he did not speak. Madge felt a little bad for crushing him. At the same time, she had to stop these ideas of them as a couple. She wasn't a couple with anybody, and she never intended to be.

She marched a little faster down the hallway and around the corner to the vestibule. Her cane thumped on the carpeted floor and echoed off the walls. And, all the time, she could hear Elmer walking behind her. When they reached the vestibule, he slipped easily ahead of her and opened the doors to the sanctuary. This time, Madge paused before going in.

"Thanks for your help," she said.

"Nothin' to it." He didn't give his little bow that time. Nor his grin.

Madge felt a little sorry about that.

Only Tom and Evelyn sat in the third row today. Madge realized they had already seen her in a strange car and would wonder about it. Before she could say anything to them, she heard Elmer coming down the aisle. She didn't even know she had memorized the sound of his steps. But she knew. She recognized the rhythm of his feet and the specific sound of the heel-to-toe tap of his shoes. It was a cocky walk, really, for a man without much to boast about.

The cadence stopped suddenly, and Madge realized Elmer stood beside her in the aisle. She waited, but he didn't move. She glanced at Evelyn and Tom, but they were paying no attention. She turned slightly and stretched her neck to see if anyone else was watching. Elmer Grigsby seemed to have all the time in the world to dawdle in the aisle, and he didn't seem the least bit worried about it.

Finally, Madge scooted down and allowed Elmer to step in next to her. She planned to drop her purse on the pew between them, but Elmer sat too quickly for that. Not so near that it felt uncomfortable, but close enough that anyone who cared to wonder would figure out the choice of seat was no accident.

She spent the better part of the worship service thinking up good explanations about Mr. Uber. She would have to admit she had ridden to church in a rented car. How could she explain that away? She couldn't outright lie and claim the Marvels had sent it. Evelyn would know Madge couldn't have pulled it off herself. She was rehearsing an explanation when Pastor Cleveland stood to speak.

"It is not good for man to be alone," he said.

Madge forgot about the car. The words seemed to bounce off the high ceiling and rumble like a shout through the room. She looked up to see if Pastor Cleveland had spoken the words directly at her. He didn't seem to be looking toward her pew, though.

"Some of the first words God said on the earth had to do with relationships. Marriage. A partnership for work and for life. He goes on to talk about relationships all through the Bible."

He flipped a few pages in his Bible. "The psalmist says that God sets the solitary in families. And that He has placed eternity in our hearts. Eternity is all about relationships. We won't take anything to Heaven with us except one another."

He held up his Bible. "The Old Testament is one long story about a family. The children of Israel, who are also the children of God. We can trace the family tree all the way from Abraham to Jesus. Everywhere we read in the Old Testament we find intriguing connections. For instance, did you realize that King David's grandmother was Ruth the Moabitess from the book of Ruth?"

Madge did not know that. Truth be told, the Old Testament was kind of hard for her. All those lists of names and the gory parts where so many people had to be killed. Catherine had loved the Old Testament. She said it was like reading her family history. She must have talked to Pastor Cleveland. That thought brought Madge back to the sermon of the day.

"In the New Testament, Jesus chose two sets of brothers and one of their good friends as His first disciples. How much more proof do we need? God loves relationships. At the very end of Jesus' life, when He was hanging on the cross, He looked at his best friend, John, and said, 'behold your mother.'"

"To Mary He said, 'Woman, behold your son.' He was taking care of family and friends even as He died to take care of the whole world, past, present, and yet to come."

Well. Madge had long wondered about that spot in the Bible. She had read it a lot of times, and she wondered why Jesus was telling Mary to look at Him. It would have been a horrible sight. But that wasn't the way it went. He was telling Mary to look at John. Telling John to take her in and make her a part of the family just as the Marvels had done for Madge.

She thought about her adopted family and wondered where they were today. Would they be out in the snow, skiing and romping? Or maybe driving. Maybe on the way home even as she sat here.

Madge felt a stab of something she thought might be called love. And then another thought dawned. It wasn't just the Marvels. It was Jack and Paige. They were hers, too. And now Joe and

Mara Lynn seemed to be latching on. Everywhere she looked right now, she saw connections. Before Madge could decide how she felt about that, Pastor Cleveland said something that made everyone laugh. Madge realized she had missed a good portion of the sermon while her mind wandered.

"So," Pastor Cleveland said. "It is not good for man to be alone. Nor for woman or child to be alone. As we step into the New Year, let's see what we can do about that."

Madge felt something brush her hand. She looked down to see Elmer Grigsby's hand holding the hymnal they would use for the last song. He held it on his lap but scooted it so close to the edge that his little finger barely brushed Madge's little finger.

She wanted to jerk back. She wanted to pretend this connection wasn't happening. She wanted to step away from something that threatened her independence much greater than a semi-adopted set of kids.

Yet, it was not good for man to be alone. Nor woman.

Madge lifted her hand and rested it on the hymnal. She would not hold the man's hand in church. But she might share his song book.

CHAPTER TWENTY-TWO

The Great Divide

On Monday afternoon, Madge heard the rumble of the garage door while she was working on a *Word Search* in the kitchen. She had started the puzzle in her sitting room, but she wasn't sure she could hear the garage door from there. So, she moved to the family room. The Christmas tree seemed to taunt her, though, reminding her she was alone in the big house.

The kitchen seemed the most sensible solution. She could putter around if she needed to stretch her legs, and she rather enjoyed having a spot at someone's kitchen table.

She would have told anyone who asked that she had no idea what time the Marvel family would return today. It could be the middle of the night for all she knew. That wasn't the strict truth, though. Mara Lynn had called to let her know they planned to start out right after breakfast.

On the last grocery order, Madge had included a pocket-sized United States atlas. She would pay Alex back for it. In the meantime, she had spent Sunday night plotting their course on the way home and calculating the time, adding in extra for bathroom breaks and meal stops.

Even with all her behind-the-scenes detective work, Madge would never have expected the family this early. She pushed away from the table and walked across the room to check on the Crock-Pot. She had dropped in some chicken and frozen vegetables to make a stew for supper, just in case they got home early.

Quinn burst through the door first. "I skied," she shouted. "And not just on the little bunny trail. I skied down the giant mountain. It looked just like the one in Aspen's painting."

Peyton tromped in next, shouting similar victories.

"No, you did the bunny trail," Quinn said. "You never went up the big mountain."

"I did. It was huge." Peyton raised her arm as high as she could while stretching on her tiptoes.

"What did you do while we were gone, Madge?"

She hadn't seen Aspen come through the doorway because the little girls were so rowdy. Now, Aspen stood looking like a model for winter sports wear. Somebody must have gotten some new clothes on the mountain.

"Oh, just the usual," Madge said.

"Did you go on any more dates?"

Madge squinted at Aspen and tried to ignore the little girls who were still arguing about who went down which trail. "What makes you ask a thing like that?"

Aspen pulled off her furry mittens and unwrapped the red scarf with slow moves. "Oh, you know, I was just wondering."

Aspen finished her sentence just as Luke came into the kitchen holding a sleeping Grace. Alex came two steps behind.

"Speaking of supper," Madge said, "I've made some stew. Should be ready in about an hour. That gives you time to get your boots off." She waved toward the laundry room where she assumed wet boots should go.

"You did have a date, didn't you?" Aspen spoke more quietly, as if talking to Madge alone.

Madge waited for one of the parents to shush Aspen and tell the girl Madge's social life was none of her business. Nobody spoke, though. They just waited.

Madge started to say that one date had been plenty for both of them. Then she remembered Mr. Uber. The hot chocolate and the Christmas lights. She didn't know if Aspen would call that a date, but she expected a girl her age could put quite the romantic spin on an evening car ride between friends.

"I'd say that's enough talk about such things." Madge turned toward the kitchen counter and kept her back to Aspen. "Now that you're here, I might stir up some muffins to go with that stew. I bought a mix just in case."

"Thanks, Madge," Alex said. "That sounds great. Come on, girls, let's get suitcases upstairs and start unpacking." Luke led the way with his bundle. The girls each grabbed a backpack and started for the stairs. Alex stopped at the dining room. "I hope you haven't been too lonely," she said.

Madge waved a hand without turning around. "Not a bit," she said.

Supper was a noisy affair. All the girls talked over one another, telling Madge about their escapades. Luke and Alex dropped in a few words here and there. Even Grace babbled on as if her late nap had given her unending energy.

Finally, Luke told the girls to start clearing the table. "You know school starts back up tomorrow," he said. "Regular bed-times tonight."

The chorus of complaints rose, but the girls started stacking bowls and spoons. As they worked on the chore, Luke stood. "I think I'll check email," he said. "I ignored a lot of stuff last week, and I'd feel better going in tomorrow if I know how many things I have to untangle when I get to the office."

Alex nodded as she took the last bite of her muffin. "I'm sub-bing at the girls' school tomorrow, so I can drive them."

"Great. I'll be up later."

"Sure."

Madge watched the interaction as the family went about their normal after-supper dance. This time, though, she was not fooled. She waited until everyone had left the room and she and Alex were alone.

"I folded that last load of laundry you had in the dryer," Madge said.

"Oh, thanks. I forgot we left anything going."

Madge shrugged. "I was looking for an extra blanket and checked the dryer."

"Did you find what you needed? I hope we didn't leave you in the cold."

"It's not me you better worry about."

Alex stopped scrubbing on the Crock-Pot and turned toward Madge. "What do you mean?" Her tone indicated that Alex knew exactly what Madge meant.

"I found the sheets from the green room. Somebody is sleeping in there."

Alex reached for a towel and then slumped onto the stool in the corner. "It isn't a huge deal," she said. "We're making good progress right now. I just feel like I still need a little space. A little time to think. Luke is fine with that."

Madge raised an eyebrow and popped a lid on the plastic container of leftover stew.

"I know it isn't conventional," Alex said. "But you know wealthy couples used to sleep in separate rooms all the time. I bet lots of them still do."

"Oh, sleeping isn't a problem," Madge said. "I can see where a person might want a bed to themselves. The sleeping in separate rooms wasn't what I'm worried about. It's none of my business, of course.

"Well, no, it isn't." Alex stood again and ran her hand along the counter as she walked toward the dining room. She kept her eyes on the counter as she said, "Where I sleep is not anyone else's business at all."

"Well, I might like to comment on that."

Madge looked up in time to see Alex take a step back. Luke had evidently come back down the stairs.

He pointed toward the table. "I left my phone down here."

Alex nodded. "How long have you been standing there?"

"Long enough to hear Madge call us out about the sheets from the green room."

Madge looked around the room for a way of escape. Before she could act on any of her ideas, though, someone pounded on the back door and then flung it open. Joe came barreling in with Mara Lynn right behind him.

"Hey, welcome home, you guys." He sent his million-dollar smile all around the room. "We were drivin' by on a grocery run and saw the garage door still wide open. Did you know you left it up, man?"

"No," Luke kept his eyes on Alex as he spoke. "Must have been distracted by all the unloading and unpacking. Thanks for stopping to tell us."

Madge felt the tension flying around the room. It finally zinged Joe hard enough for him to figure out he'd walked in on something.

"So…I guess you all had a good time, and you're pretty tired. Ready to call it a night. No time to stay up and chat with the folks who've been lying around on the sofa all day."

"Hey, speak for yourself lazy bones." Mara Lynn held up one hand in defense. "One of us took down a Christmas tree, re-packed all the decorations, and stacked leftovers in the freezer for hours."

"With your family at the house, I was surprised we had left-overs," Joe grinned when he made the comment, and Madge hoped that would break the feeling in the air.

It did not.

Mara Lynn gave Joe a light slap on the shoulder. "Be nice. I told my mother to do that same thing, and she listened."

"Yes, she did. Your mama didn't insult me one time this year. Closer to twenty-five times if I counted right."

Joe and Mara Lynn both laughed and did a little dance step around each other as if they might throw down and wrestle. Madge was glad to see somebody still having holiday fun, but she thought things might explode on the other side of the room.

After a few seconds, Mara Lynn stopped and looked at her friend. "Alex, you okay? Things are feeling a little tense in here."

"Sure. I'm just tired," Alex said. "I think Luke may be suffering from exhaustion or something. He seems a little cranky."

"I'm fine." Luke took another step into the room. "I've been fine for months. I love sleeping in the guest room of my own house. Makes me feel so special."

Madge scrunched back as far as she could in the corner. The only thing worse for her than a public display of affection was a public airing of one's laundry. She desperately hoped Luke would drop this line and go back to being fine.

Joe put his arm on Mara Lynn's shoulder. "She keeps threatening to kick me out for snoring, too, buddy. It happens."

"I don't snore."

"Okay," Mara Lynn put on her bright, sales-lady voice. The one that probably sold houses. "I can see we have stumbled in at a bad time. We'll just close that garage door on our way out." She grabbed Joe's hand and turned.

"No," Joe said as he shook Mara off. "I think we better stay for a minute." He turned toward the corner. "Aunt Madge, you think these two ought to have a little talk with friends and see if we can't sort some things out?"

Aunt Madge thought nothing of the sort. She thought somebody should clear a path and let her escape the ring before blood started flowing in this fight.

"Madge doesn't need to hear our stuff," Alex said. "She has been caught up in it long enough."

That made great sense to Madge. Yet nobody moved enough to unblock her way through. She edged toward the sink, hoping a gap would come.

Instead, Joe and Mara closed ranks. They took a couple of giant steps toward Alex and completely penned Madge in. Mara spoke over her shoulder. "Madge, do we have any coffee? The caffeinated kind?"

"We do." Madge dove for the coffee pot, grateful to have a task. Especially one that required running water at full blast. Maybe she could drown out the noise.

Instead, the interested parties remained silent until Madge had plopped four coffee cups and saucers on the kitchen table. She wished for a bite of cookie or something to make it feel more like a get-together than an ambush. Left over oatmeal muffins probably wouldn't help.

Joe and Mara sat first. Luke came into the kitchen slowly and pulled out his chair while continuing to stare at Alex. She sat last, meeting Luke's stare without a flinch.

"Okay, this is good," Joe spoke with a soothing tone. Madge wondered if he used it when he was trying to arrest violent criminals. It seemed to work. Alex and Luke both nodded and Madge saw Alex's shoulders relax. She had stood in boxing mode for quite a while.

"Now, let's see what this is all about. Who wants to go first?"

Madge wanted to go first, out the door. Especially after Alex said, "I blame Madge. If she hadn't found the sheets from the guest bed in the laundry, everything would have gone on as usual."

That was enough for Madge. She grabbed her own coffee cup and slammed it on the table. She pulled a chair to the corner and perched right beside Joe.

"Don't blame Madge," Luke said. "I'd have brought it up sooner or later. I know you still feel a need for space. But, really, Alex, how are we ever going to work things out if we live in separate worlds?"

"Having some privacy doesn't mean separate worlds. Ask Mara. I bet she'd like to have her own room somedays."

Joe raised his eyebrows and made a face at his wife. Madge almost laughed, and Mara did.

"Yeah, I'd like a room-sized closet for my shoes and a bathroom all to myself. If we ever move out of that dinky house, I'm taking the second bathroom." She squinted at Joe. "But I don't think I want to sleep in the other room. Not even if it did have a queen-sized bed. I like to cuddle around midnight."

"She does that," Joe nodded at everyone. "I wake up sometimes and the woman is all up on my side of the bed, and I'm hugging the edge of the mattress dreaming I'm gonna fall off a cliff."

They both laughed again. Madge hadn't seen a married couple interact like this since the nights she spent with her nephew Ben and his wife, Nancy. It was the same thing. Always touching. Often teasing. Quite content in themselves, though. Nothing needy about the way they intertwined. They simply liked each other. What a thought.

She realized Alex had been talking for a few minutes, outlining all of Luke's faults and the reasons she still needed time to sort out her emotions before jumping full steam back into the marriage.

Luke held his hands up in defeat and said, "What do you think about that, Joe? What can I do in a situation like this?"

"Why do you have to do anything?" Alex said. "Why can't we just let it lie for a while longer and see if things change?"

"What things, Alex? Me? You? The alignment of the stars? What do you think is going to change and make this magically all better?"

Alex dropped her head into her hands for a minute. When she looked up, she seemed less defensive. "I don't know. I truly, honestly have no idea what to do."

"I'll tell you what to do." Even Madge was surprised to hear the words coming out of her mouth. Everyone turned. Their looks of surprise might indicate they had forgotten she was in the room.

"Seems pretty simple to me," Madge said. "Put the green sheets in a drawer."

CHAPTER TWENTY-THREE
The Sounds of Silence

At breakfast on Tuesday morning, Madge decided Alex had not taken her advice. Neither adult spoke except to tell the girls to hurry or to turn down all Madge's offers for something more substantial than coffee. She spoke to the room when she explained that she would be home all day because Circle had been cancelled due to frigid temperatures. "Rather like the ones in this room," she said.

Everyone ignored her.

Luke did speak in Madge's direction as he grabbed his gear. "I'll be home late. Go ahead and eat supper without me."

"I'll have papers to grade," Alex said to Madge. "I'm subbing all week. If you don't mind heating up something for the girls, I'll grab a yogurt later."

Madge turned to the sink and mumbled to herself about grown-ups acting like children. She would put up with this for about two seconds. If people weren't talking to each other by tomorrow, she would have something to say.

She didn't, though. Tuesday evening passed exactly as the warring parties had predicted. Alex stayed upstairs all evening, supposedly grading papers. Luke came home just in time to turn off the lights as Madge shuffled off to bed.

On Wednesday morning, Madge found a similar atmosphere. Luke and Alex moved through morning rituals like a couple of frozen snowmen. Finally, Aspen spoke up.

"I assume you guys aren't speaking to each other again. Could you instant message or something to work out who is picking us up after school?"

"And who is taking us to church tonight," Quinn threw in.

"I can handle school all week," Alex said to Aspen. "Don't worry about that."

"And I'll drive to church tonight." Luke pushed a travel mug full of coffee toward his wife. "Anyone is welcome to ride along."

"Anyone might have papers to grade," Alex said. She grabbed the mug and reached for her heavy bag. Luke got it first.

"I'll carry this out," he said. "You're going to ruin your throwing arm lugging this thing."

Madge thought she saw the tiniest dent of a smile from Alex.

If Madge were poetic, she would call the day dreary. Heavy gray clouds filled the sky, but they refused to drop any snowflakes. That would have been better, it seemed to Madge, than this oppressive looming over the world as if they could send a blizzard to stop the whole city any time they wanted. Ominous.

She wouldn't have admitted to anyone that she missed the other Glory Circle sisters. She had always gone to Circle because Catherine went. After she died, Madge kept going out of habit. At least, that is what she told herself.

Madge gave herself a shake and wandered to a different window. She looked out on the wide lawn toward the street and watched for a car to drive by. Anything to break the monotony of the day.

When that didn't work, Madge went back to her room and picked up her word puzzle. The letters seemed to jump and swim and scoot all around. They would not behave and line up into words she could circle.

"Fiddlesticks." She tossed the puzzle book onto the side table and crossed her arms. This was a fix. They had ruined her for being alone. All these years of being perfectly content, and now she had developed a case of loneliness. There must be a cure for the aggravation of it.

Madge noticed the remote control lying on the table. With a couple of clicks she had transformed the quiet room into a jangle of noise, lights, and action. She didn't know who these people were or what silly game they were playing, but by golly they provided some noise.

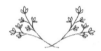

By suppertime, Madge started craving silence again. The family came home pent up from their day inside. Maybe the mountain air had done something to the girls. Madge thought they might burst before they could tell her all about their days. Even Aspen had a few comments about "stupid boys" and "heartless teachers."

"Here," Madge shoved a plate of hotdogs toward the table. "Fix yourselves some grub and wolf it down. You have to get homework done and rooms cleaned before your dad turns that bus around and loads us up for church."

"Is he here?" Alex looked up from her papers. Tonight, she had decided to work at the kitchen bar. "I didn't hear him come in."

"No," Madge squirted ketchup on a plate so Grace could dip her supper. "He called a while ago and said he would eat at the job. He'll be home in time to drive us."

"Are you going?" Aspen asked her mother.

Alex shrugged. "I've got to concentrate on this for now."

Madge looked at the stack of papers spread around the woman of the house. She thought Alex seemed a little too glad about having teacher homework that would keep her from going with the family to church.

That suspicion proved true. When Luke blasted through the kitchen door at the last second, a gust of wind hit the papers and sent them in a swirl around the kitchen.

"Grab those," Alex yelled. She leaped from her stool and snagged one sheaf of papers before they hit the floor. Aspen and Quinn joined her and corralled a few more. Luke bent to pick up the papers that had landed at his feet.

"Sorry," he said. "About being late and being a tornado."

"It didn't really matter," Alex said. "I won't be done with this until midnight, anyway."

Madge didn't intend to make a disapproving sound, but she heard it come out of her throat. Alex looked up at Madge, then down at Quinn, whose eyes resembled those of the last puppy waiting to be chosen.

"Would it help if I read some of the papers when we get home?" Luke still stood in the center of the room, holding the papers he had saved from the floor.

"Maybe, I have a rubric to use."

Madge wondered if that was some kind of new-fangled computer gadget. Whatever it was, she hoped it would put things over the top and get those two people in the same pew by seven o'clock. She had the slimmest hope Pastor Cleveland might preach about man not being alone again. Or something similar. Something to help these two get over the crunch.

In the end, Grace decided the day. She came into the room carrying her little black patent shoes and saying, "chuch" without the r.

"You rascal," Luke said. "We think you're just the baby of the family, but you hear everything that goes on in here, don't you?"

Grace held up her shoes.

"Okay, I give." Alex tossed the papers onto the counter. "We shall go to church and hope Heaven sends angels to grade these papers while we are away."

"Or elves," Peyton said. "The shoemaker had elves."

"That, my dear, would be lovely." Alex popped a kiss on top of Peyton's head, swooped Grace up with her free arm, and walked toward the staircase. "Everyone be ready in ten minutes, got it?"

"Got it," came the chorus from the kitchen.

Luke leaned down toward Madge as he walked by. "Thank goodness we got it, because I thought I was going to get it."

CHAPTER TWENTY-FOUR
Saved by Grace

Madge felt her nerves starting to jangle while the family got ready for church after supper. Her only job was to put on her socks and shoes, but she could hear lots of scuffling upstairs, and it made her jumpy. She sat for a few minutes and took a deep breath. She thought about shouting up the stairs that they didn't need to worry about being late. Cold weather would slow everyone down.

She gave up the idea, though, because they wouldn't be able to hear her well, so someone would come to the stairs and shout back at her. The whole effort would make things worse. Better to let them scurry while she waited.

Sure enough, when Madge and crew traipsed into the vestibule at three minutes till, a dozen people were still pulling off coats and boots. She looked around to see if any of the Glory Circle had arrived. She could see Evelyn down near the front of the church. Her hair still perfect despite the wind. Grace Colby probably wouldn't stir out, and no one would want Bess out in this weather. Madge did not admit to herself or anyone else that she had started adding a certain gentleman to her mental roll call. She knew Elmer Grigsby would be there. He only had a few steps to come across the yard from the parsonage. Still, she knew she was checking on him. She just didn't know how to stop.

The roll call proved to be harder than Madge expected. Elmer Grigsby still hadn't taken a seat by five minutes after seven. Madge fiddled with her song book and rearranged her purse at her feet. She looked down the row to see that all the Marvels were in place. She was glad to see Alex sitting beside Luke.

Finally, when Madge had nearly given up, she heard the familiar footsteps coming down the aisle. She waited to see if Elmer would drop into the third pew beside her or if he would go back to the lonely second pew. They hadn't really made seating arrangements official.

He walked by the third pew. What's more, he didn't stop at the second. Instead, Elmer Grigsby strode normal as could be up the three steps, beyond the rail, and into the pulpit with his son.

Madge reminded herself to close her mouth.

Pastor Cleveland stepped to the podium. "Good evening," he said. "Thanks to so many of you for braving the weather and coming. Tonight, we are going to start something I hope we can carry on through the new year. The Bible says the saints of God overcome by the blood of the Lamb and the word of their testimony. So, we are going to start taking some Wednesday nights to hear testimonies."

He looked over at his father. "My dad, who puts up with my experimental cooking and my idiosyncrasies at home, has also agreed to be my guinea pig for this project. He is our guest speaker tonight."

Pastor Cleveland nodded toward his father and extended a hand. "Please help me welcome Elmer Cleveland Grigsby, the First."

Madge joined the applause, and she hoped she wasn't clapping louder than anyone else as Elmer stepped into the pulpit.

"Well," he said, once Pastor Cleveland had taken a seat. "As you can figure, I've worried jest a bit about this night. I've known for a while it was comin', but I tried to think on other things to avoid the jitters."

He didn't look at Madge with that statement, but she felt a little rush of heat in her face, just the same.

"When I was castin' about for what to say, I got a little jumbled up. Till, finally, I decided I'd jest start out by usin' somebody's words that were better than my own. So, here it is from the great psalm writer. In number one-hundred and sixteen."

He balanced a pair of reading glasses on his nose, opened the big Bible, and thumbed through the pages without appearing to be bothered by the time it took. Madge was amazed one more time by his easy manner. She wondered how he could have gone so quickly from a bum on the street to this man comfortable in a church pulpit.

"The pains of death surrounded me," Elmer read, "and the pangs of Sheol laid hold of me. I found trouble and sorrow."

He looked up from the Bible. "This is about the best description I've ever heard for war time. You'll find that those who've been there won't talk of it much. But Sheol, that means the underworld. Hell, if you pardon my language. That is the best description of war that I can imagine. I'll leave it there, except to say that I went to the army a green kid who had never been across the state line. I came home a broke up man, hiding inside a bottle ever' chance I got. And then, I broke everyone and everything around me."

Madge felt tears pushing at the edges of her eyes. She knew if he kept talking like this, she would cry right in front of everyone. Fortunately, Elmer's voice brightened.

"But then," he said, "after about a lifetime of drunkenness, and thanks to the prayers of some of your own godly church women, I called upon the name of the Lord, as the psalm says."

Madge felt herself breathe. She felt a slight urge to shout, in fact. But she pushed it down.

Elmer closed his eyes for just a second, then bent closer to the Bible and read on. "Gracious *is* the Lord, and righteous; yes, our God *is* merciful.

"Such good words," he said. "But now get this next part. It's talkin' about Elmer Grigsby if ever anybody did. 'The Lord preserves the simple; I was brought low, and He saved me.'"

"Hallelujah," Pastor Cleveland shouted from his chair behind the pulpit. "I know we aren't a shouting people around here, but that deserves a 'hallelujah and amen!'"

Others in the room joined the shout, and before Madge realized it, she was standing and clapping with the whole congregation. Her hallelujah wasn't much of a shout, but she felt it in her bones. Once the crowd sat down, Elmer went on.

"And here we are. At a year where I expected to be dead. And, instead, I'm living better than ever I dreamed." He paused just long enough for the weight of his next words to settle.

"I 'spect there are some who wonder how one like me can walk with his head up in proper company, let alone stand in this holy place here. And they'd be right. I oughtn't to be here." He paused just long enough for the weight of truth to reach the back corners of the room.

"That's just the thing, though. I've been readin' my Bible and talkin' to my boy, and I see now that it ain't me that's standin' up proud. It's the good Lord inside me. It's that amazing grace we sing about. Nothin' I coulda done to make things right. He had to do it."

Madge nodded. She had never *amened* a preacher in her life, but she was on the edge of doing it. Elmer went on.

"The only testifying I ever knew about was done in a court of law against a scoundrel. I never had to do it, or have it done toward me, though I deserved it more times than I can tell."

He looked straight at Madge then. "I can sure and honest give that kind of testimony tonight. Elmer Grigsby the First was a drunk, and a scoundrel, and a no-good who run out on his wife and his little boy. But I'll be dad-blamed if the good Lord hasn't turned me around and set me right. It's just like the writer here said." He looked down at the Bible one more time. "The Lord has dealt bountifully with me."

Again, the applause came. It started more subdued this time. Madge supposed some people were wondering if they should clap for a man who said "ain't" and "dad-blamed" in the pulpit. Before long, though, the applause grew. People started standing again and shouting out "amen" and "good word, brother," and "preach it."

Madge clapped until her hands started to burn. She kept her eyes on Elmer, even when Alex said, "Quite a catch if you ask me."

Madge wanted to snap back with, "I'm not fishing." But she didn't. Because she knew it wouldn't be true. She had not set out to hook this man. She hadn't even loaded any bait on purpose. But she was pretty certain that she and Elmer Grigsby had gotten tangled up together for sure.

CHAPTER TWENTY-FIVE

Yes and Amen

Once the service ended, people surrounded Elmer with handshakes, congratulations, and even a few hugs. Madge was not accustomed to such a flurry. She suddenly realized that she counted on Elmer finding her after every church service and exchanging a few words. They had been doing that for quite some time now. Months? Years? She wasn't sure. Nor would she have thought that it had become something she expected.

Now that Elmer had admirers, Madge was left standing alone in the aisle. Waiting her turn, for Heaven's sake. Well, enough of that. Madge turned back to the pew and snatched her handbag. She would just walk right on up the aisle and out the door. She didn't need to wait around for any man to speak to her. Heavens to Betsy. She had people waiting on her.

Before she made two steps, though, she felt his touch on her arm. And she closed her eyes for a moment at the sheer pleasure of it.

"I 'spose I should have warned you about tonight," he said as he stepped up beside her. He reached for her heavy purse and slid it onto the crook of his arm as if that wasn't a ridiculous sight. Then he put his arm under her elbow and gave a gentle pressure to nudge her forward in the aisle.

Instead of feeling man-handled, Madge felt something very close to happy. Drat it all.

"No need to warn me. It was just church as usual."

"Well, I'm glad you thought so. Some of them other folks about made it go to my head with all their fancy words."

"Don't let it do that," Madge said. She walked two more steps and then stopped. "I'm sure to be struck dead for lying right here in the church house," she said. "You didn't need to warn me, but it was a sight more than church as usual."

She stood straight and turned so that she was looking Elmer straight in the eye. "I'll tell you the God's truth, Elmer Grigsby. It made me proud to be your friend."

It was a big speech for Madge. She had rarely said anything that mushy to anyone. Not her family. Not Catherine. Not anybody. And yet, Elmer didn't immediately seem to realize what a gift she had bestowed. He didn't smile or tease her like she expected. Instead, he stepped even closer in the aisle and spoke in a quiet voice.

"Friends, is it? Are we just gonna be friends, Pearl?"

"Well," she jerked back. "I don't know what on earth you would call us if not friends. If that isn't good enough for you, we can go back to being people who go to the same church and exchange a word now and then. Yes, sir, that will be dandy by me."

She tried hard to sound huffy, but her voice gave out with the last few words and shook just a little. She didn't know why.

Elmer's eyebrows went up just a smidgen. His countenance brightened a tiny bit. Madge didn't suppose anyone else would even have been able to notice the change. But she could see it.

"Well," Elmer said. "I see we need to have a little clearing of the air here." He guided her into the next pew and motioned for her to sit.

She did.

"It seems to me," Elmer said, "that you've been fightin' right hard to keep from admitting that you like keeping company with me."

"Now…"

Elmer held up his hand. "Jest hold a minute and let me have my say. Then you can talk all you want."

She waited.

"If I thought for a minute that it was true. If I thought I was just pesterin' and you'd like me to go away, you know good and well I'd do it. I'm not naturally a cocky man. For most of my grown life, I've kept clear of folks. But everthin' has changed for me since I started coming to this church. And you know the biggest change has come from you. Well, outside of the good Lord, a-course."

He looked as if he might reach for her hand, but thankfully, he did not. "We aren't youngsters, Pearl. If we are gonna make somethin' of this, we best stop dancin' around and be straight with one another."

Madge sat back and dropped her hands into her lap. She hardly knew what to think. No man had ever talked like that to her. Except Luke when he wanted her to use the side door at church. And Jack when he wanted her to stop driving with her suspended license.

In the last six months, Madge had been straight talked by more men than in most of her life. She brought herself back to the moment and squinted at Elmer. His eyes were brown. She liked brown eyes.

"So, as I was sayin', are you ready to stop this back-and-forth? You ready to tell people that we are steppin' out?"

She was ready. She didn't know when it happened. Didn't know how it happened, but she was ready. Madge stood and Elmer joined her. She reached out to take his arm, and together they began walking up the aisle. She walked beside him not as someone in need of assistance for a crippled hip. But like someone who was, indeed, stepping out with Elmer Grigsby.

When they reached the vestibule, Elmer walked her right up beside Grace Colby and Erma. He smiled, did that little tip of the head, and then turned to Madge and said, "I'd like to invite you to take the noon meal with me and my boy on Sunday. We'll have something cookin' in the oven, and I can walk you over after service. Me and Mr. Uber can see you home afterwards."

She heard Erma gasp. She imagined Grace Colby's frown. She stepped off the cliff. "Okay. I accept."

Elmer grinned so big she worried he might reach over and give her a peck on the cheek right in the vestibule. So, Madge reached out and shook his hand. It was a silly thing to do. They didn't normally shake hands. But she felt embarrassed and pleased all at the same time.

The handshake didn't seem to bother Elmer. He returned the pressure of her hand and then covered it with his other hand. "I thank you," he said.

CHAPTER TWENTY-SIX

A Table Before Me

"It's Psalm 23 today," Aspen said. "I know some of that one."

"Do you, now?" Madge didn't want to seem particularly impressed, even though she did feel surprise at this revelation. She also felt grateful that Paige had wrapped up another Verse-of-the-Day calendar for her Christmas. They had bought one last year on a whim, and Madge had used it to count down the sixty days she would work for the Marvels before she got her car out of hock.

She wasn't counting down any days with the new calendar.

"Maybe we sang it in choir," Aspen said. "Or it was on a Christmas card or something. 'The Lord is my shepherd,' right?"

"He is," Madge said. "And that is how Psalm 23 starts."

Aspen plopped the calendar back on the windowsill and put on her thoughtful face. Madge feared the girl might be about to ask some deep theological questions about the valley of the shadow. Fortunately, Alex walked into the kitchen and broke the moment.

"Lunch," Alex said. "I didn't make a good plan last night. Something for the slow cooker? Chili, maybe?"

Madge coughed and turned away from Alex. "I'll be taking lunch out," she said to the wall.

"Out?" Alex asked the question while she poured coffee. "You and the ladies going out for lunch?"

"Not exactly." Madge picked up yesterday's mail and flipped through it as if she would see something new.

"Then what exactly? If it is any of my business."

Madge could tell Alex was smiling even before she turned around. "I'll be taking lunch at the parsonage today."

"Oh, my," Luke walked in from the dining room just in time to hear the confession. "Visiting the preacher, huh? Isn't it more common for parishioners to invite the parson over?"

"Madge isn't eating with Pastor Cleveland," Aspen said. She stepped across the room and draped an arm over Madge's shoulder. The pressure hurt Madge's arthritis, but it was a nice pain. "Madge is eating with Mr. Grigsby the First, aren't you?"

Aspen looked at Madge with such a clear expression of certainty that Madge gave up any pretense. "I am. Although, to be precise, we are eating with Pastor Cleveland."

"Meeting the kids," Luke said. "Is this thing getting serious, Madge?"

Madge didn't scold. She just took a breath and said, "Might be."

The room suddenly took on the feeling of a slow-motion movie. Or maybe a game of freeze tag. Alex froze with a coffee cup halfway to her mouth. Luke stopped with his mouth open to say something that never came out. And Aspen stayed glued to Madge's side, her arm growing heavier on Madge's shoulder.

So many thoughts dashed about in Madge's head that she felt like little Lucy in that wardrobe book. As if she were living hours and hours of experiences in Narnia while the world on this side of the door went forward in seconds. Even with all that activity, her brain couldn't seem to form any words.

Finally, Luke broke the magic between worlds. "So, that's news." He leaned against the bar, crossed his arms, and smiled at Madge. "Do you want to tell us more?"

"Not a bit," Madge said. "I just think if a man invites a woman to his place for a meal, somebody better be thinking hard on the subject. That isn't the kind of thing you do willy-nilly."

"I suppose not," Luke said. Alex came to stand beside him and handed him the coffee she hadn't tasted yet. Luke put the cup on the bar without looking at it.

Alex looked at the ceiling when she finally spoke. "So, theoretically, we could say that you and Mr. Grigsby are ready to be seen as a couple? That you are okay with people knowing about that?"

"That we don't have to pretend you didn't go on a date with him after Christmas?" Aspen said. She pulled her arm away from Madge but stayed close.

"I suppose," Madge said, "you could say that we are keeping company."

"With serious intent?" Luke asked.

"Yes."

Madge thought about those words all the way to church. She rolled them around in her head as she crawled out of Luke's family bus and reached for the back door of the church. Aspen had hopped out with her this time and grabbed the door before Madge could reach it. Madge didn't even say thank you. She just kept walking and thinking about serious intent.

She didn't see Elmer until she and Aspen stepped into the vestibule. She spotted him in his spiffy suit and the tie she liked best, and she felt the volume turn up in her mind. "Serious intent. This is serious intent."

The words stayed so loud she could barely greet the other Glory Circle sisters. When the Marvels came in the front, she maneuvered herself between the little girls so she would have an excuse not to respond to people who tried to talk to her. She just wanted to keep hearing those words and deciding what they meant. And if they were true.

Elmer didn't catch up to them until they reached the third pew and started shuffling in. "Serious intent," Madge's mind screamed.

"Here, let me untangle this little bit so you don't trip over her," Elmer said. He took Grace's hand and twirled her just enough to move her out of Madge's way. And the noise stopped.

"Thank you." She didn't mean for moving Grace, but Elmer couldn't know that. How could he even imagine that the very sound of his voice could soothe her frenzy. When did that start? She couldn't remember.

She didn't hear a word of the sermon. She was warm and tired and scrunched in among so many people she never expected to love. Despite the excitement of the day, Madge nodded off a time or two. Finally, the last song had been sung, and everyone rose for their good-byes.

"I'll be gettin' our guest home with Mr. Uber this afternoon," Elmer said to Luke.

Luke nodded. "Not too late. She has therapy tomorrow."

"We'll be in before dark," Elmer said.

Madge knew they were joking with one another, but she didn't laugh. Now that the moment was upon her, she was ridiculously nervous. The walk to the parsonage took about five minutes. But it felt long and leisurely. Holding Elmer's arm. Strolling as if they had no place to be. Thinking about how nice it would be to sit and enjoy their meal.

The nerves stayed under control until Pastor Cleveland opened the door and welcomed them in with a wide sweep of the arm. "This is such an occasion," he said. "I never in my wildest could have dreamed up this one."

They stepped into the tidy room, and Madge looked around. She had never been further in the parsonage than the back porch. The ladies had helped with cleaning and unpacking for new preachers back in the day. Madge had always thought the outside work was more fitting for her, since she hadn't been born in church. The preacher's kitchen felt a little too personal. Heaven help the woman who had to make up his bed.

"Pull up a chair," Pastor Cleveland said as he ushered them inside. "Our party is complete now, and we can take out the roast beast. Let's all pray I turned the oven on."

He swooshed into the kitchen and left Madge and Elmer standing on the edge of a tight circle. Madge stepped back when she realized the dining room was full. Jack and Paige. Tom and Evelyn. And Bess. Sweet, addled Bess.

Elmer must have sensed her concern, because he leaned in and said, "We tried to pick out folks that make you feel easy. Just thought it might be nice to have some background babble so's you and me could talk kinda to ourselves if we wanted."

"Good idea," Madge said, although she barely meant it.

The meal turned out mostly perfect. Madge didn't know the pastor could cook. He admitted to having a little help with some shortcuts from the grocery story. "The vegetables were all cut up and seasoned," he said. "I just dumped them in a pan."

"Very sensible," Evelyn said. "A man shouldn't have to feed the sheep and then feed his guests within the hour."

Everyone gave polite laughs and went back to the delicious potatoes and carrots some grocery store girl had seasoned to perfection. After the pie, which also came pre-cooked, everyone adjourned to the living room. Madge immediately noticed the two matching recliners pulled close together with lamps and tables on both sides. She liked the look. In fact, she could imagine herself sitting in one of those chairs with Elmer in the other while Vanna spun the wheel every night.

She shook herself back from the daydream and realized Elmer was nudging her toward a place on the small sofa in the corner. They sat, and Madge pulled a cushion from behind her back. She started to put it between them, but that seemed a little rude.

Elmer reached over and helped her out, dropping the pillow at his feet.

In the end, they didn't talk much. Madge sank into the sofa and felt the comfort of it on her weary bones. She listened to the sound of easy conversation all around her. Of friends chatting, of stories told. And she caught herself smiling more than once. Elmer leaned his head toward her. "You look natural here."

"Oh, shoot." Madge wiggled a little to keep from sinking further into the cushions. "Pastor Cleveland just knows how to make people feel welcome. That's all."

"He does that," Elmer said. "You probably can't imagine what it was like for me the first few nights here in a warm house. I kept watching the door, calculatin' how long it would take me to cross the room, snag my coat, and get out and down the steps. I was right jumpy."

"How did you get over that?" Madge thought she could use a little instruction on conquering jumpiness.

"Well, it was my cat, to tell you true. That animal had been as stand-offish as you can imagine. Never gave me the time of day hardly. But once we traipsed in here, he started actin' like a regular house cat. Rubbin' up around my legs. Askin' for his food with a polite little mew. He even started to purr."

"He could feel the welcome, I suppose." Madge looked at the gathering of friends as she spoke.

"That he did. I finally figured if the cat was determined to stay, I could give it a try myself."

"Did it take long?"

Elmer shrugged. "Not long in relation to how things had gone in my life. But long when you are feeling itchy about a thing." He leaned a little closer. "You know that feelin'?"

"I do."

CHAPTER TWENTY-SEVEN
One Giant Step

Madge had never struggled much with Mondays. She knew some people dreaded the beginning of the week like a trip to the dentist. For her, the weekends had never held any great attraction. Saturday had always been the day to clean her house, do the wash, shop for groceries, pay some bills. Nothing too exciting. Before she started going to Mt. Zion, she lolly-gagged on Sundays. She slept late, ate something cold, and then slept again in the afternoon, sometimes right up to supper. A few of her jobs through the years had been pretty tough, and they wore her out.

Even so, she had never experienced what people called the Sunday night blues. She didn't long for another day off to do chores. Now, suddenly, she found herself dreading Monday because it was a day that stretched out with no plans. When on earth did she get attached to a social life?

Madge gave herself a good shake once the family got out the door. She had plenty to do. Stretch her legs, read her Bible, clean the kitchen. "What's gotten into you?" she asked herself out loud. "Stop moping around because you're on your own. You've been that way for decades."

When she finished wiping a dishcloth across the kitchen counters, Madge sat at the bar and ran her finger along the marbled design. "Admit it, woman. You've let a man get under your skin, and now you can't even wait one full day until you see him again. You are pouting because you know he won't come calling today. Silliest thing in the world."

She decided to check the mailbox. Not because she expected any mail, but because it would give her something to do. She trudged along the sidewalk and took her time pulling out the bundle and sorting through it. She supposed it might be nosey of her to look through the Marvel mail, but she convinced herself she was just making sure there was nothing for her.

She was wrong. Three pieces of mail were addressed to her. A brochure for a walk-in tub, a notice from Medicare, and an envelope with a yellow sticker showing that it had been forwarded from her home address.

Madge tossed the brochure into the trash and stacked the family mail on the counter. She poured a cup of coffee before she pulled out a chair at the table to peruse her mail. The Medicare paper made no sense. They never did. She tossed it across the table. "I'll show it to Paige. She'll know what it says."

The other envelope had been postmarked before Christmas and must have been delayed in the forwarding. Madge opened it slowly and pulled out the card from her nephew Clyde. Obviously, Ben had not kept him up to date on her whereabouts. Clyde's wife had probably written the nice sentiment. In a few scrawled lines at the bottom, Clyde had added:

"Still think you'd better move out here near us. Don't want you spending another winter on your own out there. We'll talk."

"No," Madge said as she folded the card. "We won't talk about that. I'm not on my own at all. Not a bit." She tried to pretend, even to herself, that she had the Marvel house in mind with that statement, but the image of two easy chairs beside a fire kept popping into her mind.

Madge did manage to live until Tuesday. She thought Paige drove a little slowly, and she didn't mind a bit getting out in the upper lot. She grabbed her cane and handed Paige her pocketbook before she pulled herself out of the car. She scooted across the sidewalk fast enough that Paige hadn't even gotten back in the driver's seat before Madge reached for the church door.

It was locked.

Madge tried a second time, thinking maybe the door had frozen in the night. But it didn't budge. She turned toward Paige with a shrug, and Paige waved her back toward the car.

Once Madge was tucked back inside and could feel the warm heat on her toes, she looked at the stubborn door. "What a mess," she said. "I suppose it will be the front steps today."

"No," Paige turned the wheel and started out of the lot. "You will sit right there in your seat while I run inside and get someone to unlock. Then we'll drive back up here. You aren't climbing those steps. Not on my watch."

So, that is exactly what they did. Which meant Madge sat for way too many quiet minutes in the car at the foot of the steps. She wondered if Paige would find Elmer. She wondered if he was even inside the church at all. Maybe he had gotten sick. She wondered if someone else would have a key to the back door. Finally, she wondered if she would get inside the church before Circle ended or before her need for a bathroom became embarrassing.

Paige came scampering down the steps after enough time for Madge to get completely worried. She waved a key as she slid into her seat. "Got it," she said. "Grace Colby knew where there was a spare key in a drawer."

"How did she know that?"

"I've no idea, but I'm glad about it." Paige whipped into the upper lot and scrambled out of the car. She pulled Madge's door open before Madge had gathered her wits or her purse.

"Let's go," Paige said, "They will start without us."

"Are you leaving your car up here?"

"I am. I'm pretty sure there is no one around to complain. The vestibule and sanctuary were both dark. No lights in the offices. We Glory girls are on our own."

Madge didn't quite match Paige's enthusiastic stride as they walked across the darkened gym. They used Paige's cell phone like a flashlight, but it only gave off a small glow. Nothing like Elmer's good flashlight from the closet. The memory of that first walk reminded Madge that something was definitely wrong. She couldn't imagine Elmer would fail to show up this way.

Or maybe he would. Maybe her opinion about men in general had been right all along. Maybe they were all insensitive jerks who thought only of themselves. Maybe this particular man hadn't changed after all. Maybe she would tell him exactly what she thought if she ever saw him again.

It took several minutes for Madge and Paige to find chairs and greet everyone and tell the story of the back door being locked. Evelyn picked up her gavel as if she were going to start the meeting, but Grace Colby interrupted. "I knew that Elmer Grigsby was shifty. I've been waiting for him to show himself true, and now he has. Off on a drunk somewhere, I expect."

Madge opened her mouth and was about to slap that idea into the next county when she felt Paige's hand on her arm. "Oh, I don't think we need to make assumptions," Paige said in a sweet voice. "We don't have any evidence that Mr. Grigsby has gone back to the bottle."

"Well," Erma said, "I hate to speak ill, but once alcohol gets hold of a person, it is nearly impossible to escape. I had an uncle with that trouble. My dad ran a general store, and he would never sell Uncle Bill any hair tonic. He would drink a bottle straight down once the bartender cut him off down the street."

"Hair tonic?" Grace Colby crossed her arms. "What on earth do you mean by hair tonic?"

"Oh, you know," Erma waved as if a bottle might materialize before them. "Men rub it in their hair to slick it down. Or they used to. Maybe nobody wears it anymore. My dad carried a couple of different kinds. They smelled nice, but they were almost straight alcohol. One of them carried a warning on the label that the user should not smoke until his hair was completely dry."

Madge tried to erase the picture in her mind of Elmer Grigsby's slicked back hair catching fire from a cigar. Fortunately, Elmer didn't wear his hair slick as far as she could recall. It looked kind of soft and natural.

"I don't think we have to worry that Mr. Grigsby is out drinking hair tonic," Evelyn said.

"Oh no, not at all." Bess jumped into the conversation with a serious expression. "Madge would never keep company with a man who drank hair tonic."

Every head turned. Every voice stopped. It seemed to Madge that the next moments went by in slow motion as she cleared her throat, reached for a tissue, and tried to think of what to say next.

"Well," she finally said, "that is quite an idea, Bess. I don't think..."

A sound filtered into the room from the far end of the hallway. The sound of a man whistling a carefree tune. Madge loved that sound.

She cleared her throat again. "I don't think we have to worry about Mr. Grigsby," she said in a strong voice. "He's probably just running a little late today."

Sure enough, the man himself stepped into the open doorway within moments. "Well, ladies, I sure do hope you can forgive a fella for this terrible mix-up today."

"Nothing to forgive, Mr. Grigsby," Evelyn said. "We were a little worried about you, though. Hoping you weren't ill."

Much throat clearing around the room followed that comment. A few people mumbled their agreement.

"Oh, no. Not a bit sick," Elmer said. "But it was the darndest thing. Electricity went off over at the parsonage. Must have happened in the night 'cause neither one of us noticed it. Just a little bit ago, my boy noticed that his watch and the kitchen clock were off by almost an hour." He turned directly toward Madge and finished his speech. "I'm sure sorry for the trouble my tardiness must have caused."

Madge wondered how much he had heard before he started to whistle. Did he know the ladies doubted him? Did he think Madge felt the same way? Or did he wish she had stuck up for him better? Questions came at Madge's mind like mosquitoes on a hot night. She tried to flick them away, but some of them stung just the same.

When she couldn't stand it anymore, Madge spoke up. "You didn't cause us any trouble. We've just been sitting here wasting time with silly prattle. Probably ought to get the meeting going if we want to get out of here by lunch time."

Evelyn picked up her gavel, and the ladies all swiveled in their seats as if to give attention. All the ladies except Madge. She stood, right in front of everyone, and turned toward the door.

"I thought you might like to come for supper on Saturday," she said to Elmer. "We've got a nice roast."

"Well, that sounds about perfect to me," Elmer said. He gave her the imaginary hat tip. "I'll be around about six if all goes well."

"Good," Madge felt the pressure of every Glory Circle sister staring at her. "The little girls will be glad to see you," she said to Elmer as he walked away.

Suddenly, Madge felt an irresistible tug to quit being a coward. "I'll be glad to see you," she yelled down the hall.

She heard his footsteps turning the corner. Then she heard him whistle.

CHAPTER TWENTY-EIGHT
To Tell the Truth

"So." Alex put her coffee on the table Thursday morning and sat near Madge. "Tomorrow is Luke's birthday."

"Well." Madge stopped working on her puzzle book and folded her hands. "First I've heard of it."

"I know. We agreed years ago to stop making a big deal out of our birthdays. We were so busy. And the budget never stretched."

"Did the budget get better this year?"

"No. The budget is definitely worse."

Madge nodded and pushed her book aside. "So, what do you have in mind?"

"Nothing grand. I thought maybe a few people over for pizza. Order a cake."

Madge liked the plan. Maybe Alex was trying to make up for being something of a jerk about sleeping arrangements. Maybe the trip to Aspen had finally done its job.

"I thought Joe and Mara for sure. Maybe Jack and Paige."

"Good party," Madge said. "Just enough to keep things lively without such a big crowd you can't hear anybody talking.

"And Mr. Grigsby, of course."

"Oh, I don't know about that. You don't have to invite him to everything. And I had already asked him for Saturday. If that's okay." Madge realized she had failed to mention her impromptu invitation.

"Saturday's great. I'm glad you asked him. A man gets tired of making all the moves, you know."

"Fiddlesticks. It wasn't a move." She stopped then as she ran the events back through her mind from Tuesday morning. The ladies talking bad about Elmer. Madge failing to defend him until the last minute. "Might be more of an apology."

"Well, either way, it will be nice to have him for dinner again. Let's ask him for Friday night, too. That will even out the numbers."

It turned out Elmer was happy to be number eight at the grown-ups' table on Friday night. Everyone grabbed a paper plate and loaded it down with pizza and chips before snagging chairs in the dining room. The little girls prepared to devour their pizza in the kitchen. Aspen stood in the doorway between the two rooms, a perfect picture of the tugging time between young woman and child. She looked at Madge as if asking for help.

Everyone else had already started trying to out-talk one another about how happy they were to see the weekend. Madge looked from Alex to Elmer and wondered what to do. After a few seconds, she scooted her chair a few inches his way and pointed to the extra chair in the corner. Aspen sent Madge a smile and claimed the chair. While she maneuvered it into place, Elmer reached over and put his hand on the back of Madge's chair. "Scoot on over here," he said. "I've got plenty of room."

The little girls finished before the adults had hardly begun. Peyton and Grace wandered off to play until cake time. Quinn, though, slid quietly onto the edge of Aspen's chair and leaned in on her elbows.

Madge realized the girl had been staring at her for a few minutes.

"What?" she said. "You need me to get you something in the kitchen?"

"No. I was just wondering something."

"Spill it," Madge said.

"Is Mr. Grigsby your first boyfriend?"

Aspen reached out and put a finger over her little sister's lips. "Quinn. That's personal."

"I know." Quinn pushed the hand away. "Madge doesn't care."

"Well," Madge hesitated long enough for Luke to break into the conversation.

"Madge doesn't have to tell us her romantic history. That is none of our business." He piled another piece of pizza onto the one in his hand. "Unless she wants to."

Everyone turned toward Madge.

She had told this story to very few people in her life. One of them had been Aspen. At the time, she had thought it might help the girl cope during a hard time. She didn't know if it had worked. And there was Elmer to consider. Should he hear all the gory details like this? In front of so many people?

"Go ahead, Madge," Aspen said. "Tell us about Mr. DuPree."

Madge looked at Elmer. He gave the smallest nod as if he were bracing himself for whatever revelation would come.

"Well, let's see." Madge tried to go back in her mind and sort out details that mattered from those that didn't. "DuPree was a salesman who came through our county. A fancy man, my dad called him. He wore a checkered suit and carried a real leather briefcase. He told stories about city life, about what a person could do there, how women had jobs in tall buildings and wore perfume to work every day. For somebody who had been dressing chickens all afternoon, those stories were some kind of magic."

"Why do you dress a chicken?" Quinn asked.

"Not in clothes," Madge answered. "That's the word for… for getting them ready to eat."

"Oh…" Quinn narrowed her eyes. "You mean you'd been killing chickens all day?"

"I had." She decided to leave out the part about singeing, plucking, and cutting up for canning.

"Anyway," Jack said, "Mr. DuPree was talking…"

"Right. That's about the whole story, really. He talked a lot. Made some big promises. And got me to climb out the window and run away with him one night just after I turned sixteen."

Gasps around the table followed that announcement. Madge heard real live audible gasps.

"Sixteen?" Joe recovered first. "That woulda been against the law."

"Sure. It was." Madge tried to focus on a picture across the room and keep herself removed from the story. As if she were just the narrator and not the leading lady. "That's what saved me in the end. Mr. DuPree dumped me a few days later, and my dad was able to get the marriage annulled because of my age and not having permission."

"What about the law?" Joe asked again. "Did your dad file charges against that no-good?"

"He didn't." Madge took a breath and tried to shake out of the moment. "He thought it was good riddance. Said he didn't want to ever see the man again. Not even to send him to jail."

She brushed away a crumb on the table. "And he never wanted to hear another word about him. So, he didn't."

"Oh, Madge," Alex looked across the table with tears in her eyes. "I'm so sorry, so deeply sorry that you were treated that way. So sorry."

Madge blinked and concentrated on breathing slowly. She would not let that man get the best of her now. She would not break down in front of everyone. How many years had she kept him locked up in a dark place of her mind? How many times had the thought of him threatened to jump out and scandalize people around her? How many times had she evaded questions, made general comments, or outright lied to avoid this moment?

She felt a pressure on her hand and realized Elmer had slid his over on top of hers. He squeezed more gently than Madge thought a man could do.

"The man was a worthless dog," Elmer said. "Ought to be shot for it. And yet," he wrapped his entire hand around Madge's. "I'm eternal glad he skipped out and left the prize for me."

"Bravo!" Paige shouted. "Bravo, Mr. Grigsby. That is exactly right." The silence around the table turned to cheers as everyone added their salute to Elmer's statement. What had been a horrible experience just moments ago gave way to laughter and congratulations.

"Let's have cake in Madge's honor," Luke shouted.

Madge hardly knew what to think. She had considered so long what it would feel like to get this secret out in the open, now that her folks were gone and couldn't be shamed by the admission. She never expected a celebration.

CHAPTER TWENTY-NINE
To Have and to Hold

The enthusiasm from Friday night had completely evaporated by Saturday morning. Madge felt as grumpy as an old setting hen after the eggs had been gathered. She fussed around the house, looking for things to do, then fussed some more when she couldn't do what she wanted. When a stack of plates slid out of her hand and thwacked the counter, Alex finally stepped in.

"What do you think about a little nap, Madge? Rest up for the evening so you can enjoy your guest?"

"I don't need to be told to take a nap like baby Grace," Madge said. She grabbed plates and started restacking. "This cane gets in my way, but by golly, I'm not a daft old woman or some kind of cranky baby. I just didn't have a good grip."

Alex held up both hands in surrender. "Okay. I give. You don't have to take a nap. If you want to be tired and out of sorts tonight, that is your business."

Madge retreated to her room. She sat in the soft chair, picked up her puzzle book, and muttered about bossy people messing in her life. She grumbled and mumbled until the next thing she knew, she was waking from a long nap in her chair.

Once they all sat down for supper, she had to admit to herself the nap had saved her. She felt more alert. Not quite spry, but at least able to keep up with the conversations that flitted around the table. By the time Alex and Luke stood to clear the table, Madge felt quite relaxed. It had been a good night. She tried to think of something nice to say, but Elmer spoke first.

"I wonder, Miss Pearl, if you would do me the honor of a short walk."

Madge looked out the window. The gray overcast day had given way to a raw evening. A little wind. A few drops of rain. Certainly not the kind of night for a walk.

"Just out on the porch, if you please," Elmer said. "I'd like the air."

She supposed that would do. The man had lived much of his life under the stars. Maybe houses crowded him too much. Especially houses filled with noisy girls.

Madge pulled the Mizzou jacket from the coat rack and waited while Elmer got his own coat and hat in place. He left the gloves in his pocket. Like a true gentleman, Elmer held the door and motioned for Madge to go first. She stepped out and instantly knew she was in trouble. She heard giggling as the door closed.

Someone had gotten the summer chairs from the garage and placed them on either side of a small table. Candles glowed from the center of a winter flower arrangement. Real flowers, out in the night air. They would freeze in minutes. Before she could say so, Elmer guided her to the first chair.

He remained standing. The far-away streetlight glowed behind him, making him look like someone from a movie with his dark coat and nice hat. Madge tried not to be silly, but the man looked good.

"Pearl," he said. "I expect you know what I'm up to. I promise this plan was in the works long before that story you told last night. I thought about puttin' it off, because I didn't want you to think this was out of pity or something. It is none of that. Do you understand?"

Madge nodded. She could not speak. Not even to tell Elmer Grigsby to stop what he was about to do.

As if in slow motion, Elmer bent his knee and knelt in front of her. He put one hand on top of her cold fingers. The other hand he slipped into his pocket.

Madge hoped he was reaching for his gloves.

But no. He brought out another blue velvet box from Austen's. "I thought hard about givin' you this one for Christmas and savin' the necklace for another day. But this way around seemed like the right order."

He opened the box and revealed the ring. A pearl. With stones that looked like diamonds. All glittering and bright and enough to make Evelyn jealous, Madge thought.

"Miss Margaret DuPree, will you do me the honor…"

She stopped him. "Don't be an old fool. What are you thinking? People our age don't get married. They don't even keep company. We can't carry on like this. Now get up off the porch before you catch your death."

"I can't."

"Oh, for the love of Betsy. I'll help you." She reached for his elbow.

"No, I mean I can't. I can't get up until you say yes. We both know it is meant to be. We've known it for some time. I don't pretend to be any kind of a catch, but I promise you this: You will never be lonely. You will never be ashamed. You will never be short on any bit of love as long as I'm alive."

Madge sank against the cold chair. She had been lonely. She knew it but couldn't admit it, not even now. The thought of living out her days with a man beside her seemed atrocious, though. A man in her kitchen. In her front room watching television. A man in her bedroom, listening to her snore, and whatever else that would mean. The thoughts made her cringe and want to pull back. Yet, something unimaginable kept pulling her forward.

"All right. Yes. I'll take the ring. Just to get you up off the porch."

"Wait," he held up his hand. "Not just the ring. You'll take me? To have and to hold? In sickness and health? For richer or poorer? Till death do us part?"

Madge knew she would have to say these words again. If this train kept roaring down the track, she would have to repeat this vow in front of more people than she cared to count. How could such a big decision come down to such a tiny moment?

People flashed through her mind. Those who would vote "yes" if they were standing on the porch. All the Marvels. Jack and Paige. Probably Pastor Cleveland.

Then she thought of all the "no" votes. All the Glory Circle sisters, except maybe Bess who might think it was romantic. Emily for sure. And Emily would represent Catherine in the vote. Madge wasn't exactly sure what Catherine would have said. She had mentioned more than once that a good husband was a true comfort in old age.

Catherine's husband had died, though. He left her rich, but terribly sad. She never really recovered. Would it be worth the trouble to get attached to a man at this age when he might up and die on a person at any minute?

Madge knew the answer. It didn't matter what might come next month or even tomorrow. She had already grown attached. The imaginary crowd of witnesses evaporated. Madge looked at Elmer, still waiting on one knee. He managed to look relaxed and confident even though she felt him starting to shiver. She decided to have mercy and end his suffering.

"Against all my better sense, Mr. Grigsby, I do."

CHAPTER THIRTY

Two Steps Forward

Madge tried to think of any excuse to avoid church the next morning. She couldn't go without wearing the ring. Or the pearls, for that matter. To go without them would be to deny Elmer, and she could not do that. Not anymore.

To walk into the church house with a man's ring on her finger, though. Madge didn't know if she could do it. She never imagined it. Never dreamed it. Never wanted it in all her years of singleness.

No. The last part was a lie. She had been telling it to herself for decades, and she almost believed it sometimes. But deep inside the most secret parts of her, it had never been true.

She had been the only one in their circle who never had a man. At least, not a man she could bring up in conversation. She didn't even have a man to complain about when everyone was fussing about theirs.

After several failed attempts to dress, Madge finally emerged from her room wearing the blue sweater and a new pair of slacks Paige had helped her order from a catalog. She pulled on her coat, buttoned it up tight, and added a pair of stretchy gloves that had been stuffed in the closet. She wore the ring and the necklace, but nobody could see them if she chose to stay wrapped up. And it was cold today. A soul might want to wear their coat and gloves all the way through church.

She knew the plan would fail, but she thought she might be able to hold out at least until she got down the aisle. That part worked. The Marvels arrived early, wonder of wonders. So, Madge was saved from walking through the gymnasium with Elmer or meeting him in the vestibule. Instead, she walked into the sanctuary with Luke on one side and Alex on the other. She kept her coat buttoned and her gloves in place.

Once everyone was settled with ample room beside Madge for Elmer, Alex reached over. "I'm sorry. I can take your coat and gloves back to the coat room. We rushed you."

Madge shrugged away. "No bother. I've got a bit of a chill. I'll keep them on."

"All that porch time last night," Luke said. "I told Elmer he better warm you up afterwards, but he said it wouldn't be proper."

"Luke!" Alex shook her head.

Madge gave him the side-eye. "Watch yourself, mister. Talking that way in church could get you struck by lightning."

Luke leaned back and stretched his arms across the back of the pew. "Nah. The good Lord invented romance. He's all for it." He winked at Madge, but Alex turned at exactly the same moment and caught the wink before it traveled down the pew.

"Luke!" This time she gave his arm a little tap. Madge noticed that Alex didn't pull away immediately, though. She let her hand rest on Luke's arm.

Just as Madge was ready with a comeback, she heard Elmer walking down the aisle. She glanced to the left to see if all the Glory Circle sisters had arrived. They had. Every woman sat in her usual spot, staring straight ahead as they waited for the choir to filter into place.

Madge decided to risk the moment. She unbuttoned her coat as Elmer crawled into the pew. She pulled open the collar as he sat beside her. She wondered if the pearls at her neckline would be glowing in this light. They felt as if they were glowing.

She pulled off the glove on her right hand and smoothed it on her lap. She waited just a beat, but it was enough. Elmer reached over and took her left hand. Slowly, with a gentleness she would never expect in a man, he pulled off her glove. He touched the bare hand for just a moment, then left the glove in her lap.

The earth did not open to swallow her. The pews didn't even quake. In fact, no one in the third pew, nor even in the entire congregation, seemed to notice that Madge DuPree was wearing a ring.

She waited a few seconds. No response from anyone. When she knew it was almost time for Pastor Cleveland to come down the aisle, she cleared her throat. She turned and spoke toward Bess, who was seated at the end of the row, beyond Grace Colby, Erma, Evelyn, and Tom. "Good to see you this morning, Bess. Hope the cold isn't too much for you."

Everyone turned, as she knew they would, and with one swift move, Madge reached up to brush the hair out of her eyes. It was a move Evelyn would make without thinking. A move that always made her diamond rings and silver bracelets sparkle and dance. Madge had practiced it in the mirror about twenty times, but she never thought she'd do it.

"Madge," Evelyn said, "is that a new ring?"

Madge had also practiced the "oh, this is nothing" response several times. What came out of her mouth, though, was. "Brand new. Got it last night."

Grace Colby leaned closer to look. "From the handyman, I suppose."

Elmer reached over Madge and held out his hand. "The one and only. Feel free to congratulate me on my catch."

Grace accepted the handshake, but her face didn't change.

Erma, however, shoved her hand forward. "Well, isn't that the nicest thing?" she said. "I would never have guessed it, but I'm sure you will make a good couple. All will be well, I'm almost certain."

And so it went down the line. They couldn't reach one another well, not even when Tom stood to let Evelyn and Bess slide closer. Finally, they gave up any sense of decorum and all huddled around the happy couple.

It was quite a display of emotion before everyone settled back in their seats. Madge straightened herself, twisted the ring so the pearl showed better, and then looked toward the front. Pastor Cleveland must have come in and walked right past them. She hoped he already knew. She hoped he was happy.

On Monday, Madge asked Alex for a ride. "Sure, where do you want to go? I have some errands this morning."

"Jack's office."

Alex raised her lovely eyebrows, so Madge elaborated.

"I need to make sure my affairs are all straight if I'm gonna get hitched."

"That's a good idea. You'll want to line everything out." Alex took the last gulp of her coffee and swooped a stack of papers and notebooks into her open bag. "I'll grade papers while I wait for you."

Madge hesitated. This being toted around by other people was such a nuisance. She didn't want Alex sitting out in the waiting room with Paige while she and Jack talked. She thought it might take a while and knowing someone was waiting would make her fidgety.

"Why don't you just drop me off and then run your errands? I'll wait with Paige till you get back."

Alex put a hand on her hip and appeared to consider the option. "So," she said, "You don't want me hanging around in Jack's office. Are you afraid I might decide I have business there?"

The thought hadn't entered Madge's mind. Until now. "Do you?"

"Of course not. We cancelled the divorce papers when you were in the hospital. You knew that, didn't you?"

Madge knew it. She felt a little glad that her commotion had brought Alex to her senses on that account. She didn't think, though, that the problems had gone away with the papers. She didn't know exactly what kept the Marvels from living up to their name, but she would sure like to see them patch it up.

"I knew about the papers," she said as she hoisted her handbag. "But I also know some people aren't sleeping in the same bed."

Alex started toward the back door. "I don't believe that is any of your business."

Madge followed, leaning on her cane more than she wanted to in the moment. It conflicted with her plan to be pushy on the subject. "My business or not, it isn't going to set things right between the two of you. I may not have been married more than a week, but I've learned some things from casual observation."

Alex tossed her bag into the car and walked around to help Madge in. "Truly, I promise you, Luke and I are not thinking of divorce anymore. Your home here is perfectly intact. We just need to work a few things out."

"And how are you doing that? Where is the working part?"

Madge knew she should probably let it go. Alex had a short endurance when it came to personal conversations. This one had gone on past her usual point. Even so, Madge wanted to get in one more good shot before retreat.

"Come on in and wait at Jack's office if you want. And sleep wherever you please. But when things get hairy around here again, don't count on me to explain to your girls."

Alex slammed her door, pressed the switch, and let the grumble of the garage door answer for her.

When they arrived at Jack's law office, Paige supplied the sunshine they had been missing. She tapped her pencil on a vase full of fresh flowers as she greeted Madge. "See what I got this morning?"

"Well, I'll be," Madge said. "Has the boy figured some things out finally."

"The boy certainly has," Jack said as he entered the room. "He has figured out that some nice grandmotherly ladies can be total con artists."

"Hey," Paige said. "That's enough mean talk about Madge."

"Oh, did you think I meant Madge? Why would you jump to that conclusion? Did you have evidence to support such a conclusion? Why, yes, you did."

He smiled as he spoke, but Madge didn't like the way this visit was beginning. Recounting her trespasses would not help the case she hoped to build.

"She represented herself as a housekeeper," Jack said, "although she had no experience or credentials."

"Not true," Madge said. "You asked for references, not credentials, and I gave you my nephew's card. I cleaned his house every time I visited."

She pulled her purse up higher on her shoulder and stepped around the desk toward Jack's office. "I've come here on official business, if you don't mind."

"Well, by all means," Jack said. "Miss Rosedale, please hold my calls." He took Madge's arm and led her to a chair in his office, swinging the door shut with his foot.

Once she and Jack had taken leather chairs on opposite sides of the desk, Madge pulled a peppermint from her purse. She expected her mouth might get dry before this conversation ended.

"So, I expect you've heard the news."

Jack pointed toward the ring on her finger. "Big news, and I like it. I think Elmer is a good man."

"He is. I don't know why he thinks we ought to hitch up this way, but I've run out of ways to back him off."

"When is the big day?"

"Oh, not for a while yet. I don't expect to walk in the back door at my own..." She had never said the word before. She knew that accepting the ring meant having a ceremony. A wedding. They hadn't talked about the where and when of the thing. Maybe he was thinking a quick service over at the parsonage. Or down at the courthouse. Maybe he didn't expect her to walk down the aisle at Mt. Zion at all. That would be a great relief. She couldn't think of herself as a bride.

"So, you are getting married." Jack nodded for her to keep talking.

"Right. Married. So, before we go off and do such an outlandish thing, I need to get my affairs in order."

"We can take care of that." Jack reached for a note pad on his desk and posed to start writing. "Update your will, I imagine. And the power of attorney we did at the hospital. You will want to put Mr. Grigsby's name ahead of mine. You may have assets you want to keep separate for the sake of your nephews. I don't think we need a full prenup, but probably some conversations. Most of those things can be included in your will."

Madge stared at the man. Maybe he was better at his job than she first thought. "Yeah, sure. We can talk about all that. But the real reason I'm here is pretty simple. I want my driver's license back."

Jack lowered his pen. "Your license?"

"That's right. That judge took my license away when we had the hubbub about the ice cream truck."

"The one you crashed into with your car."

"The one that was parked too close to traffic."

"Across two lanes from where you should have been."

Madge did not like the direction of this conversation any more than she liked the direction of the one-way streets downtown. "Okay. Let's forget what happened in the past. What can we do now to get back the license?"

"Well," Jack tapped the pen against his chin. "It is probably just suspended, not revoked. Did the judge make any conditions, like going to traffic court or anything?"

"Not that I remember," Madge said. "He slapped a lot of money on my bill. By the time I paid it, I couldn't afford all the repairs to my car. So, it's still in hock at the shop. Ben and Nancy offered to help get it out when the time comes. I'm fixing to send them a little note saying that the time has come. Just a loan, you know."

"Okay," Jack started writing in his notebook. "I'll have Paige run down the details. We'll see where things stand."

He put down the notebook after a few scribbles, crossed his legs, and leaned back in gentleman lawyer fashion. Madge thought he looked decidedly more grown up in that pose. He should use it in court.

"I can't promise, you know."

"I know."

"And I'm not even sure it is a good idea."

Madge wasn't fooled by his casual tone and relaxed style. She knew they were both a trick to throw her off her game. She watched cop shows on television. The lawyers were always smooth like this just before they pounced.

"What do you mean about not a good idea?" She crossed her ankles and tried to match his relaxed stance. Her handbag kept slipping, though, and she ended up clutching it like a life preserver.

"I just mean that I think you've been doing well living at the Marvels and letting them drive you around. With your hip surgery and, well, your age in general, maybe it isn't such a good idea to be driving your own car."

Madge let her purse drop. She uncrossed her ankles, sat straight in the chair, and narrowed her eyes at Mr. Charles Jackson Oakley. "I'm not paying you for your ideas," she said. "I'm hiring you like a regular person and telling you I want a job done. Now, are you interested, or should I go on down the street?"

Jack waited a few seconds before answering. Almost long enough to make Madge get nervous. After an uncomfortable stretch, he said, "Okay. I'll look into it."

"Thank you." Madge stood with more trouble than she had hoped. It made it hard to seem aloof. "Just have your assistant send my bill."

With that, she swooped out of the office the best she could with a crippled wing.

CHAPTER THIRTY-ONE

One Step Back

Madge had never been a list-maker. She preferred to let things unroll naturally. When she shopped for groceries, she walked the aisle and grabbed whatever she could afford. Sometimes a good cut of steak looked pretty nice, but she generally went for burger. Although, in recent years, the cost of hamburger had gone up so much she usually mixed it with oats and egg to make it stretch.

This new development in life had her thinking of lists on Tuesday morning. While she waited for Paige to arrive as her chauffer, she searched the house for a notepad like Jack had used in his office. When the search failed, she pulled off yesterday's calendar page and flipped it over.

She couldn't remember if she had read the verse from yesterday. It was something from Psalms, she thought. She turned the page over and read out loud, "We can make our plans, but the Lord determines our steps."

"Good joke," she said to the Almighty. "I'm making a list anyway. It will give You something to work with when You decide to rearrange things."

She wrote a large number one on the page, but nothing came to mind. Earlier, she had felt a multitude of details swirling in her mind. Now they had evaporated. As if she didn't need to worry about a single detail. Like where she and Elmer would live. "Number One: My house or the parsonage? Or somewhere else." She planned to ask Elmer that question next time she saw him. She couldn't really imagine Elmer in her house. In truth, she couldn't imagine herself there anymore. She had only been in the Marvel house a few months, but she already dreaded the thought of going back to the old house with its scarred linoleum and tiny bathroom. She had gotten spoiled, and she knew it. Saw it coming and couldn't stop it even if she had wanted to try. She and Elmer could not live in the blue room at the Marvel house, though. It wouldn't do, even if they asked her to stay on as a nanny/house-keeper.

Madge knew the title was a joke. She hadn't been much of either. Anyway, housing was a big question. She couldn't move into the parsonage. Thinking about it made her queasy. She would never fit into a preacher's life.

That made her stop and stare out the window. Good heavens. She would be a stepmother. To the preacher.

The thought rocked her so hard she considered calling the whole thing off again. She recognized her pattern, though. When things got a tiny bit uncomfortable, she reverted to denial. Pretended she didn't want to marry Elmer Grigsby. Didn't want him sitting at her table for supper each night. Didn't want to share his company on drives to church or walks to the store. Didn't want to lie down in the same bed at night and…

"Whoa, there, Betsy." Madge spoke to herself with a sharp voice. "Let's move on."

She did want those things, though. Madge admitted the truth to herself for one tiny minute. She had been lonesome to belong to someone since the morning DuPree lit out and left her behind.

Madge was spared any further ruminations by Paige shouting from the kitchen. "Ready to go, Madge? I'm here."

Madge thought Circle would be a good distraction from all the fol-de-rol of a wedding. She could not have been more wrong.

Paige started the instant they got into the car. What did she plan to wear? A dress or a suit? What color? Did they want a big wedding with the whole congregation or something smaller? Maybe a wedding at the parsonage, even.

Everyone at Circle had an opinion on those questions, and they posted them before Madge could take her seat.

"Here at the church, I assume," Evelyn said. "We could set up a lovely reception in the fellowship hall. Do you have colors in mind? I always like to tint the icing a little for the groom's cake. The bakery right here on Forty-second does a nice three-layer. We had one for our fiftieth anniversary."

"Maybe you want pie instead," Erma said. "My great-niece got married in the summer, and they had a pie supper at their reception. It was delicious. So many varieties. We all baked our specialty and brought it along. I took a Dutch apple. My mother's recipe."

Madge had no relatives to contribute pies, even if she thought that would be a great idea. Ben's wife, Nancy, might bake something. Alex would order something from the store along with her weekly list. No one, though, would be at home baking on wedding eve with fond thoughts of the couple.

"No pies," Madge growled.

"Maybe you want a destination wedding," Paige said. "Those are all the thing now. We could all go to Florida and watch you get married on the beach. That would be a lovely break from this winter weather."

No one spoke for a few moments. Madge was wondering what kind of shoes she would need to wear if she got married on a beach. All that sand.

"Oh, I don't think so," Bess finally said. "Some of us are past our prime for bathing suits. I'm not sure Madge could pull it off."

The image of the Glory Circle sisters in beach attire was more than any of them could take. A few giggles started spreading around the room.

Amazingly, Grace Colby saved the day. "Let's forget the destination for now." She crossed her arms in her trademark pose and stared at Madge. "What's the date?"

"We haven't decided yet." Madge felt herself leaning back as if trying to get out of this conversation all together. Maybe she could make an excuse to ask Paige to take her home early. She kept right on talking, though, as her mind scrambled.

"Not soon. I'm sure it won't be soon." She gripped her cane and cast about for some reason to change the subject. Her cane. Brilliant plan. "I refuse to walk in the back door for my own wedding," she said. "So, we won't be getting married before I can walk up the front steps like normal."

This set off a flurry of side conversations. Evidently, no one thought Madge should wait that long. A person her age could die before she healed enough to get married. That would be a terrible fix.

"Can we just change the subject?" Madge yelled over the chaos. "When we decide a date, we'll put it in the church paper.

"Very well," Evelyn said. "Let's move on now, ladies, and get ourselves in focus. Is there any new business this morning?"

"Yes," said Erma tentatively. "Where will you live, Madge?"

They rode home in silence. At least for the first ten minutes. Once they passed over into the Cherry Hills neighborhood, Paige spoke. "You aren't really going to make Mr. Grigsby wait, are you?"

Madge pulled her purse closer as if it might shield her from these infernal questions. "I don't know. We didn't talk about it."

"But if he wants to marry soon, you'll consider it?"

Madge started to speak, but Paige pulled a hand from the steering wheel and motioned for her to wait. "You do understand that we'll all be sitting in the sanctuary. When they pull open those gorgeous doors and you step into the aisle, no one will know which entrance you used."

Madge closed her mouth.

CHAPTER THIRTY-TWO

And Then...

Elmer called on Wednesday since he had missed Madge at Circle. Trouble with the furnace had kept him in the basement all morning. "I'd have liked to catch a look at you," he said. "Even if it did make me fluttery for a spell."

Madge had never been accused of making a man fluttery before. She didn't know what to do with the information. "Did you fix the furnace?"

"I did."

She could almost feel him smiling through the phone. They sat for a while, neither of them speaking, and Madge realized that she felt no need to fill the silence. No need to ask a question or make a statement or prod the conversation on in any way. She just wanted to sit in her chair, look at the snow out her window, and feel connected through the mysterious magic of a cell phone.

"Since I missed you, I sent a little something in the mail," he said. "You be watchin' for it. Don't let those little girls get to it first. They are sweet, but this is for you."

"I'll watch," she said.

She had no intention of being goofy about the mail. Yet she kept finding reasons to loiter near the front window in the next couple of days. She knew Alex would never relent to Madge going out to fetch the mail with snow on the ground. Even so, Madge hoped that her shout of "mail's here" would be enough to send Alex out for it.

On Thursday, she shouted the bulletin toward the laundry room where Alex was folding towels. "I'll go out in a minute," Alex shouted back. "Almost done with this load."

She came through the dining room a few minutes later with a neat stack of towels taller than her head. She plunked them on the table and reached out to steady the tower. "Probably should take these in two loads," she said.

Madge tried not to count the steps as Alex carried the first load upstairs. She tried not to check her watch before Alex returned for the second load. Finally, all the precious towels were finally in their appropriate cupboards and Alex could concentrate on the mail. Instead, she plopped in front of the computer.

"Weren't you going to get the mail?"

Alex kept her eyes focused on the screen. "Yeah, in a minute. I wanted to check this one thing online before I get sidetracked. A job lead, I hope."

A new job for Alex was certainly more important than whatever little trinket or message Elmer might have sent her on Tuesday evening. Maybe he didn't even send it on Tuesday. He didn't say when he sent it. And it might not be anything to worry over like this. Probably a joke he'd cut from the newspaper. Or some bit of news from the church bulletin he thought she hadn't seen.

"Maybe I could get the mail," she said to Alex's back.

"Okay," Alex laughed and pushed away from the desk. "I get it. You want the mail. Are you expecting a love letter or something?"

"Probably just bills," Madge said. "No matter to me when you bring it in. I don't care a bit." She moved away from the window.

"I'll be right back." Alex grabbed her coat and shook her head as she opened the door to the icy wind.

Madge watched her progress down the long sidewalk to the mailbox. Alex struggled with the latch and then pulled several pieces of mail from the box. At the last, she reached far inside and came out with a small parcel. Madge tapped her cane toward the front door.

Alex handed her the box, along with a few pieces of mail, without saying a thing. Madge took the treasure to her room and shut the door. She rarely shut the door, and she knew it would make Alex wonder, but she didn't care. A man had never sent her anything in the mail before.

Madge tossed the other pieces of mail aside, even though she noticed one of them was a note from Emily. She pulled the brown paper away from Elmer's package and then held a small, heart shaped box in her hand. Madge lifted the lid to find four pieces of the fancy candy Elmer had shared with her before.

A little early for Cupid season, she thought. But she popped a piece into her mouth just the same. While she chewed, she opened the card.

"Dear Pearl," he had written inside the flowery card. "Will you be my Valentine next month? And forever? Let's get married on February 14th. What do you say?"

Madge spit her candy across the room.

"Lord have mercy," she said as she heaved out of her chair and looked for a tissue. She retrieved the candy before it made too much of a mess on the carpet and dropped it into her trashcan. "What is the man thinking? Valentine's Day? That's a month. Barely a month. Not even a month. Who does he think I am? Some lonely heart who will come running for any man who buys me candy and toots his horn? I can't get married in a month. I won't even have my car back by then."

She stopped protesting long enough to look at the card again. It had a nice verse. A famous poem, probably. "Grow old along with me," it said on the front, "the best is yet to be."

"Too late for that, bub. We grew old long ago."

She sat holding the card for a few minutes and dared to pop a second chocolate into her mouth. It was scandalous idea. Way too soon. No way she could climb the steps. And yet, she had already started picturing herself in a light blue suit like the one Evelyn wore last year for Easter. A white hat maybe, with a little rose bud in the band.

Before she could get completely carried away with silliness, Alex knocked on the door.

"Madge, Jack is here to see you. With Paige. May we come in?"

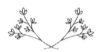

They crowded the room more than Madge could have imagined. It always felt so roomy to her. Now, though, with Paige seated on the footstool, Alex on a kitchen chair she had brought along, and Jack leaning against the door jam, the place felt claustrophobic.

She knew Jack had bad news about her license. She could tell by his face. The poor guy could never play poker. Paige looked like she was about to cry, too, and Alex stared at the floor. Madge wished they would just get on with it. She wanted to eat the rest of her candy and read her card again and think about something besides the awful mess with her car and the courthouse and the nuisance ice cream truck.

"You can't get it done," Madge said to Jack. "They've tied your hands I suppose, on getting my license back."

Jack nodded. "It's a tangle. I'm not saying we can't get it done, but not right away."

"Figures." Madge put the candy on her table. "Always red tape when you go to messing with lawyers. No offense."

"None taken." Jack cleared his throat and shifted his position. The women kept looking like someone had died.

"It's not the end of the world," Madge said. "Jack will fight 'em. He'll get it done."

"There's more," Jack said. With those words, Alex turned and looked into the hallway, as if she couldn't face Madge for the more.

Madge lifted her shoulders and braced herself for bad news. "Spit it out," she said to Jack.

"I had to do a search of some records," Jack said. "I was hoping to find some information that would help me build a case for leniency with the court."

"And?"

"And I learned something that is going to be pretty hard to take."

"What's that? Was I adopted?" Madge used her best sarcastic tone to try and lighten the room.

"No." Jack waited one beat. "You're still married."

CHAPTER THIRTY-THREE

To Believe God

All the air in the room suddenly sucked out in a giant whoosh as if a vacuum had been switched on overhead. Madge felt herself swirling away with the air even as she heard Jack's voice still spouting out details she could not absorb. Images whirled around her like debris in a tornado. Elmer's candy box and any future with him went first. Tattered bits of the DuPree marriage certificate followed. One white glove from the pair she had bought at the dime store ten minutes before her courthouse wedding. The yellow tie DuPree had worn.

Even as she felt her mind trying to flee the room, or the world, Madge wondered why she remembered that tie. Such an ugly tie for what should have been a lovely day.

"Madge, do you understand?"

The voice belonged to that nice Miss Paige Rosedale. Madge knew it did. Knew she should come back into the room and answer the question. Paige had been a good friend. But Madge could not come down from the ceiling. From the floating feeling of being far above all the commotion in the blue room below. Just floating here with memories like clouds.

"Madge! Are you having a stroke?"

Jack's voice brought her back. Down to the chair. Down to the earth. Down to the cold, hard, horrible truth he was trying to tell.

"I tore it up," she said.

"What?"

"The paper that named me Margaret DuPree. I tore it up the minute I got home. After my dad said he would take care of everything."

"Well." Jack came and knelt by her knee. He took one of her hands as if he were a doctor telling her she had only days to live. "He didn't take care of it. No one ever filed for annulment. Ever."

Madge wanted to fly to the ceiling again. Or out the window and above the trees. Her common-sense-self had fully returned, though. She could not make her mind bend like Bess and take her away from the truth.

"Probably didn't have the money," Madge said.

Jack nodded.

"And he probably thought it didn't matter," she said. "Nobody else would ever want me."

Paige wiped at her tears and took Madge's other hand. Alex turned and revealed her own blotchy face. She pulled a tissue from her pocket.

"I've already started the research," Jack said. "The trail grew a little cold looking for him, but we should be able to claim desertion if nothing else. It will take some time, but we should be able to fix this."

Madge squeezed his hand. Just a small squeeze, but a big gesture for her. "Never mind," she said to Jack. "Don't waste your time. I knew this was a hairbrained idea, and now it's proved. I'm done with the whole thing." She pulled her hand free and swept the box of chocolates into her trash.

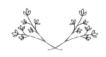

Jack and Paige stayed in the kitchen with Alex a long time. Madge had refused their arguments and finally asked them to leave her alone and let her rest. She didn't sleep. Instead, she stared out the window and thought hard thoughts despite her best attempt to be numb.

She never had expected much from life. She had, in fact, gotten much better than she probably deserved. Any girl who would run off with a man like that ought not expect to be treated like a lady again. She hadn't expected it, either. She had worked like a horse the rest of her life. Did a little swearing here and there. A lot of smoking. She never took to drink, but mostly because it cost too much, if truth be told. She had lived rough, worked hard, and planned on being the loud-mouthed, red-headed Madge DuPree the rest of her life.

And then, out of nowhere, Mt. Zion Church. Not that church had saved her. Not in the heavenly sense. She knew Jesus had done that. Mt. Zion, though, had been the megaphone God used to get her attention. Catherine started the whole thing by inviting her to a ladies meeting. She remembered that day. It had been such a lark.

Mrs. Catherine Benson with her fur trimmed coat and her real leather purse had climbed onto the bus at the stop on Thirtieth Street. Madge wouldn't know the lady's name for a few blocks. She had always kept her handbag on the seat to prevent anyone unsavory from joining her. She looked up that day, though, and saw the uncomfortable look on the elegant lady's face. Most of the seats were full.

Madge took pity and picked up her purse. It was the best move she ever made. They talked a little, Catherine going first. She explained about her husband dropping her off downtown and telling her he would send a car for her before noon. The car never came, though, and she had waited two hours. Her feet were nearly frozen. She expected it had been a mix-up of some kind. Went to the wrong address probably.

In the end, Catherine had decided to become the mistress of her own destiny and had walked to the bus stop. She seemed quite proud of herself.

Although Madge had wanted to laugh at Catherine that day, she saw something in the other woman's face that made her realize taking care of herself that way was as big an achievement as Madge landing this new job at the factory. Two women living wildly different lives, they were both fighting the same fight. Survival. Independence.

Before they reached Catherine's stop, she handed Madge a pink ticket. "We're having a luncheon for some ladies who are new to our church," she said. "Won't you come join us? It is this Saturday. I bet you'd enjoy a change of scenery for the weekend, wouldn't you? No commitment. Just a few ladies chatting. And some delicious food."

To this day, Madge didn't know why she had done it. Why she brushed her wild hair into a bun, added a hat, and traipsed all the way down to Forty-second and Maple. She remembered standing at the bottom of those steps and feeling like she was facing the Great Wall of China. She would never have gone in at all if Catherine Benson hadn't shown up at the bottom of the same steps. They walked in together. Not quite arm-in-arm, but more together than with anyone else in Madge's entire life.

They stayed that way until Catherine died.

"Madge," Alex stepped into the memories and brought Madge back around. "Could you eat some soup?"

"No. Maybe later."

Alex nodded. She started to walk away but turned again. "It hasn't been for nothing, you know."

"What's that?"

"Your life. The journey. However, you want to put it. Your common sense, which probably comes from some of these hard knocks, it's a treasure. It has helped us."

Madge doubted that statement. She felt pretty sure she had muddled this whole thing pretty badly. From the slight exaggeration about her qualification for the job to her fall on the ice that made her dependent instead of dependable.

"It's true," Alex said. "I hadn't mentioned it yet, but we put away the green sheets."

She walked away with that statement and left Madge sitting with her mouth open for a witty response. She couldn't think of one, though, so it was good Alex walked away.

"Well, how about that," she said to the empty room. "Somebody wins."

The rest of the day went on as if the household was in mourning. Which it was. Madge sat in her room, feeling like the deceased party. The other three sat in the kitchen, drinking coffee and talking in subdued voices, so as not to wake the dead. The hardest part would be telling Elmer. She wanted to do it over the phone, to avoid seeing his eyes and hearing the whistle go out of him. She knew that was cowardly, though. Late in the afternoon, she asked Jack if he would drive her over to the parsonage.

"I will," he said. "Are you sure you don't want me to go in first. Soften the blow for you?"

"Maybe," Madge said. "We'll see how much of a chicken I am once we get there."

Her courage grew as they got closer to the church. Something about that solid building gave her courage to face whatever might come in her wobbly world. Jack walked her to the door of the parsonage and then went back to wait in the car.

Madge supposed they would be about ready to sit down for supper. Terrible to ruin a man's appetite this way. She pushed the buzzer.

The look of pure delight on Elmer's face when he saw her standing on the porch made Madge almost turn and run. Knowing she would trip over the cane and land on her face made her stay put.

He invited her in, but she couldn't go. She could not step into the warm room with the two chairs and the inviting fire. She could not walk into the home Elmer had won after his long, hard life and smash things up again.

"I've come with bad news," she said. "I'd rather tell it to you here and let us both move on without a bunch of sentiment."

Elmer stepped out on the porch. He shivered with his head uncovered and only his shirtsleeves against the chill. She wanted to send him back inside but decided a quick slash would be the most merciful way to kill the thing.

"I'm married," she said. "Didn't know it. Never intended it. But there we are. I'm a married woman and continuing to step out with you would be a sin. If there is any justice in this world, Jack will find it and straighten the mess out. For now, though, I'm lawfully and awfully still Mrs. DuPree."

She tucked the pearl ring into his hand and turned to run, the best she could.

"Now, jest a minute," Elmer said. He stomped across the porch and blocked her path. "I don't rightly know what yer talkin' about, but I know it don't matter one whit to me. If there's some paperwork Jack's got to do, let him do it. If this fellow DuPree wants to fight me for ya, I'll fight him. But you take this ring and put it right back on your finger where it belongs. I've not come this far to be waylaid by some legal loophole."

With that, he took her hand and slid the ring over her arthritic knuckle without a bit of struggle.

Madge didn't know what to do, how to respond. "But I'm married," she said.

"Only on paper." He still held her hand. "Only on a scrap of paper somewhere in a dusty record book and it don't amount to a hill of beans. Jack will take care of it."

"I'm not sure he can," she said.

"Well," Elmer gave her that cocky grin, the one that said saved-by-grace-and-proud-to-be-here. "I reckon we'll have to appeal to a higher court then. We'll just have to believe God."

"Believe Him?"

"Sure, He says Himself that He is good. And that He is a re-warder of them that seeks Him. We've sought. He'll reward."

Madge hoped with her living soul that it would be that easy.

CHAPTER THIRTY-FOUR

Walking by Faith

She wanted to believe God. To believe everyone when they told her this thing could be fixed. By the time she arrived in the vestibule for Sunday morning service, though, her ability to persevere seemed thin. She had worked so hard just to reach the point of surrender. It had gone against everything in her to accept Elmer's attention. To return his affection out loud had been like doing the high jump at the Olympics. Now, everything felt ruined.

Thank Heaven she hadn't fallen in with a bunch of loudmouths. Jack would be sworn to secrecy for lawyer and client stuff. Paige had not peeped a word. It seemed like Luke and Alex would stay away from the subject at church, too.

Madge twisted the ring around on her finger a few times. She wondered what Pastor Cleveland thought of her now. Surely Elmer had told him. As if he could read her mind, or her soul, Pastor Cleveland came down the aisle at that moment. He paused at the third pew and greeted the family.

When he leaned down to shake Madge's hand, he said, "So glad to see you this morning. And every morning. I'm believing with the two of you."

He moved on before Madge could answer. Elmer took his place on the pew a few moments later. "Been sleepin' good?" he asked.

"Not particularly."

"Figured as much. I'm sleeping better than ever. You'll get there. It'll be all right." He slid his hand over and covered hers.

Madge tried to relax. She tried to match his calm. She tried to think about the Almighty, about the angels, about anything at all besides that man DuPree. She failed.

She didn't hear a single song, and she would probably have missed the entire sermon if Pastor Cleveland hadn't started out with an announcement.

"I wanted to make sure you all know," he said, "that I'm going to be out of town for a few days. I'll be attending a conference in St. Louis starting on Tuesday night. After that, I've been asked to do a couple of talks at the seminary. I'll be gone about ten days total. One of the deacons will bring a message next Sunday. I think they are fighting over who gets to preach. It will be so good you'll never want me back."

A couple of the deacons called out their opinions on that before Pastor Cleveland continued.

"Someone will be in the church office a few hours each day, but it will be hard to get messages to me. So, you all just look after one another the next couple of weeks, okay? Visit the hospital if someone gets sick. Loan out your car if someone gets stuck. Come up with bail money if someone goes to jail."

Most people laughed at that, and Madge even smiled.

"Also," he said, "I'd appreciate it if some of you checked in on my dad now and then. He is a tolerable cook these days, but I'd feel better knowing you all are looking in." He cleared his throat, and Madge took the pause to jostle Elmer with her shoulder as if to make good on that. He jostled back.

"Taking care of one another is the subject of my sermon," Pastor Cleveland said. "This week will be a good excuse for everyone to put it into practice."

Madge didn't hear another word.

She and Elmer exchanged the usual chit-chat after church. Grace Colby, Erma, and Evelyn soon crowded around as if Elmer Grigsby was a special guest for the morning. Evelyn made a firm date that she and Tom would bring supper over at the end of the week.

Madge stood back and watched the flurry. She wondered when the sudden change of heart caused the ladies to see Elmer as a worthy member of the congregation. Of course, maybe they didn't. Maybe they saw him as a project.

The thought riled her, so she pushed her way into the tight circle. "Speakin' of food, didn't Bess say she was hungry? You know she gets weepy if she doesn't eat on schedule."

Evelyn did her usual intervention and steered Bess with slight pressure under her elbow. "Let's go see if Tom is ready. Maybe some lunch on the way home."

Soon, everyone had wandered away, replaced by the Marvel family.

Aspen put her arm around Madge's shoulders. "We will take care of Mr. Grigsby, won't we?"

"Are you offering to cook?"

Aspen didn't have time to answer before Jack and Paige joined the group. "Aspen cooks?" Jack said, "When did that happen?"

Madge expected the teenager to slam back with a zinger. She could do it. Instead, she pulled her arm away and shrugged. "I'll get your coat," she said to Madge.

No one else seemed to notice the obvious dodge. They kept right on chatting about how Elmer could fill his empty days.

Madge watched Aspen walk away, her shoulders slumped. At the last second, Aspen turned in the doorway to look at the group. She caught Madge staring at her. Madge raised an eyebrow to show she knew something was up. Aspen shrugged again.

It was Monday night before Madge had a chance to follow up on that exchange. Aspen had stayed in her room Sunday evening, and Madge still wasn't doing steps. Monday morning was typically chaotic. After supper on Monday, though, Madge took control.

"Aspen and I will take kitchen duty," she said.

"We will?"

"Yep. I think it's our turn."

"That's great," Alex said. "I need to make some changes to tomorrow's lesson plan."

"Good by me," Luke said. "I have pressing business in the family room with the remote control." He ruffled Aspen's hair as he walked by. He also winked at Madge, and she decided he probably recognized a woman with an agenda.

They had the dishwasher emptied before Aspen finally spoke. "So, what's on your mind?"

"More things than you need to handle," Madge said. She dropped silverware into the basket. "The main one right now is this: Why are you mad at Jack?"

Aspen stopped working, but she did not look at Madge. "What makes you think I'm mad?"

"You slammed an imaginary door in his face yesterday."

"Yeah," Aspen leaned against the sink. "I guess I did."

"So?'

"So." Aspen tapped the counter. "So, I didn't know before that Jack was the bad guy."

"In what story?"

"Ours." Aspen got louder. "The one where our parents tried to ruin our lives by splitting up, and the judge tried to teach them a lesson by giving the house to us kids."

Madge tried to decide how much she really wanted to dig into this hash. Not much, to tell the truth. Yet, she couldn't stand Aspen having the wrong idea about Jack. He had pulled her out of a couple of bad moments, and her future hung in his hands right now.

"It wasn't like that," she said.

"No? Seems pretty like that to me."

"Well, you don't know everything," Madge said. "I know you think you do, but you don't. That story had a lot of crooks and turns you never knew about. It still does. But Jack never set out to take your house or split up your parents."

"How would you describe his job, then?"

"His job was to make sure your mom got a fair deal in the divorce. She wanted to sell the house, so it was his job to help her do it."

"Exactly."

"But when he got to know you guys, he pretty much stopped doing his job."

"He did?"

"Yep. I expect he dragged his feet a while on the paperwork. And after I fell and everybody came around, he pretty much stopped the whole case."

"I didn't know that."

"'Course you didn't. You ought to take those ear plugs out now and then." She flipped one of the cords dangling from around Aspen's neck.

Aspen reached over and smacked a sloppy kiss on Madge's check. The moment was so unexpected that Madge almost stumbled back. She didn't know what to do with a kiss from a teenager. Or from anyone, for that matter.

"You are a pearl," Aspen said. "We lucked out when we got you."

She tossed the last crumpled napkin toward the trash and then bopped out of the room, humming.

Madge stood at the sink for a while. She knew she had made Jack out to be something of a hero, because she couldn't stand for Aspen to think otherwise. She hoped she wasn't putting too much faith in Jack for herself. She did trust the Almighty with her eternal soul. She supposed that she trusted Him with her day-to-day the best she could. But, at a time like this, it sure helped to have a good lawyer in the family.

CHAPTER THIRTY-FIVE
In Sickness and Health

On Tuesday, the plague struck the Marvel house. Madge didn't know if it was strep throat, whooping cough, pneumonia, or a combination of all three. She only knew the household sounded like a hospital ward. Coughing, hacking, wheezing, crying. Lots of crying.

Quinn succumbed first, just before daylight. Madge couldn't hear everything that happened upstairs, but the sound of Quinn crying came straight through the floorboards and woke her. She had her slippers on and her robe in hand before she remembered she couldn't make the stairs. At least not on her own. So, she waited in the dark until she heard the door open from Alex's room. Then the padding of feet. The crying stopped, but the coughing increased. It seemed to be coming from two rooms now.

Madge went to the foot of the stairs and listened. Definitely Quinn and Aspen coughing. Then Peyton started to cry followed by sounds that were gruesome. Madge heard Luke crossing the hall.

When she heard Alex call out for a thermometer, Madge couldn't take it anymore. She grabbed the bannister and took one step up. Then two. It seemed after a while as if she was climbing the stairs in time with the coughing. When she reached the top, she was tempted to stop for breath. She didn't feel any more pain than usual, though, so she pressed on to the little girls' room.

"Give me Quinn," she said as she entered the room. "One of you check on Aspen." Luke turned toward the hallway, coughing as he went.

"I'll get something for the fevers while you stay with them," Alex said.

Madge scooted over on the side of Quinn's bed and pushed the hair back from the hot forehead. By stretching out her arm and leaning just a bit, she managed to perform the same service for Peyton. Both girls continued to cough every few minutes.

The night turned into morning with all the adults in the house staying busy getting drinks, patting backs, singing songs, and trying not to admit if they felt a tickle in their own throats. Around breakfast time, Aspen wandered into the little girls' room and curled up at the foot of Peyton's bed.

"Is it the plague?" she asked. "Should we send for Doc Baker?"

Madge had seen enough *Little House on the Prairie* shows to get the reference. She didn't think it was a bad idea. If either Alex or Luke started coughing, she planned to hang a white flag from the mailbox and hope someone sent help.

Alex leaned against Quinn's padded headboard. "I think we should probably make a trip to urgent care. These fevers aren't coming down much."

Luke leaned over and touched Quinn's cheek. "What do you think they have? It sounds awful."

Alex rubbed her hands across her eyes. "Last fall, when things were a mess, did you happen to remember to take the girls in for their flu shots?"

Luke frowned, and Madge closed her eyes. "Why would I think of that?" he asked. "I never do that stuff."

"Right. I was just hoping it might have come up."

"It didn't. I can't imagine how it would. Didn't they have checkups or something before school?"

"Grace did. But it was too early for shots. We get those in October, usually."

"So, you think this is flu."

"I do. Not stomach flu. Influenza. The kind that can be dangerous if you develop breathing problems. I saw a post yesterday saying there were several cases in the school district."

She turned to Madge. "Oh, my gosh. Did you get a flu shot, Madge? Even if you did, you better get downstairs and away from these kids."

"Balderdash," Madge said as she wiped Quinn's head.

"You were going to clean up your language," Quinn said without opening her eyes.

"I'll do it when you get well."

Mid-morning, the entire family loaded up in Luke's vehicle, wrapped in warm coats and looking like miserable snow people. While they were gone, Madge decided to make a phone call to Paige and let her know she wouldn't be going to Circle. They probably shouldn't even meet during flu season. Old people died of the stuff. Maybe she would call Evelyn, too.

"Oh, I'm so sorry to hear about the girls," Paige said. "Jack is down, too. Probably the same stuff. He is coughing hard enough to break ribs. Serious body aches. He says he would have to get better just to die."

"That's bad," Madge agreed.

"I'm afraid I didn't take him too seriously," Paige said. "I may have indicated he was being dramatic."

"Thought he was just man-sick, did you?"

Paige laughed. "I guess so, though I've never heard that term."

"You'll learn it," Madge said, "if you hang around with a man long enough. Anyway, I'm going to call Evelyn. You tell Jack to stay in bed. Take him some chicken soup but leave it outside his door. This stuff is contagious."

After Paige agreed to conditions, Madge pressed the button to end the call. Then she called Evelyn, who had gotten her immunization in mid-October and felt perfectly fine and well-covered. Madge had skipped the shot this year in all the hoopla, and she kind of regretted it now. She would just have to take her chances. She did not, however, admit any of that to Evelyn.

They agreed Circle should be cancelled in light of the spreading illness. None of the ladies could afford a bout with the stuff. Evelyn would take care of details, and Madge should just take care of herself.

She would do exactly that. After one more call. Madge had never called a man on the telephone before. She had caught on that manners had changed. Paige called Jack all the time. Girls on the television called boys every whipstitch. In Madge's day, though, the gentleman did the calling. Not the lady.

This felt rather urgent, though, so she dug in her purse until she found the church bulletin from Sunday. Sure enough, the parsonage number was listed. She counted seven rings before Elmer answered.

"The pastor is out," he said after giving his greeting, "but I'll help ya if I can."

"You can," Madge said. "You can help me by staying put today and not going over to open the church. We've cancelled Circle due to an attack of influenza."

"Well, that sounds pretty serious."

"Oh, I doubt it. But we decided not to take any chances."

"Are you sick?" Elmer asked.

"No," Madge rather growled her answer. "I don't get sick."

It was a big brag, and she knew she might regret it. Even so, she growled on. "We'll be going under quarantine as soon as they get back from the doctor. So, you don't try to come over here. I won't be at church, either. Probably good timing."

Elmer paused a rather long time before he answered. "Getting kinda bossy about things, aren't you?"

She could hear the smile in his voice. She knew he was kidding, but she decided to pretend otherwise. "I'm bossy all right. Just ask anybody who has known me more than a minute. And I don't plan to change. I've lived all my life as my own boss."

"And it's worked right well for you, I can tell."

Still smiling. The man could be irritating.

"I'm hanging up now," she said. "You just stay put."

"Whatever you say, Your Highness."

Madge pulled the phone away from her ear. She could hear Elmer laughing as he said, "Good-bye."

She was wrong about the quarantine. She heard Luke's car pulling into the garage just before noon. Aspen came through the door first and held up a white paper sack.

"It is not the plague," she said. "Just plain old bronchitis. We got drugs."

She kept on walking through the kitchen into the dining room and up the stairs before Madge could think what to say.

Peyton and Quinn came next. "Mine is cute bronchitis," Peyton said. "Probably cause I'm cute."

"What was mine?" Quinn asked.

Alex came into the kitchen and started pulling off coats. "Acute bronchitis, Peyton. But you are cute."

"And so is this pretty pink medicine," Luke said as he handed Madge the bag. "Refrigerate, I think."

"No, that one doesn't need to go in the fridge." Alex spoke with the confidence of a former drug salesperson as she took the bag from Madge. "I'll put it in the upstairs bathroom so we remember to give it to them at bedtime."

"So, not influenza," Madge said.

"Nope." Luke opened the fridge. "Are we out of soda?"

Madge reached in and pulled a can out from behind a huge head of broccoli. "Ever think of going on the wagon?"

"This is the wagon." Luke stopped with the can in his hand. "I'm sorry, Madge. Are you sensitive about things like that now? About drinking jokes, I mean."

"Why would I be sensitive about that?" Madge reached into the fridge and pulled out her own soda. She rarely drank the stuff, but she felt determined to change this conversation. She popped the tab and listened to the fizz. "Nothing to be sensitive about. Did anybody ever accuse me of being sensitive?"

Before he could answer, Alex came back in the room. "Even though we don't have flu," she said, "the nurse at the clinic said it is everywhere. You should be really careful if you're going out. Wash your hands frequently. Stay away from people who are coughing. That kind of thing."

Madge nodded. "I don't plan on going anywhere."

CHAPTER THIRTY-SIX

Sunlight and Shadows

At first, Madge thought a few days of enforced rest would be good for the whole family. Instead, the pink medicine worked quickly, and the little girls got bouncy. Aspen did not enter the bouncing stage. Instead, she got crabbier as the week wore on.

As predicted, both Luke and Alex started coughing by Thursday. That didn't keep them from going to work, though. Or, more precisely, to take turns going to work. Neither of them thought Madge should be left in charge of a hospital, so they took turns staying home for nursing duty.

When Friday night arrived, both spouses collapsed like heaps of over-worn clothes. Alex sprawled on the sofa while Luke stretched out in his recliner.

"Do we have any soup?" Luke called toward the kitchen where Madge was working on macaroni and cheese for the girls.

"Or tea," Alex said. "Hot tea with honey would be really helpful."

Madge paused with her rough hands on her hips. She didn't hire on as a nurse. This was not in the plans or the job description. And yet, she couldn't ignore the fact that she was the only person left standing.

"Yeah, we got both," she shouted back toward the dining room. When the words stopped echoing, she pulled open the cupboards and got busy.

Paige called on Saturday night.

"Anyone still alive at your house?" she asked Madge. "Jack has rallied. He thinks he might live, especially if I will drop off one more tub of ice cream and the video game that just came out this week. I might have to stand in line a little while for the game."

"That boy is going to have you plumb wore out with his fetchin' and totin'."

"Yeah," Paige answered with some dreaminess in her voice.

"We're still alive over here," Madge said. "Bronchitis all the way around, evidently, for everyone but me."

"Let's go to church tomorrow, then." Paige's voice brightened. "Here I was feeling sorry for myself with this empty weekend, and now you have given me hope. Maybe we can even take Mr. Grigsby with us and go out to lunch."

Madge waited. She didn't want to go out with Elmer again. Not while things were so tangled up. Yet, the thought of sitting with him in a nice café, having Paige with them to lift the mood, sounded rather nice.

"We'll just play it by ear, shall we?" Paige kept her bright tone. "I'm going to run by Jack's place now. I'm glad it isn't the flu at your place. Hope everyone recovers soon."

They did not recover soon. Madge awoke on Sunday morning to the sound of tag team coughing as usual. She crept around in the kitchen getting her breakfast so as not to wake everyone. She put some stew in the slow-cooker and left a note for Alex explaining lunch had been started. She didn't know for sure when she would be back.

She took more time than necessary getting dressed. Putting the pearl necklace on under her sweater, then taking it off, then putting it on again. By rights, she should give the pearls back. But if he wouldn't accept the ring, he surely wouldn't accept the pearls. She took them off again, tucked them into the blue box, and shut them inside a drawer.

Paige knocked just as that job was finished. They drove quietly for several blocks, listening to music, admiring the sunshine. Paige took advantage of a long stoplight to bring up the subject of marriage.

"They say marriage is hard work."

"Seems true," Madge said. "Though mine has pretty much been a breeze."

"Ouch." Paige frowned before she nudged into the intersection.

"Not much of a joke was it?"

"No," Paige sounded sad. "Nice try, though." She waited another block. "I'm wondering, though, how much work it is to be married, to stay married, for dozens of years like some people do."

Madge felt she was the last person on earth to give marriage advice. She searched her memories for tidbits she had heard from happily married couples like Catherine and her late husband. Or her nephews and their wives. Even Tom and Evelyn seemed to sail on fairly calm seas. Finally, she remembered something Joe had said about Mara after pizza that night long ago.

"Somebody told me once, that it isn't the falling in love that matters. It's the staying."

"Right, but how do you know you can do that?"

"Well," Madge struggled for the smooth words Joe had used. She reached for her own interpretation. "You just decide. Every day. Maybe every hour. You just decide to stay put, to work it out, to give more than you take, and to love the sucker no matter how old and ugly he grows."

"Well, that's romantic."

"You didn't ask about romance."

"No. I didn't."

Madge looked at the traffic picking up around them. "I'll tell you one more thing before you need to concentrate on your driving. This is one lady who is too old and crotchety for any romantic foolishness."

Paige grinned and whipped into the next lane. "I think Mr. Elmer Grigsby disagrees."

Madge didn't argue the point, because she wanted to arrive alive. She worried it over in her mind a good bit, though. She didn't see any way out of this but to stop it cold turkey. That is how she gave up smoking, finally. She tried to drag it out at first, cutting back every few days. That always failed, though, because she could talk herself into one more puff for every reason in the world. When she finally decided to be done, she tossed them into her trashcan. After about an hour, she went back out and poured vinegar on top of the trash so she'd quit being tempted to pull them out.

It was time to pour vinegar on this romance. She pulled up her proverbial stockings and got ready to face the man. She would tell him straight out, first thing. Before any of the music or singing or praying could get her all soft and gooshy again. The minute she laid eyes on Elmer Grigsby, she would tell him "fare-thee-well" for good.

Elmer was not at church.

He wasn't waiting at the back door of the upper lot. In fact, no one had turned on the lights, and Madge had to borrow Paige's flashlight cell phone to make her way inside.

The hallway felt ice cold, as if no one had turned on the heat. Madge didn't feel any warmth at all until she reached the vestibule. She saw Tom coming up from the basement.

"Don't know what to think," he said to Evelyn. "I assumed the thermostat was programmed to come on automatically. But evidently someone does it manually every week. The furnace is working."

"Who takes care of turning up the heat?" Evelyn asked.

"Elmer Grigsby, I expect." Grace Colby might as well have spit the words. She had her back to Madge and couldn't have known the words carried to her. It was quite a change from the praise they had all sung last week.

Madge stopped walking. She wanted to defend him, wanted to explain that he had probably gotten sick like so many others. Wanted to run out the back door and over to the parsonage to see if that were true and to wipe the hot sweat from his forehead. Instead, she stood still with her crippled leg and her wobbly cane.

Evelyn spoke to Grace. "I hope he isn't unwell. So many are down with the flu this week." Ever the ambassador, Evelyn nodded toward the sanctuary as if to indicate Grace should lead the way. She did.

Tom spoke once more. "Good thing I brought my keys today or we wouldn't even have gotten in."

Evelyn looked over her shoulder and raised one eyebrow at Madge before disappearing through the doorway.

"What was that all about?" Paige reached out to take Madge's coat.

"I think I'll keep it. Chilly in here this morning."

The sermon was probably good. Maybe even great. Madge felt a little surprised to see Tom rise from his seat just before service and walk toward the pulpit. She knew he was a deacon, but she never thought of him that way. He was just Evelyn's husband.

He started with a story from his childhood. Something about baseball and wise words from his father. Madge's mind kept wandering to the parsonage. Tom ended with a call to action, suggesting everyone find someone who needed a word of encouragement this week and handing it out like his dad had done for him.

Again, Madge thought that he had probably done a good job. Maybe he should have been a preacher instead of a banker. Evelyn would probably have given up her diamond bracelet and brooch for the sake of the gospel.

That rabbit trail only took her right back around the tree to Elmer. He would never shower her with diamonds, but the pearl ring was mighty nice. She touched it and felt sorry all over again for the way she had to harden her heart. And she would, too. Just as soon as she knew he wasn't dying of pneumonia.

"I'd like to check next door," she said to Paige once the crowd had thinned.

"Yes, I think we should."

The chore was not easy. Madge needed a little help navigating the sidewalk covered with melting snow. Once they reached the porch, she knocked. Hard.

After no one had answered from several knocks, Paige went around to the side yard and Madge walked to the back door. She peered inside and could see that the house was dark. She didn't know much about the parsonage and wasn't sure which windows were bedrooms. Upstairs, probably. She thought of throwing rocks to get his attention, but that seemed silly.

Instead, she took out her phone and for the second time in her adult life, she called a man. Her jitters over the call were unfounded. She got a recorded message that the person with that number had either traveled outside the service area or had turned his phone off.

Drat.

Madge slid over to the kitchen window and tried for another vantage point. Suddenly, she caught sight of the cat. He licked the last bite from a food dish that must have been recently full. A bowl of water sat nearby.

Paige came around the corner just then.

"Well, he isn't dead," Madge said. "He's fed the cat."

"I suppose he's just sleeping," Paige said. "If he's sick, that's the best thing to do."

Madge stuck her hands and her phone into her pockets. "Might as well leave him be then."

"I think so," Paige put an arm around Madge. "We can try calling him again later."

CHAPTER THIRTY-SEVEN
The Cat's Meow

Madge did not call Elmer again. The effort of searching for him on Sunday had been almost too much for her troubled soul. She turned him over to the Almighty, although she did plan to have a few words with him when she got to Circle on Tuesday. She wasn't sure how these things worked, but the man ought to let somebody know if he was sick.

Madge rehearsed the words as she took the few steps from Paige's car to the gymnasium door. She didn't want to sound like a nag. She just wanted him to understand that other people got concerned when he didn't show up at church. She gave the church door a good jerk in case the ice had it frozen. She almost pulled her shoulder out of socket. The door was locked.

Madge tried the door two more times before she went back to the car.

"Locked?"

"Maybe frozen," Madge said. She must have pulled too hard on the door. Her breath came hard, and her heart was pounding.

"I'll pull around front and run inside. I'll find someone to un-lock it, and then we'll come back."

"Don't run," Madge said. "No need to fall. We're early, and he might just have gotten sidetracked with the furnace or something."

"Right." Paige did not sound convinced.

While she waited in the car, Madge ran through all the possible explanations. She started with the furnace idea. She gave it no credence, yet she named it. She added the thought that he might have had a stroke and died in the night. At their age, anything was possible. In a less dire circumstance, she assumed he was sick and needed looking after. He might simply be chatting in the vestibule with the other ladies and hadn't noticed the time. They might laugh about this. Someday.

Paige didn't appear to be laughing as she hopped down the steps and into the car. "Mr. Grigsby didn't open the church or turn up the heat. Do you suppose he is sick?"

"Must be," Madge said. "Maybe we should check on him after the meeting."

"Or before?"

"After." Madge refused to look like a silly woman chasing a man. She had made a vow about that in the ugly hotel room after DuPree fled with all their money and the last of the chocolate cookies they had bought as a wedding supper.

The ladies had assembled by the time Paige and Madge entered the room. They took two chairs near the door, and Madge tried to look unconcerned. The last thing she needed was people making assumptions or conjecturing about her life.

"I hope dear Mr. Grigsby hasn't gone off on a drunk," Bess said.

Of all the mornings for Bess to know her up from her down, this was the worst. Madge couldn't even work up an angry defense. Partly because of her fond spot for Bess, and partly because she had been thinking the same thing. God help her.

"I'm sure he is just feeling under the weather," Evelyn said. She spoke to Bess, but she made eye contact with Madge. "So many people have been sick this week. He probably knew I carried an extra key for emergencies, so he didn't bother any of us with the details."

"Oh." Bess nodded and looked off in the distance. "That's good then. I'd hate for him to sleep on the streets tonight. It is so cold."

"He wouldn't feel the cold," Grace said. "Booze heats you up."

"Is that right?" Erma leaned around Bess and spoke to Grace. "Alcohol raises your body temperature?"

"I think we can change the subject now." Evelyn held up the little gavel and looked around the room as if calling tardy children to order. "Let's discuss the date for the spring bazaar."

Immediately, the room took on the sweet buzz of worker bees with a bazaar to plan. Things to crochet. Items to bake. Slogans to create.

Madge thought she might die.

Instead, she sat straight and kept nodding her head now and then to pretend she was paying attention. After a few minutes, Paige touched her arm.

"Let's sneak out, shall we?"

Madge followed when Paige slid from her chair to the door and out into the hallway. Paige made the trip in what looked like one fluid movement. Almost like a cartoon character who slinks out of the room by becoming one with the wall. Madge hadn't been one with anything except her arthritis. She made it to the hallway, though.

"Want to go check?" Paige asked.

Madge didn't bother with an answer. She just stomped down the hall as fast as her two legs and a cane would go.

They drove around to the parsonage. The day was gloomy, but no lights showed in any windows. Paige tried the front door again, while Madge took the back. When neither opened and no one answered the bell, Madge put her hands against the glass and looked into the kitchen.

She could see the cat walking in circles around his empty food dish and yowling every few seconds. "Should we break the window to open the door?"

Paige stepped forward. "I don't think we'll have to be that dramatic." She pushed aside some snow with the toe of her boot until she could see the doormat. She pulled back the corner and was rewarded by a sight better than hidden gold. An extra key. So predictable.

Paige opened the door. Madge had obviously gotten too cold out on the porch, because her hands were shaking. The cat dived under the side hutch the minute they walked into the room. Madge felt glad they didn't have to bother with the creature while they searched the house.

She didn't exactly hold her breath, but she took shallow breaths and tried to be completely silent. Her cane rapping on the floor made that impossible. She went forward with trepidation. The idea of snooping around in a man's house felt worse than the thought in the tiniest crevice of her mind that they might find Elmer sick. Or dead. Or drunk.

She didn't know which one would be worse. Well, dead, of course. It was the only one that couldn't be fixed.

It turned out Madge had seen most of the main floor on her first visit. She had seen the kitchen, small dining area, living room, and bathroom. One more door opened to a nice office with lots of books. Again, two chairs were pulled close to a table with a lamp. Madge tried to imagine Elmer sitting there. Did he read books now? Had he been a reader before the war? What would he have been reading in this room?

Paige pulled the door shut before Madge could explore more. "I should go upstairs while you wait down here. Why don't you sit in the living room?"

Madge nodded and returned to the main room. Obviously, she couldn't go up the steep staircase. Just like she couldn't climb the steps at Mt. Zion for a wedding next month. She could not.

And she wouldn't marry any other way. Climbing the steps probably wouldn't matter now.

She tried hard not to be maudlin. Better that he showed his true colors now, before she got hitched in the traces with him for good. She could just cut her losses now. Back to the Marvel house as nanny and housekeeper in a couple more weeks. She could earn her salary again and get her debts paid off. The minute she got the keys to her Oldsmobile, she would be out of there and off on her own. Maybe she would go visit the nephews for a while. Maybe even go to Florida. She could drive to Florida.

"No sign of anyone." Paige hopped the last two steps. "Beds are made. Things are tidy."

Madge wanted to slap herself for wondering what the bedroom looked like where Elmer slept. She jerked her mind back into line. "Well, we can't wait around for him to show up." She tried to stand with a dignified humph. It came out as more of a groan.

As they crossed the dining room, Paige said, "Do you think he might have jumped in and gone with Pastor Cleveland at the last minute?"

As if to answer, the cat scooted out of the kitchen and wrapped himself around Madge's ankles. She managed to remain upright by grabbing onto Paige. The varmint cat yowled and meowed and continued to tangle himself in her ankles.

She reached down with one hand and scooped the animal up under her arm. "And left his cat without food? I don't think so." She almost managed to march as she walked out the back door, cat under one arm, purse over the other. Cane gripped at an odd angle and offering no aid whatsoever.

"What are you going to do with the cat?" Paige pulled open the car door and grabbed Madge's purse to help her in.

Madge handed over the purse and managed to plop into the seat without sitting on the cat's tail. She looked at Paige without a grimace. "I'm gonna feed him."

CHAPTER THIRTY-EIGHT
The Worst of Times

"Shall we drive around a block or two?" Paige sat with her hands on the steering wheel, staring ahead.

Madge kept both hands on the yowling cat. "No. We're liable to be scratched to pieces before we get home. Let's go."

The going was not smooth.

"What's his name?" Paige asked over the loud wailing.

"Cat."

"That's original."

Madge gave her a look. It was the best she could do. What did she care whether a man named his cat or not? In fact, what did she care about the silly cat? They'd probably need to take him to the animal shelter in a few days. Nobody could put up with this kind of racket for long.

She didn't plan to pet the cat. It must have been a natural instinct of some kind. Before they had gone three blocks, Madge realized she had started running her hand down the slick fur. And the cat had stopped complaining. He stretched his back in a great arc and then curled into a fur ball on her lap.

"Well, look at you," Paige said. "The cat whisperer."

Madge wouldn't have been more surprised if she had tamed a lion at the circus.

They all three remained silent for the rest of the drive, except for the soft sound of purring.

When they reached the Marvel house, Paige said, "I think you better let me carry him."

Madge agreed and lifted the limp animal up toward Paige. He did not approve of the change in position, and he made his preferences known. Loudly. Thank goodness the girls were still at school. Madge would have time to find a box in the garage and pen the cat up before they got home. She would put some milk in with him. Under no circumstances whatsoever would the cat be allowed in the house.

"I can explain," she said to Alex a few hours later.

The little girls sat on the kitchen floor cooing over Elmer's cat as if he were a baby. Aspen knelt nearby, flicking a piece of string for him to catch.

"You can explain why we suddenly have a cat?" Alex didn't exactly look angry, yet Madge didn't think the look was happy, either.

"Well, it's a long story. Some of it might not be meant for all the ears."

Alex waved toward the hallway. She tapped Aspen on the shoulder as she walked by, and Aspen said, "I've got it."

Once they reached the blue room, Madge poured out the whole story. Of thinking Elmer had gotten sick. Of checking on him Sunday and the cat looking fed. Of going back today and realizing Elmer wasn't at home. Probably hadn't been for days.

"I couldn't leave the cat to starve," she said. Even then, she tried not to admit to herself what that statement meant about Elmer.

"Do you know where he might have gone? Would he have left with Pastor Cleveland after all?"

"I asked that same thing," Paige said from the hallway. "I couldn't leave Madge alone this afternoon, so I worked from the dining room table. I hope you don't mind."

"Sure, no problem."

"And I'm so sorry about bringing the cat here. My apartment has a rule."

"It's okay."

Alex didn't look okay, and Madge realized the look on her face was worry.

"Do you think we should call the police?" Alex said to Paige.

Before she could answer, a door slammed in the kitchen. "Hey, anybody home?"

The girls erupted in shouts, telling someone all about the new cat in the kitchen. The entire box of bedlam seemed to be heading in the direction of Madge's room. In a few seconds, Joe, Mara Lynn, and the girls all crowded into the room. Joe held the cat.

"We just dropped in to see if anybody wanted to order pizza tonight. But now I've gotta know what you got here, Aunt Madge? I didn't know you liked cats."

"Hate 'em," Madge said. "This one probably needs a good home if you're interested." As she said it, Madge knew it wasn't true. Not anymore. If something had happened to Elmer Grigsby and she was never going to see him again on this earth, she was certainly going to keep his aggravating cat.

Alex took Joe's arm and tried to steer him back into the hallway. Madge stopped them.

"Don't bother hiding around corners to talk about it," she said. "I've been thinking all afternoon, and there are only a couple of possibilities."

Everyone leaned in, or at least it felt that way to Madge. "Either Elmer has gotten so sick that he called for an ambulance, and he's in a hospital somewhere. Or," she looked straight at Joe, "he's off on a bender."

She felt like everyone took a deep breath at once. As if they were taking in air for the arguments they planned to throw at her conclusions. Joe put an end to it.

"Could be either way," he said. "You are right about that." He kept petting the cat who had draped himself over Joe's arm like a towel. "You ladies better start calling hospitals. They can't release any information since you aren't kin, but you can give them the pastor's phone number and ask them to call him if Elmer is there."

Alex nodded, and Paige started taking notes on her phone.

"I'll take a drive," Joe said.

"Where are you going to look?" Madge wasn't sure she wanted to hear the answer.

"I know places," he said. "I've spent time in most of them."

"I'm going with you." Madge reached for her cane despite the corporate complaint that went up all around her.

"Now, Aunt Madge, I can't take care of you and look for Mr. Elmer at the same time. What if somethin' happens to you? We're gonna be stretched thin taking care of the two of you."

"I'll take care of Aunt Madge."

She hadn't seen Aspen enter the room. She had no idea how much the girl had heard. Yet, there she stood in all her almost-thirteen-year-old determination. Madge barely had time to think about Aspen calling her "aunt" before the conversation continued.

"I'll take care of Aunt Madge," Aspen said again. "We'll wait in the car while you go into the bars. That way she won't be alone."

"I know you want to help," Joe said. "But I can't take a teen-ager and a nice lady into the neighborhoods where I'm going."

Alex stepped in when Aspen was about to protest. "Your dad will be home in an hour. I think we should wait for him."

"Good idea," Joe said. "An hour probably won't make that much difference. You girls start making calls. Aspen and I will sit with Aunt Madge." He handed the cat to Aspen. She sat at Madge's feet and transferred the cat to Madge's lap.

Madge let her hand rest on the purring back, and the hour passed without much talking. Joe seemed content in silence. That was a good trait in a man. After about thirty minutes, Aspen said, "Want to listen to some music? It helps me sometimes."

"Sure," Madge said, although she didn't think rock and roll would soothe much.

Aspen took the remote and made a few clicks. A soft piano sound floated from the television. Blue skies, white clouds, and fields of poppies filled the screen. Madge realized the music was a hymn.

Luke took more than an hour getting home. Traffic. A wreck on the interstate. And he didn't know the fate of the world, or at least Madge's world, waited on him at home. Alex evidently gave him an update during the short walk from the garage to Madge's room. He stepped inside, squeezed Madge's hand, and scratched Cat behind the ears.

"Let's go," he said to Joe.

Madge stood more easily than she had in months. She slipped Cat toward Aspen and said, "I'll get a jacket." She expected someone to scold, but nobody spoke. Evidently, her determination had been communicated to Joe through telepathy as they sat waiting. He must have understood that he would lose this tussle should he decide to take it on.

Aspen stepped into the closet and came back with Madge's jacket. "I'll get you a scarf and some gloves," she said. "Maybe boots. What size do you wear?"

Madge's feet were decidedly too big for any boots in the house. They settled for sending along two blankets and an extra pair of heavy socks. Along with strict warnings that Madge was never to leave the car.

Madge tried not to think about the Christmas drive with Elmer and Mr. Uber. This night was the exact opposite. Snow had been pushed into huge piles along the streets. Exhaust from traffic turned the mounds mostly black now, with glimpses of snow here and there. Instead of the fairy land she had seen on her ride with Elmer, she felt like she was trapped in a horror film. She never watched that stuff, but she had seen previews. Everything was dark and grimy.

A few blocks toward downtown, the streetlights popped on. However, they did nothing to change the atmosphere. They didn't sparkle like the lights on display when she and Elmer had sipped cocoa. What a ninny she had been. What a silly, light-headed ignoramus. People her age did not live in fairy tales.

"I'll go in," Joe said as he pulled the car to the first curb.

Madge looked at the neon light flashing in the window of the small building. A man in a huge overcoat stumbled out the door as Joe went in. The man walked a few steps, leaned against the wall, and hunched forward. Madge realized he was about to take care of business. She put a hand over her eyes and wondered how long to count.

"Sorry about that," Luke said. "Try looking at the city skyline instead. Over there." He pointed in the opposite direction.

Madge looked. She was not impressed.

Fortunately, Joe came out the door within seconds. He paused long enough to say something to the guy in the street, then slid back into the car.

"Did you give him a warning?" Luke asked. "Against public indecency?"

"Nah. I told him about a shelter on Seventh Street. They got a good AA meeting there."

Luke grinned and nodded. "I'm a jerk, aren't I?"

"Little bit. Sometimes." He turned the car into the street. "Guy probably won't go, but I know I tried."

"Yep."

They repeated the scenario so many times Madge lost count. Dingy bars on dark corners with various forms of ragged humanity stumbling in and out. Each time, Joe stopped and talked to someone. Madge saw him handing out cards a time or two.

"Did you give that guy money?" she asked once after she saw an exchange.

"No, Aunt Madge. Never give a man in that situation money. It will just go back into the till at the bar. I keep fast-food cards in my pocket. I told him to get a burger and warm up."

"You're something," Madge said.

"And so are you. That's why we hit it off so good."

After that, Joe talked some while he drove. He talked about how hard it had been to clean up his act, how he couldn't have done it without the Holy Spirit. They were mostly the same stories he had told at the pizza place that night a million years ago. Madge knew he was telling them to her to give her hope. He could have saved his strength, though. Hope left her six bars ago.

A little after midnight, Joe pulled over under a streetlight. He turned around and spoke to Madge. "That's about it," he said. "We've seen all the obvious spots with no luck. Now, that could mean he is sleeping it off in a dumpster somewhere. Or it could be better news. It could mean he just got cold feet and went off somewhere to think a spell. Maybe he is perfectly fine and will show up in a day or two."

"He didn't get cold feet," Madge said. "It's not his way." How she knew the way of a man who had come so recently into her life Madge could not have said. She knew, though. Elmer Grigsby did not have cold feet.

CHAPTER THIRTY-NINE
And so It Goes

When Joe's headlights flashed across the Marvel's driveway, Madge first thought a mound of dirty snow had slid off the roof and landed on the porch steps. Then she wondered why someone had dropped off an army bag full of dirty clothes. It took a few seconds for the coat to become familiar in her mind.

After all the intoxicated souls Madge had seen that night, one more didn't bother her, except she thought she would recognize this face when the boys rolled him over.

Joe said something in a voice so low Madge couldn't hear it, and Luke jumped out of the car before it stopped moving. She realized they hoped to get to Elmer and spare her the worst of the sight. She would have none of that. Madge reached for the door handle, but Joe had somehow locked her in. She pounded on the window.

"Now, now, Aunt Madge." Joe held up both hands in surrender. "I'm gonna let you out. Just give Luke time to settle things a little bit and see what we're up against."

He turned to look over his shoulder for a moment. When he turned again, he reached for the door and offered Madge his hand. "Here you go. Take it easy. Slick spots underfoot."

She took it easy. She wanted to make each step take about a year because she could not imagine what she would say when she finally faced the man. She could not decide if she would ever be able to forgive him or to explain to him how awful it was to be cut to pieces a second time in life. She just didn't know. So, she took small steps, checking for ice, but mostly checking her heart.

She knew it would probably do no good to talk tonight, anyway. He would need time to sober up before the showdown. Maybe the boys could take him home and pour some coffee into him. Madge was suddenly glad Pastor Cleveland was out of town. He wouldn't have to see this mess.

She had nearly reached the porch before Joe stepped aside and stopped shielding her. Luke backed off. Then, wonder of all wonders, Elmer Grigsby stood straight and clear in front of her. "I'm sorry I worried you," he said in his normal, sober, wonderful voice.

Madge hiccupped. She knew it meant she was about to burst into tears, so she took control. "What kind of lunatic are you?" she said. "Drive a woman mad this way. And what about that wild cat? He would have starved if I hadn't gone over there. What were you thinking?"

"I trusted you'd feed him," Elmer said. "My phone give out because I forgot to take along the cord. I'm not used to the new-fangled gadgets. Then I found I didn't have a single number stored up in my head. I'm not used to such things. Haven't had a phone in years. Nobody to call, you know."

She knew. She didn't want to give him any mercy, yet she did understand. She suddenly realized she didn't have telephone numbers memorized either. She counted on that silly contraption to keep track of them for her. She'd have to fix that. Write down Alex's number somewhere. And Paige.

She stopped wandering when she remembered she was mad. "Well, where in tarnation have you been?"

Elmer smiled. "I've been a bad influence," he said. "I've never heard such language from you."

"Balderdash, then. How do you like that word? Just tell me where you've been. You've had all these people worried to death."

"I reckon we could go into the house," he said. "Warm up a smidgen while I tell the story."

She considered. Part of her wanted to demand a full explanation right here under the winter sky. Right here where God could see them clear. That seemed useless, though, since she counted on the Almighty to see all the way through to her heart every day. A roof wouldn't bother Him.

"All right," she said. "Let's go inside and hear the story."

Alex jumped from her chair when Elmer walked through the doorway. She took half a step forward and said, "You look frozen."

"I've been sittin' on yer doorstep for a while now."

"Why didn't you come in?" Alex said as she threw an afghan over his shoulders.

Elmer pulled it close, which is when Madge realized he was shivering.

"Hadn't worked out in my mind exactly how to handle the thing," he said. "I'd have come to it before long; my toes were goin' numb."

"Good grief," Alex said. "Come on in. I'll get coffee. Somebody grab another blanket."

In a few minutes, Elmer sat in Luke's chair, tucked up with blankets and a hot cup of coffee in his hands. He took a couple of sips before he put it on the table beside him. "Well," he said. "I'm sure sorry I worried you folks. But I had all the faith in you." He looked at Madge. "I knew you'd work out that I'd gone somewhere, and you'd take care of my cat."

"After we called all the hospitals," Alex said.

"And visited a few bars," Joe added.

"Oh." Elmer leaned back in his chair with his hands on his knees.

Madge couldn't look at him. He'd had faith in her to feed the blasted cat, but she'd shown no faith in him at all. She had assumed the worst right away. Expected him to abandon her and go back to his old ways.

"You would think of that, I 'spect." Elmer looked at a distant spot on the wall. "I'd almost got used to bein' a human, so I didn't stop to think you all would lean toward finding me in the gutter right away."

"No," Alex moved closer to his chair. "No, it wasn't like that at all."

"Yes, it was." Madge said. "It was exactly like that, and I'm ashamed of myself. You've never given anybody a bit of reason to expect such a thing. We gave up on you at the first bump. Or, at least, I did."

Elmer turned to face her.

Madge watched to see what his expression would be. Was he mad? She probably would be. Or disappointed? Or maybe embarrassed. She couldn't read his expression at all.

"Well, then." He started to grin, just a little at first. It broke into a wide smile showing all those good teeth. "I reckon I've got one up on you, then. We'll have to be gentle with each other while we're learnin' this stuff."

She hadn't expected that. Forgiveness. Mercy. Handed out as easy as candy at Halloween.

"Maybe it would help Aunt Madge if you told us where you've been," Joe said.

Madge thought that would help a great deal. Yet, she couldn't imagine an explanation that would make things go back to where they had been before.

"I've been to Kansas," he said. "Looking for a man named DuPree."

"What on earth?" Everyone started asking questions at once. Why had he gone? How had he gotten there? What did he expect to accomplish? Was he out of his mind?

Madge asked no questions. She just let the words run in and out of her mind. She felt them like the soft blanket on her bed at night. "I've been to Kansas to look for DuPree." She didn't even worry about what would come next. She just reveled in the wonder that Elmer Grigsby was taking care of her. She came back into the conversation when he started talking.

"I didn't know how long Jack might be out of commission," he said. "I heard he got sick, and this wedding certificate thing was bothering me. I took a bus."

"A bus?" Alex seemed to still be just on the edge of mad about the whole thing. "You went all the way to Kansas on a bus?"

"I did. You know they don't go straight through, neither. I sat up all night and rode most of the next day. Stopped in every little town between here and there. At one stop, we were supposed to get off and eat our supper, but I didn't know how much money I might need for the search, so I stayed on."

Madge listened to the conversation, but she felt as if she were sitting in the next room. Able to hear but not join in. Finally, when the rapid-fire questions slowed up a bit, she spoke.

"Did you find him?"

They were hard words to speak. Hard words to even consider. If Elmer had found DuPree, it might mean the path was clear. After the way she had behaved tonight, though, she wasn't sure she could take the steps. And could she believe that Elmer would never end up on the streets again? Did she have enough faith in either one of them?

If he hadn't found DuPree, it would mean her nightmare continued, and a good man might have caught his death trying to help her. Either way, Madge wasn't sure she could go forward. She looked up from the hands she was knotting in her lap. Elmer had reached into his overcoat and was pulling out a paper.

"In the end, I didn't have to fight him for you."

"Good." The thought was silly. But gallant. No one had ever been gallant for her.

"I went to the county courthouse lookin' for your wedding papers," Elmer said. "Right nice young woman workin' behind the counter. When I told her what I needed, she started tapping those keys, squinting her eyes, and all of a sudden, she yelled, 'Bingo!' Then, lickety-split, her machine spit out this piece of paper."

He pulled back just as he was about to hand it to Madge. "Maybe it can be my weddin' present to you."

Madge closed her eyes. She wasn't sure she wanted to see the paper nor do the work that might be required. After a few seconds, she opened her eyes. Everyone was staring at her. It would be cruel to ignore something Elmer had worked so hard to dig up. She took the paper.

It looked like a copy of a newspaper clipping. She frowned and looked closer.

"Take your time," Elmer said. "It's right interesting."

DuPree had died twenty years ago from a heart attack. The writer included several awards he had won as a salesman and listed the organizations he had joined. Madge was not mentioned.

She was glad about that, but a little sorry, too. The man was survived by no one except a few distant cousins who weren't even listed by name. He must have lived a solitary life. How sad.

The sadness surprised her. She didn't owe the man any grief. Nor had she ever felt the need to be peopled. If she had died two years ago, before coming to the Marvels, her obituary would have read much the same.

"At least they left my name out of the paper," she said.

"Out of that one, at least," Elmer grinned a sort of ornery grin. It made Madge wonder what scandal he had uncovered. What tale had been told to a local reporter somewhere. Maybe the desk clerk had been interviewed. Or the judge who married them.

She braced herself for the embarrassment while Elmer pulled another paper out of his coat.

"They left you out of the obituary. I don't suppose anybody knew a thing about you. Except maybe these folks." He handed the paper to Luke, as if someone else should interpret.

Luke unfolded the paper and read for a moment. "It's a life insurance policy from his company." He looked up at Madge. "He listed you as beneficiary."

"What?" Madge felt hot and scratchy. She pulled at her sweater. "He did what?"

"He named you as next of kin," Luke said. "Probably had to put something when he filled out this paper. It's signed in 1969."

"It's still good," Elmer said. "I checked."

Madge wanted to cry for the second time in an hour. The scoundrel DuPree had not forgotten her completely. He had not abandoned her without another thought. Somewhere in his devious mind, her name had come to the surface when a secretary asked who they should list as next of kin.

She knew how those things happened. You fill them out when you are young and strong and never really expect anyone will use them. She'd done the same thing when she opened a Christmas Club account one year. She knew she wouldn't die before December, so she didn't give a second thought about which nephew to list.

This, though. This was something else.

"You have Jack call the lawyer in Kansas," Elmer said, "and that amount at the bottom of the page is yours to claim."

Madge reached out for the paper. It hung between them for a moment before Luke let go and Madge pulled it into her lap. Twenty-five thousand dollars. The man had sent her twenty-five thousand dollars from the other side of death. She had a fortune.

CHAPTER FORTY

Fol de Rol

Madge didn't notice the others leaving the room until she looked up from the insurance paper and found herself alone with Elmer. He was smiling. "Nothin' in the way now," he said. "We can go right ahead with wedding plans."

"Are you sure?" Madge asked. "One-hundred percent, no-turning-back, stuck-together-for-life sure?"

"I am." He stopped smiling and leaned toward her. "Have you got the jitters?" He asked.

"Maybe. How about yourself?"

"Not a bit," Elmer said. "I feel sorta solemn. Big responsibility to say the words. But I mean 'em from my heart, and I'm trustin' the Almighty to help us."

"Don't you think this is a bunch of nonsense, though?" she said. "Two old people like us?"

"Well," he said, "I never thought to do it. No sirree, I never did. But just about the first time I laid eyes on you, with that fiery hair and those snappin' eyes, I knew I was done for. It took some months of clean livin' before I could put it into straight thoughts. But after a while I sorted it out. I knew I wanted to live out my days with you whether they be many or be few. I'd like to think you want to do the same."

Madge stared at the insurance paper. DuPree had been a skunk. No doubt about that. And she thought he had ruined any chance of her ever letting another man turn her head or her heart. Evidently, she had been wrong about that.

She looked up again, straight into Elmer Grigsby's sweet and craggy face. "Fiddlesticks," she said. "You know I want to marry you. I've wanted it lots longer than I ever cared to admit."

"Let's get hitched on Valentine's Day like we planned," Elmer said.

Madge nodded. "Lord, help us," she said.

Elmer touched her hand, "Oh, I'm countin' on that."

On a clear Saturday morning, one week before the big day, Madge found herself surrounded in her bedroom by Alex, Paige, and the Marvel sisters.

"I don't need a fussy wedding shower," Madge said.

Alex held a white sash with "Here Comes the Bride" in gold letters. Paige waved a sparkly tiara.

"I'm not wearing those things," Madge said again. "They can go straight to the dress up box for the girls."

"At least wear the flowers," Aspen said. "Mr. Grigsby sent them."

Madge looked at the wrist corsage made of pink sweetheart roses. She had never in her entire life worn a corsage of any kind. She had always thought, if the occasion arose, she would want one just like this. How did the man know?

Aspen didn't wait for an answer but slipped the flowers over Madge's stiff hand. She had expected the roses to make her hand look silly. A hand so old and wrinkled shouldn't wear a creation meant for young girls. Instead, the flowers seemed to cast a pink glow across her entire hand. She held her hand up and marveled at how the age spots had almost disappeared.

"I'll get the door," Alex said. Madge hadn't even heard it ring. She was still admiring the flowers when Alex returned. With guests.

Madge looked up and then gasped. "Catherine?"

"No. Oh, I'm sorry. I didn't mean to shock you," the woman said. "I'm Elizabeth. Catherine's sister. The youngest one."

Madge gripped the arms of her chair. "Oh, yes. You came to visit a long time ago. You were younger."

"Yes, weren't we all?"

"You look just like her." Madge wasn't sure she had said the words out loud until Elizabeth smiled. She had Catherine's smile.

"I'll take that as a great compliment," Elizabeth said.

Madge suddenly realized what a mess everything must be.

"You have to forgive us," she said. "We're in the middle of a lot of fol-de-rol around here."

"Yes, I know," Elizabeth said. "That is partly why I'm here. Some friends decided to drive up on business this weekend and asked if I'd like to come along."

"Well, that's nice." Madge had never been good at small talk, and this was one of the smallest kinds. She felt her heart beating faster while she tried to figure out what things she should talk about with Catherine's baby sister. She had lots of things she wanted to say and ask, but she had no idea where to start or how to get there. Did a person just jump in on such personal questions?

"Emily told me about your situation here with the Marvels," Elizabeth said.

"Oh, that Emily," Madge said. "She keeps her hand in everything, doesn't she? If she didn't have such a good heart, I'd call her a busybody."

Elizabeth nodded. "She also mentioned the 'fol-de-rol' you are going through right now."

Madge felt her face getting hot, and she looked around to see if her water glass was anywhere nearby. "Lot of foolishness, isn't it? A couple of old people acting like youngsters. If we are going to do such a thing, we could have at least snuck off to the courthouse instead of messing with flowers and dresses and such."

"I think the flowers are lovely." Elizabeth motioned toward the corsage. "And that's sort of why I've come, really." She pulled a white box out of the bag she had carried with her.

"We have a tradition in our family that we sisters always provide the 'something borrowed' for one another when we are brides. I know, if Catherine were here, she would have gone to her drawer and selected the perfect one for you. I inherited her collection, so I thought it only proper to come and do the honors."

She looked up suddenly and stopped with her hand on the lid. "Oh, you may have something borrowed to carry already. Or you may not want anything."

Madge sat silent. She had never imagined herself a bride. Never in all her years. And this. A tradition handed down from sister to sister. It choked the words right out of her.

"I don't get it," Aspen said. "What's borrowed mean?"

"Oh," Elizabeth let her hand drop on the box. "It's an old tradition among brides. On our wedding day, we each have something old, something new, something borrowed, something blue, and a lucky penny in our shoe. It's just a silly game, really, that is supposed to bring good luck. We don't even believe in luck. We depend on Providence. But we've always done it out of tradition."

"Perfect," Aspen said, "Because Madge is wearing blue. It's her best color. And her pearl necklace is sort of new."

"Her shoes are old," Quinn said. "She doesn't want new shoes because she doesn't want her feet to hurt while she stands at the altar in front of God and everybody."

"Very sensible," Elizabeth said, while Madge wished the girls hadn't listened so closely to every conversation.

"I'm sure we can find a penny," Aspen said. "Or maybe we can get a shiny new one from the bank. Then she could have it as a keepsake with her wedding year on it."

"Wonderful ideas, all." Elizabeth smiled as if she had just helped to arrange the entire wedding. "And now, for the something borrowed. If you are interested, Madge? I think Catherine would have liked you to have one."

Elizabeth opened the box and started laying out fancy lace handkerchiefs. There were more than a dozen in various shades of blue, pink, white, and ivory. Some had flowers. They all had fancy stitching.

Madge leaned over and picked up a small kerchief. It was all white with a simple border. In the lower left corner, CB was stitched in blue curls. "She did this one herself, didn't she?"

"I think so," Elizabeth said. "It looks like her hand."

Madge smoothed the hanky across her knee and ran her finger over the letters another time. "Thank you," she said. "Thank you very, very much."

She wasn't going to be able to squeeze another word out around the choking in her throat. Fortunately, Elizabeth was in a big hurry and had a car waiting outside.

"I'm going to pop in on Emily," Elizabeth said. "Then downtown to meet up with my friends. We drive back tonight." She stood and looked around the room. "The house looks quite different, doesn't it?"

Madge nodded.

"And yet," Elizabeth said, "it feels exactly the same."

Madge walked to the door with her guest, crowded slightly by the little girls. While everyone else was distracted with farewells, Madge stepped away and turned toward her room. Once inside, she closed the door and leaned against it, breathing in the silence. She put the hanky in the drawer beside her Bible, touching it one more time. She wanted to wrap it in tissue paper to keep it spotless for the big day, but she didn't have a scrap of the stuff around. She would have to ask Alex to look for some.

Three hours later, Madge had enough tissue paper to wrap the entire house. Or so it seemed. They held the shower in the same room where the Glory Circle met every Tuesday, but Madge would not have recognized it. Balloons, streamers, paper lanterns, even tablecloths with flower centerpieces.

"We did it up right, didn't we?" Paige asked the question, but the ladies all nodded.

"You sure went to a lot of work," Madge said. "Don't know if it was worth the bother, but you sure put some time into it."

She couldn't admit how it made her feel to be treated this way. Royal maybe. Sort of like she imagined a queen might feel on a normal day. But there was nothing normal about opening packages wrapped in glossy paper with filmy ribbon. Nothing normal about the stack of towels, dishes, candles, and do-dads mounting up beside the clouds of tissue paper.

Even the Marvel sisters got in on the fun. An envelope full of pizza coupons from the little girls. Quinn's idea. Aspen had chosen a blanket in the exact shade of blue from Madge's room at the Marvel house. "To remind you," she said.

As if Madge needed reminding. She almost hated to leave the place now that she had unpacked.

"I suppose you'll be moving back to your house after the wedding," Erma said. "The blanket will be nice to spruce things up a bit."

Madge hadn't wanted to mention this part. She felt like she would be putting on airs to admit it. Yet, she couldn't lie straight out to Erma.

"Not exactly," she said. "We put my place up for sale last week, and we already have a buyer."

"Oh," Erma leaned forward and seemed to bring the entire room with her.

"We had a good realtor," Madge said. "Friend of the family. She helped us find a little place just a few blocks down from the Marvels. That way I can still help out now and then when the girls need something."

"We can walk there," Quinn piped in. "Anytime we want, right Madge?"

"Anytime you have permission from our house and theirs," Alex said.

"Right. Anytime." Quinn smiled at Madge as if the whole world had just been made right. Madge thought maybe it had.

"Here," Aspen said. "Open the last present." It was huge and included a simple card signed by Paige and Alex.

Madge pulled away the paper, and Aspen helped her fold back the flaps on the box. Together, they pulled out two big fluffy pillows. Exactly like the ones she had been sleeping on and coveting for the last few months. Before Madge could say thanks, Aspen pulled out another package.

This one held a set of sheets. The expensive kind.

"See," Aspen said, "We had a theme."

"I see."

"Everything you need for your new boudoir," Paige said.

Madge pulled out the final package at the bottom of the box. It was small, wrapped in white paper, and mysteriously soft. She opened it slowly, wondering if it might be a nice throw for the foot of the bed.

She took hold of the silky blue fabric and pulled out for everyone to see a frilly new nightgown with a matching robe. The Glory Circle sisters giggled all around the room.

CHAPTER FORTY-ONE

Those Who Trust in the Lord

"We could still drive around to the other door. Nobody would know." Luke stood beside the car while Madge considered.

The steps had never looked so tall. She had hoped to practice a time or two before the wedding, but they hadn't pulled that off. She couldn't explain to anyone why it was so important to climb the mountain of steps and walk in the front door of the church for her wedding. She wasn't even sure she understood. She thought about the options one more time.

"I can do it," she said.

Luke helped her from the vehicle while Alex came around from the other side.

"I'll carry your bag to the dressing room," she said. "You just concentrate on the steps."

They had come plenty early so the event wouldn't be witnessed by guests. Or so they thought.

Madge took Luke's arm and walked up the first three steps as if she had never broken a hip or sprained an ankle. She paused for breath, more from the emotion of the thing than the actual walk. When she glanced up to read the words above the door, she discovered a crowd.

Eleanor and Tom. Grace Colby, Erma, and dear Bess. All standing at the top of the stairs, ready to assist, she supposed. Or maybe just to offer moral support for the climb. Madge didn't often look for signs or deep meanings in life. They tended to disappoint. This time, though, she thought the Glory Circle sisters waiting at the top of the stairs on her wedding day was about the best sign a person could get. She felt her eyes stinging and knew she would start to blubber if she didn't change her concentration. That would never do.

"Let's get going," she growled to Luke. "I don't want to stand out here all morning for people to gawk."

In truth, Madge had looked at herself in the mirror so many times that morning she felt almost embarrassed. Aspen had done something magical with the wild, red hair. Paige had helped with face powder and a new lipstick. Madge stood fast against rouge, which Paige called blush, or mascara. Alex added a couple of shots of expensive perfume. By the time they were done, Madge definitely felt less homely than usual.

They had mounted several steps while Madge recalled the morning. The next time she stopped for breath, the friends at the top were almost close enough to touch. Although Madge didn't intend to do any such thing.

When her foot reached the final step, Bess clapped and said, "Oh, you've done it! You've climbed all the steps and can go right inside as a proper bride. I knew you could."

Before Madge could protest, Bess threw her small arms around Madge and gave her a surprisingly strong hug. Everyone else crowded around with congratulations and best wishes. Even Grace lost her sour expression long enough to give Madge her regards for the day.

"Okay," Luke finally said. "Let's get the bride into the church and get this show on the road."

"Hurry," Evelyn said. "We must get her into the dressing room before Mr. Grigsby arrives. He mustn't see her before the ceremony."

Madge realized that was the thing she wanted most in the middle of this silliness. She wanted to see Elmer. To hear his voice. And she wanted that before she could walk down the aisle in front of the whole church. She said so to Luke.

"It breaks tradition," Luke said. "I'm not sure you want to do it."

"I'll do what I please," Madge said. "I don't give a hoot about tradition. I want to talk to the man."

Truth be told, she wanted to grab hold of Elmer. She wanted to touch his solid hand. Feel him steady her for this walk down the aisle in front of God and everybody. She didn't admit that bit of weakness to the Marvels, though.

"Let's get to the dressing room," Alex said. "Then you can decide."

They didn't have many weddings at Mt. Zion, so the dressing room was mostly used for people who were getting baptized. There were no seats, although someone had put a rickety folding chair in the corner.

Finally, a soft tap sounded on the door. "Pearl, are you in there?"

"I'll wait in the vestibule," Alex whispered. She pulled the door open just enough to slip out, leaving Madge alone in the dimly lit room.

"Are you there?" Elmer said again.

"I am."

"Feelin' trembly?" he asked.

"Maybe. You think there's a big crowd?"

"Don't worry about the folks," Elmer said. "You just grab hold of Luke's arm and fix your eyes on me down at the front. Then you walk straight to me. Pay no mind to anybody else. Can you do that?"

"I can do it," Madge said. She had been right about hearing Elmer's voice. He steadied her.

"Here comes the music now," he said. "I'm gonna take my place. You just let Luke bring you to me. Okay?"

"Okay." She waited to see if he had walked away or if he had more to say. Somewhere down the hallway, she heard him whistle.

Alex pulled the door open a crack. "Ready?"

"No. Not at all. But I guess it's no use fighting anymore. I did buy this suit."

"Right." Alex offered her hand, led Madge out, and handed her over to Luke.

As Madge and Luke stood waiting for the little girls and Aspen to line up in front of them, Luke said, "Did either of your nephews feel left out? Did they want to walk you down the aisle?"

"Nah. We never went in for much sentimentality. I expect they are in the pews somewhere."

"Well, we don't have to get sentimental now, either," Luke said. The way he sniffed and screwed his face up made Madge doubt the sincerity of his remark. She didn't comment, though. She just held tight.

Ushers threw open the double doors and the wedding music flooded out into the vestibule. Paige took Jack's arm and tossed Madge a kiss before they walked down the aisle to take their places on the front row. They sat on the groom's side, just to even things out.

Alex gave Madge one more brave smile before she stepped into the aisle. She looked positively regal in her new black dress. Aspen looked over her shoulder and gave Madge a thumb's up before she followed her mother.

After a few beats, Quinn said, "Now!" The three little girls stepped into the sanctuary and began tossing rose petals into the aisle. Madge tried not to wonder how expensive that moment had been because she did like it. Even though she had called the idea a lot of balderdash in the planning stage.

The music changed. The crowd stood. And Luke applied a gentle pressure to Madge's arm. She thought for a brief moment that she had forgotten how to walk. Then her foot went forward, and they were off.

The front looked so far away. But then she saw Ben and Nancy smiling at her halfway down. Beside them, her other nephew, Clyde, gave a little wave. Further on, Emily nodded as if to draw her forward.

A few more steps and they reached the spot where Madge could see the ladies in the third pew. Beaming. It was the only word she could think of to describe Bess, who probably thought they were all still twenty-five and starting lives at the beginning.

Then she looked ahead to see Elmer. He wasn't smiling, and that worried her for a minute. Then she realized he was blinking hard and chewing on his lip. The man was about the cry.

Madge speeded up, and Luke matched her. They reached the altar in a few steps, and Madge dispensed with ceremony. She reached out, took Elmer's hand, and pulled him over to stand side-by-side. Pastor Cleveland looked down with a giant grin on his face. He started with the dearly-beloveds and said a few more words before he asked, "Who gives this bride in marriage?"

They had talked about this. Madge didn't need anybody giving her away at the altar. She wasn't somebody's property. She thought they had agreed to strike that part from the ceremony. Before she could protest, Luke and Alex spoke.

"We do," they said in unison.

"And we do," the little girls practically sang.

"As do we." That came from Ben. Or Clyde. Maybe both.

"Paige and I give her," Jack said.

"Same for Mara Lynn and me. Aunt Madge, marry the man." The congregation laughed, and Madge recognized Joe's voice.

Then all across the room, people added their voices. "We do," echoed from the stained-glass windows to the pews and up into the wooden rafters all the way to the balcony.

Finally, Pastor Cleveland held up his hand. "Thank you," he said. "I believe we have determined that everyone in the room is in favor of this marriage." He looked at Madge and Elmer. "Please step forward."

She had expected the next part to be hard. All the words to repeat. All the vows to keep. But with each word, it grew easier and easier to promise Elmer Grigsby that she would love, honor, and cherish until death did them part. She hoped that would be a very long time.

They had also talked about the kissing of the bride. Madge had said a strong no to being kissed in front of the whole crowd. It would be the first time in more than half a century, and she didn't want to miss the mark or anything. Elmer had agreed, or so she thought. Yet, after the final "I do," Pastor Cleveland leaned forward and said softly, "Dad, you may kiss your bride."

Madge felt the heat rush to her head. Her heart pounded, and her breath came hard. Elmer smiled. He lifted her hand as if they were in slow motion, and he touched his lips to her fingers as if he was greeting a queen. Madge felt the shock of it all the way to her toes.

It felt so good and so unexpected that Madge reached out, grabbed his face, and planted a giant kiss on his smooth cheek. The crowd broke into applause and Elmer put his arms around her. As he pulled her close, he said, "See, we'll get the hang of it."

The rest of the morning passed in a blur. Cake, punch, speeches, toasts. Madge started to feel tired and overwhelmed after the first twenty minutes. Eventually, Alex came to the table and sat beside her. "I think you two should get out of here," she said. "This crowd could party all day."

"Good plan," Elmer said. "You got the suitcases?"

"Luke took care of them. You have fun on your trip, and we'll see you next week. Pizza party at our house when you get home."

Madge accepted Elmer's hand and waved her bouquet as they stood. She gave the flowers a toss, trying not to make it too obvious that she aimed directly for Paige. In the hubbub that followed, Madge and Elmer slipped out the door of the fellowship hall and stood in the vestibule once again.

"Where's Luke?" Madge said. "Or did you call Mr. Uber to drive us to the train?"

"It's all taken care of, my girl." Elmer motioned toward the tall doors. They opened as if by magic, though Madge knew someone must have been standing outside. A car started honking below them.

Elmer and Madge walked out and looked down from the top of the steps. Jack stood leaning against the getaway car. It was decked with streamers and had "Just Married" written on the windows. Tin cans rattled in the breeze behind the back bumper. Even with all the disguise, Madge recognized the car right away.

"My Oldsmobile," she said.

"Good as new." Elmer took a step, but Madge stopped him.

"I don't have a license yet."

"Nope," he gave her that cocky grin and tipped his head. "But, no worries, my Pearl. I do."

AUTHOR BIO

Kathy Nickerson is an author, speaker, and eternal optimist who writes from her home in the Midwest. She has been married to her country doctor husband for more than forty-five years. They are the parents of four children, who grew up to become their best friends and who have given them sixteen grandchildren, so far.

She is the author of five novels, including the award-winning *Thirty Days to Glory*, which is the first in the Glory Circle Sisters series. She has also written short stories, flash fiction, magazine articles, and an e-book on parenting. She also blogs on her website www.kathynick.com.

You can find Kathy's books through the website or by visiting www.amazon.com/author/kathynickerson.

Kathy's favorite accessory is a microphone. She loves to talk about faith, family, and fun in a variety of settings. She has spoken at women's conferences, libraries, churches, schools, and community events.

You can learn more about Kathy's writing and her reputation as an Eternal Optimist at her website www.kathynick.com or by connecting with her on social media:

www.facebook.com/kathynick
www.twitter.com/kathynick
www.instagram.com/kathynick